On the Edge

Rebecca Deel

Copyright © 2017 Rebecca Deel

All rights reserved.

ISBN: 1979818797
ISBN-13: 978-1979818797

DEDICATION

To my amazing husband.

ACKNOWLEDGMENTS

Cover design by Melody Simmons.

CHAPTER ONE

Grace Rutledge glanced in her rearview mirror. Her stomach knotted. The bright headlights remained. Probably a coincidence. Highway 18 was the main road between Otter Creek and Interstate 40. She'd spent an enjoyable afternoon with her best friend from college, shopping in Pigeon Forge, Tennessee. Chances were good someone else from Otter Creek was also on the way home on this cool spring evening.

She forced aside the uneasiness she felt. Hanging around the man she'd been dating for almost a year made her see danger everywhere. Trent St. Claire, a Navy SEAL who worked for Fortress Security, was constantly expecting trouble wherever he went.

Grace's lips curved. What trouble would find her in the backwater town of Otter Creek? Although criminal activity popped up around town, their police department was populated by officers with extraordinary skills and backgrounds for a town this size.

Another glance in the mirror showed the headlights had moved closer to her sedan. Thirteen miles to go. Grace gripped the wheel tighter as she pressed harder on the accelerator, hoping to create distance between her and the other vehicle.

She breathed a sigh of relief when the lights faded. She'd worried over nothing. That's what she got for spending so much time with a Navy SEAL.

Grace's heart skipped a beat at the thought of her dark-haired boyfriend. Tall, dark, and deadly, that was Trent St. Claire. He hid a soft heart from everyone but those closest to him, and Grace was happy she was included in that number.

Trent had deployed on a mission a week earlier and Grace missed him so much she ached. She hoped he missed her, though not to the extent that he endangered himself or his teammates. Trent St. Claire was fast becoming as necessary to Grace as breathing.

Bright light illuminated the interior of her car. Grace looked in the mirror again, gasped. Oh, man. The vehicle behind her bore down on her. This guy must be going twenty or thirty miles over the speed limit.

She sped up again, going as fast as she dared on this winding stretch of the highway. Hopefully he'd go around her since he was in such a hurry. Grace hated this part of the drive to Otter Creek, especially at night. Blind spots were plentiful, and it wasn't uncommon for wildlife to cross the roadway. She'd narrowly missed hitting a deer two weeks ago.

Another check of the mirror. "Go around, buddy," she murmured. "I'm not going faster than this. And if you don't slow down, I'll be seeing you at the hospital." The driver behind her kept coming.

Grace eased her car to the right, praying the driver would take the hint and scoot around her. No such luck. Cold sweat broke out on the back of her neck. She wished she was driving Trent's vehicle. His SUV was reinforced with armor. She could use the protection now. Her lips quirked. Maybe she'd talk to Trent about reinforcing her car.

What was this guy's problem? Grace cast a worried glance over her shoulder. The view didn't look any better than it did in the mirror. She might be in real trouble. This driver wasn't falling back or zooming past. Grace had never seen a driver this aggressive. She felt targeted, hunted, which was crazy. As far as she knew, she hadn't cut him off or done anything to make him angry.

Not afraid to admit she was scared, she grabbed her cell phone and called the second number on her speed dial. No use calling the first number. Trent might still be out of the country. She didn't know when he would return. She never did.

"How are you, sugar?" Rio Kincaid's voice stilled some of her bone-deep fear. Trent's brother-in-law was the medic for one of the Fortress teams based in Otter Creek.

"Rio, I need help." Even to her own ears, her voice was tight.

"What's wrong, Grace?"

"I'm on Highway 18, about 12 miles from Otter Creek. There's a vehicle behind me and the driver's pretty aggressive. I've sped up, eased over, and he's still coming. He's close enough to blind me with his headlights."

"Is there a place for you to pull off the road and let him pass you?"

Grace scanned the roadside in front of her. She wished the lighting was better on this road. Another glance in the mirror told her even if she found a place, the vehicle was too close. "I can't, Rio. If I slow down, he'll hit me."

Through the phone's speaker, Grace heard the sound of doors slamming and an engine starting. "Grace, it's Quinn. Rio has you on speaker. I just called the police. They have an officer not too far from your location. He's already en route, sugar. So are we. We're at PSI, so we're close to the highway."

"I may be overreacting. If so, I'll apologize now for wasting your time."

"Never apologize for being cautious," Rio said. "Always trust your instincts, Grace. If Trent was here, he'd say the same."

"I feel better just talking to you guys."

"Keep both hands on the wheel, sugar."

Like she would do otherwise. Grace had seen the results of automobile accidents in Memorial Hospital's emergency room. She didn't want to be a patient in her own hospital.

The screaming of an engine yanked her gaze from the road to the rearview mirror. The trailing vehicle raced toward her. No hint of swerving around her slower-moving vehicle. "Rio!" Her friend's name was the only word she got out before the vehicle slammed into her car.

Grace screamed as she fought to keep her car on the road. Why was he doing this? Why did he just go around her?

"Grace!"

"He hit me."

"What's he doing, sugar?"

She couldn't breathe much less talk.

"Grace," Rio snapped. "Breathe. Talk to me. We can't help you if we don't know what's happening."

That command broke through the tidal wave of fear. She dragged in air. "He hit my car and dropped back."

"Is he still there?" Quinn asked.

Another quick check. "Yes." She moaned. "He's speeding up again, aiming right for me."

"Get over to the right as far as you can, sweetheart."

"He won't pass me."

"Just do what I told you."

Grace eased her sedan further to the right. "I'm mostly in the emergency lane."

"Good girl. If he hits the left rear panel of your car, the momentum will turn you around the other way. Use your snow driving techniques and don't over correct. More than anything, do not panic."

Easy for him to say. "I'll try." Another glance behind her. "Here he comes."

"We're not far, sugar," Rio said. "Just hold on."

The vehicle slammed into her bumper again, backed off and charged forward, this time aiming at her driver's side. Was this creep going to force her off the road or spin her around like Quinn suggested? "He hit my bumper again and is aiming toward the driver's side."

"Remember the instructions I gave you," Quinn said. "We're five minutes out, Grace."

Five minutes. She could handle five minutes. Couldn't she? No choice. She wanted to see Trent again, feel his arms around her, share another kiss. She had to survive to win that reward.

The dark-colored pickup truck pursuing her swung wide, then veered toward the back panel of her car. Just as Quinn had warned, her car spun around. The wheels caught gravel, lost traction, and continued spinning toward the ditch between her side of the highway and the oncoming traffic.

Her car slid over the edge of the ditch. Grace cried out as the car tumbled down the incline. Airbags exploded and fine dust filled the cabin, blocking her vision. Her head slammed against the door as the car came to a jarring stop.

Grace was vaguely aware of Rio calling her name as she slumped to the side and into darkness.

CHAPTER TWO

Trent St. Claire dropped into a seat in front of his boss's desk. What was taking Maddox so long? Normally, Trent would already be out of here after the debriefing from his unit's latest mission, a successful snatch-and-run of a thirteen-year-old boy held hostage in Venezuela. The boy's father, a wealthy CEO of an American clothing manufacturer, made the mistake of taking his son on a business trip to an area known for ruthless men intent on making a quick buck at the expense of foreigners unwise enough to venture into their territory.

He rubbed the back of his neck, anxious to leave Nashville. He missed Grace something fierce. He'd had a tough time keeping his mind on the job, unusual for him. Thoughts of the beautiful woman who populated his dreams had filled his mind in idle moments and threatened to distract him during the op. Only discipline from his SEAL training enabled him to maintain his focus during the critical phases of the mission.

Trent needed to do something about the incredible Grace Rutledge. If he didn't want to lose her, he'd have to man up and tell her how he felt. So why did the prospect of baring his soul make him break out in a cold sweat?

He blew out a breath. Some Special Forces soldier he was. Afraid to tell a sweet nurse that she was indispensable to him.

The door to the office flew open and his boss strode in. At the sight of Maddox's expression, Trent stood, expecting the worst. Had the boss brought him into the privacy of his office to ream him out for a misstep on the mission? If so, he didn't want to take the dressing down sitting in a chair. Whatever caused the scowl on Brent Maddox's face wasn't good.

His boss circled to the other side of his desk and waved Trent to the seat he'd abandoned. "Sit, St. Claire. This won't take long."

Oh, man. His gut tightened. "I'd prefer to stand, sir."

Maddox's eyebrows rose. "You in a hurry or something?"

Or something. "Yes, sir."

"Sit down, Trent." Irritation filled the CEO's voice. "Tell me about the Hendrix boy's father."

He blinked at the unexpected demand as he returned to his seat. "Damon Hendrix is a class A jerk. He treats A.J. like the boy's a great disappointment. He's also verbally abusive."

"Physical abuse?"

"No evidence that I saw."

Maddox grunted. "Verbal abuse can be just as destructive."

Trent cocked his head. "Why are you asking about Hendrix?"

"He's complaining about the way the retrieval was handled. Says your team was too slow and were rude to him."

Outraged, Trent clenched his fists. "Too slow? We moved on the thugs' hideout as soon as we received the right intel. The longest part of the operation was getting out of Venezuela. As I explained, we ran into a few problems." Gun-toting terrorists bent on killing all of them.

Maddox waved aside Trent's explanation. "You did exactly as you were trained to do, Trent. You and your unit did a fantastic job considering the faulty information Hendrix gave you."

"So this is about the confrontation with Hendrix when we returned the boy?"

"The guy's an idiot. I'm surprised you didn't deck him."

In truth, Trent had almost laid the father out for verbally lashing his traumatized son. At no time had he ever seen a victim blamed for his own kidnapping, but that's exactly what Damon Hendrix had done to A.J. "I wanted to," he admitted. "Didn't want to cause trouble for you."

A snort. "I appreciate that." Maddox's mouth curved into a shark-like smile. "Now I can double our normal fee."

Trent whistled. Fortress Security wasn't cheap. In fact, his company's fees were already steep. "Hoping to never do business with Hendrix again?"

"If A.J. needs us, we'll be there. The father, however, will pay through the nose for our services."

Some of the tension in his muscles eased. "Then why the private meeting?"

"Your team has been deployed multiple times in the past six months. How much time have you had off?"

"Enough." Not as much as he wanted to spend with Grace, but he wasn't suffering from burnout. He refused to acknowledge the fatigue that dogged his every waking hour.

His boss narrowed his eyes.

Before Maddox could respond, Trent's cell phone signaled an incoming text. He glanced at the other man, eyebrow raised.

"Go ahead."

He checked the screen, an invisible band squeezing his chest at the message from his brother-in-law. *Call me immediately.* Trent put through the call. "Is Darcy okay?" he asked as soon as Rio Kincaid answered.

"She's fine. It's Grace."

His breath stalled in his lungs. No. He couldn't lose her. "Is she all right?"

"She was forced off the road and crashed in the ditch on Highway 18, about 8 miles from town."

"Rio, please." His voice broke. Losing Grace would kill him. Though he hadn't found the courage yet to tell her, Grace Rutledge was it for him. If he couldn't have her, he would be spending the rest of his life alone. There was no other woman for him but Grace.

"She's banged up, but alive. I don't know anything else since I'm not family. The medical staff won't give me more information without her permission and she can't give it right now."

His blood ran cold through his veins. The hospital staff wouldn't keep Trent from her side. He'd call in every favor he had to clear the way. No one was keeping him from her. "I'm leaving Nashville now. I'll be there as soon as I can." He ended the call and shoved his phone into his pocket. "I have to go. Grace was in an accident."

"She okay?"

"Hurt. Rio doesn't know how bad." He glowered. "The medical staff is stonewalling him."

"Go to the airport. One of the pilots will fly you to Knoxville. Have one of Rio's teammates meet you at the airfield."

Relief flooded Trent. "Thanks, boss." The sooner he was at Grace's side, the better. He paused. "I'm off duty, sir." Unspoken was his plan to stay off duty until Grace was well, however long that took. Fortress owed him several days of vacation.

"Understood. Go. I'll clear the way for you at the hospital."

Trent pushed the speed limit all the way back across town to John C. Tune airport. As soon as he was buckled in, the pilot powered up and taxied down the runway.

Throughout the flight home, he went through different scenarios and made various plans to deal with each possibility, depending on the severity of Grace's injuries. That Rio hadn't been able to find out any information worried Trent. The medic was well known and well liked in the medical community in Otter Creek.

No matter. He'd find out what he needed to know and help Grace as she recovered, however long that took.

Just when he thought he'd have to get up and pace off the tension, the pilot announced the plane was approaching the airport. Thank goodness. As soon as the stairs lowered to the tarmac, Trent grabbed his Go bag and hurried from the cabin. Cool air slapped him in the face as he jogged toward the black SUV idling nearby.

He stowed his gear in the storage area, jogged around to the shotgun seat and climbed in. "Go," he ordered Quinn Gallagher, Rio's Durango unit teammate. "Any updates?"

"Sorry, man. All we're getting is they're still evaluating her."

"What happened to Grace?" That question had been plaguing him for the past two hours. Had some yahoo cut her off or had she tangled with a deer and lost?

"She called Rio about eight o'clock, told him some clown was following her too close on Highway 18. While we were on the phone with her, the scumbag rammed into the back of her car twice, then executed a Pit maneuver. When we found her, the car was sitting on its roof and she was hanging from the seatbelt. Fire department had to use the jaws of life to cut her out of the mangled mess." Quinn glanced at him. "Her car's totaled, Trent. Might be an excellent time to upgrade her ride."

He intended to do that and more. Grace's safety was his top priority. He never wanted to live through this kind of terror again. And when he caught up with the scumbag who ran his girlfriend off the road? Well, he wouldn't soon forget Trent's face or his fists.

CHAPTER THREE

Trent strode into the emergency entrance of Otter Creek's hospital and angled toward the elevators. Rio had sent him a text with Grace's room number while he and Quinn were en route. On the third floor, he skirted the medical personnel going about their business.

He turned the corner and spotted his brother-in-law talking to a nurse in the hallway. "Rio," Trent said as he drew closer. "How is she?"

"Asking for you." The medic smiled. "She's fine, Trent. Concussion, stitches on her arm and leg, bruises, but she's okay."

"Thank God," he murmured. The relief was so great he staggered against the wall. He'd been so afraid of losing her. That sweet lady had him good.

"Whoa there." Rio grabbed his arm, steadied him. "Where is your much touted toughness, frog boy?"

"Shut up, Army grunt." He scowled, his cheeks heating. "I know it's past visiting hours, but I want to see her."

"It's not a problem. Ethan worked it out." Another grin from his sister's husband. "After Maddox called in a favor."

He inclined his head to the door at his back. "Go on in, Trent."

He sent a pointed look to the other man. "Nothing short of another world war will make me leave her side."

"Wouldn't expect otherwise. The hospital personnel know you're staying with her."

Straightening from the wall, he covered the last few feet in seconds and pushed open the door to Grace's room. She reclined against the elevated hospital bed, her blond hair disheveled, skin marred with scrapes, bruises, and bandages. She'd never looked more beautiful to him than she did at that moment.

Trent crossed to her bedside and wrapped his hand gently around hers. When she stirred and opened her eyes, he smiled. "Hi, beautiful."

Grace smiled. "Trent. You're back."

He lowered the bed rail and sat by her hip, careful not to jar her. "My team returned to Nashville a few hours ago. How do you feel?"

"Decent, considering."

"Do you feel up to telling me what happened, baby?"

She gave a slight nod. "I met Nicole in Knoxville for lunch and we spent the rest of the day together shopping in Pigeon Forge. It's been a long time since I've had a chance to do that with her."

"Nicole's your friend from college, right?"

"That's right. She was in Knoxville for a convention and stayed an extra day. Anyway, on the way home, I noticed somebody following me. I didn't think much about it at first, just thought it was someone else from Otter Creek. At first, he stayed with me, hanging back, but not too close."

"He?" Trent interrupted. "The driver was male?"

She bit her lip, drawing his attention to her mouth. Man, he was more than addicted to her kisses, couldn't wait for her to heal enough for him to revel in the taste and texture of her mouth. Yep, he was a goner. He just hoped he wasn't in this deep by himself.

"I never saw the driver. I assumed he was male. About fifteen miles from home, I noticed the headlights moved closer. When I sped up, so did he. That's when I called Rio."

He squeezed her hand. "I'm sorry I wasn't here to help."

"You did help me."

"How?"

"You insisted I save the phone numbers for Rio and his teammates as emergency contacts. Because of your forethought, I had someone to call on for assistance."

He'd been gone so much in the last few months. Maddox was right. Trent needed some time off. Hopefully, the teams training at PSI would be ready to take some of the load from the current Fortress teams. "What happened next?"

"Rio and Quinn told me to move to the right as far as I could, then gave me instructions on what to do if this guy hit me. Their tips worked." She grimaced. "It was bad luck I hit a patch of gravel and tumbled into the ditch."

"Get a look at the vehicle that hit you?"

"Black pickup truck. Late model Chevy."

"Did you see the driver or a plate number?"

She shook her head. "I was too busy keeping my car on the road, not that I did a great job. Rio told me the car is totaled."

"We'll get you something else." Something bigger and safer.

"I don't understand what I did to make this guy mad, Trent. I've never seen anyone that aggressive before. He was the poster child for road rage."

Fat chance this was a road rage incident. So what did Grace stumble into during the past week to make her a target? Whatever it was, he'd find the clown responsible for her injuries and make him pay.

"When do you have to leave?" Grace asked, voice soft.

"I'm not."

Her eyes widened. "But you always have to leave town for the next mission."

Ouch. Without meaning to hurt him, his girlfriend hit him right in the heart with that statement. "Not this time, Grace. You are my priority. I already told Maddox I'm taking time off to be with you."

"I don't want to interfere with your job. I'll be fine."

He cupped her cheek with his palm. "Baby, you aren't interfering. I want time with you. It's my choice to take a leave of absence."

"But what about your job?"

He smiled. "The job will be there when I'm ready."

"And your team?"

"They're taking time off as well. The PSI teams should be ready soon and can pick up the slack." He hoped. If not, he'd ask Maddox to send another team until he was positive Grace was out of danger and he tracked down the creep who hurt her. "You're important to me. Let me do this for both of us."

A smile curved her beautiful mouth. "Thank you, Trent."

He leaned down and brushed his mouth over hers, then settled in for a longer, deeper kiss though it was still gentle. The last thing he wanted was to cause Grace more pain. When he finally drew back, Trent traced her swollen lips with his forefinger.

"You should go home now and rest. You must be exhausted."

He was miles past exhausted. "I'm not leaving you." He held up his hand, forestalling further protest. "If I was in that bed, would you leave me to go home and sleep?"

"Of course not, but it's not the same. I wouldn't be dealing with jet lag." Her gaze swept over his body. "I didn't even think to ask if you and your teammates were okay."

"No injuries this time."

She sighed, settled deeper into the pillow. "And the mission?" she murmured.

"Successful."

"I'm glad."

He raised her hand, kissed her knuckles. "Rest now, babe. I'll be here when you wake." In the meantime, he would be watching over her. Since she had a concussion, he assumed the medical personnel would check her periodically through the night. That meant another night with little sleep for him. Grace's safety was all that mattered to Trent. He'd sleep later.

Once Grace slept, he slipped into the hall, not surprised to find Rio standing watch at the door.

"She okay?" his brother-in-law murmured.

"Sleeping."

"Best thing for her."

"You staying?"

"For now. Quinn will spell me in three hours."

Trent's tight muscles loosened. "Thanks."

"No thanks needed, man. Grace is yours so that makes her one of ours to protect."

He nodded. "Cops have any leads on the truck that ran Grace off the road?"

"Stella said there was black paint transfer on Grace's car."

"How many black pickups are in Dunlap County?"

A wry smile curved Rio's lips. "Seems like every other household has one."

That's what he'd been afraid of. This was a rural community though the population was skyrocketing.

Pickups were plentiful in and around Otter Creek. "Have you contacted Zane?"

He shook his head.

Finally something he could do. "I'll take care of it." Trent inclined his head toward Grace's room. "Stay with her while I talk to Z." Trent pulled out his phone and punched in his friend's number after Rio slipped inside the room.

"Yeah, Murphy."

He glanced at his watch, grimaced. "It's Trent. Sorry, Z. I didn't notice the time."

"It's fine. How's your lady?"

No surprise that Zane knew about Grace's accident. He suspected Maddox passed the word to the tech guru in case Trent needed Zane's help. "Banged up, but she'll recover."

"Good to hear. What do you need?"

"For you to hack into traffic cams."

"Hold a minute." Following a muffled conversation and a couple of thumps, Zane was back. "I'm ready. Where was her accident?"

"Highway 18, about 8 miles from Otter Creek."

Keys clicked. "Time?"

"Around 9:00 this evening."

"Hold." More keys clicking. "What kind of vehicle does she drive?"

"White sedan."

His friend grunted.

Yeah, he got it. Grace's car wasn't safe enough. Not a problem anymore. "Quinn says her ride's totaled. I'll talk to Bear about taking care of her." Bear was Fortress Security's car guru and the man who retrofitted all their vehicles with bullet-resistant glass and armor plating. By the time Bear finished with Grace's new vehicle, she'd be as safe as possible without Trent by her side.

"Good. You planning to keep her?"

He blinked. "Why do you ask?"

"Look, I don't want to tell you what to do."

"But..."

"But you're gone a lot."

Trent stiffened. "What have you heard?"

"Rumors."

Rumors about Grace? Was she tired of spending so much time alone? His gut clenched. "Spell them out, Murphy."

"Just a whisper here and there from a few of the PSI trainees. They're quite taken with her."

He growled, literally seeing red. "She's mine."

"No ring on her finger," Zane pointed out. "Some trainees think that makes her fair game."

"I'll take care of it. Who are they?"

Zane laughed. "Are you kidding? You might kill them and then Claire would have to visit you in prison. My wife isn't going near a prison, my friend."

"Murphy, I want their names. One of them might have been involved in Grace's accident."

A snort from the communications guru. "You don't believe that for a minute. But just on the off chance that you're right, I'll send the names along with any camera footage I dig up."

"Need anything else from me?"

"Yeah, a promise not to get caught if you tangle with Grace's wannabe admirers."

"They won't be telling anyone anything."

A sigh from his friend. "That's what I'm afraid of. Don't forget Otter Creek's police chief is Special Forces. If something happens to those guys, he'll look at you first. I'll get back to you when I find info we can use."

"Thanks." Trent ended the call and scowled, thinking of the information Z passed on about the PSI guys. Once he got the names, he'd find a way to warn them off that didn't involve a confrontation with Ethan Blackhawk. Trent didn't want to push Grace if she wasn't ready to commit. On the other hand, he didn't want to lose her by being too slow to act, either.

He sent a text to Maddox, updating him on Grace's condition. Figuring his boss would be asleep, he didn't expect an answer for hours yet. He was surprised when his phone vibrated seconds later with the boss's response to take as much time as he needed and to let Maddox know if he could help.

Trent blew out a breath. His boss was a good man and he valued his people. If no one had been available to help Trent with Grace, he knew Maddox would have made an appearance along with his new wife and daughter. Fortress's CEO didn't travel without them unless he was on a mission or Alexa was in school.

Shoving his phone into his pocket, Trent returned to Grace's side.

"I'll be outside," the medic murmured as he passed. "Rest."

Right. He'd be lucky to sleep more than a few minutes every hour. Trent settled back against the chair and tried to find a comfortable position for his six-foot-four frame.

Minutes later, a nurse opened the door to check Grace's vital signs and ask her questions. When she left, Grace held out her hand. "Come here."

Trent stood and leaned close. "What do you need?" He'd move heaven and earth to get anything she wanted.

"You." She inched across the bed to the opposite rail, then patted the mattress beside her. "Come on. You'll never rest in that chair."

"You don't need to take care of me."

"Trent, every time I close my eyes, I see those headlights bearing down on me. Maybe if you hold me, that will stop."

Even in the low light, he recognized the stubborn set to her jaw. Fine. He could hold her until she went back to sleep, then return to his post. Trent climbed onto the bed, stretched out on his side, and gathered her close.

With a sigh, Grace settled her head on his shoulder and closed her eyes. "Trent?"

"Yes?"

"I missed you."

He pressed a kiss to her temple. "Missed you, too. Sleep, love."

A little after three o'clock, a commotion in the hall woke Trent from a light sleep.

"No way, man," his friend, Quinn Gallagher, was saying to someone in the hall. "You don't get inside that room without a hospital ID."

"I'm supposed to take her for X-rays."

Trent frowned. Why would they need to take X-rays now? Grace had been in the room for hours. They should have done that kind of evaluation when she'd first been brought to the emergency room.

"Still not happening without that ID."

"Yeah, okay, I forgot it in my locker. Be right back."

"I'll be here."

Trent eased away from Grace and crossed the room to the door. He stepped into the hallway, glanced around. No one but Quinn. "Everything okay?"

"Don't know." Quinn frowned. "A guy came by to take your woman for X-rays, but he didn't have an ID. He's supposed to return."

Grace's nurse walked down the hall toward them. "Does Grace need anything?"

"She's asleep," Trent said. "A guy came to take Grace for X-rays. You know anything about that?"

The nurse looked puzzled. "I'll check on that." She walked to the desk and keyed in information. Minutes later, she returned. "There's no new order from her doctor for X-rays. Must be a mix up."

Trent and Quinn exchanged grim glances. "I'll see if I can find him." Quinn sprinted down the hallway.

Returning to Grace's side, Trent gathered his girlfriend close. After making sure his weapon was within easy reach, he eased Grace's head to his chest and pressed a soft kiss to her temple.

That was no mix up. Someone had targeted Grace again. The question was, why?

CHAPTER FOUR

"When can I get out of here?" Grace asked.

Dr. Anderson chuckled, his blue eyes twinkling. "Why, Nurse Rutledge, are you complaining about your accommodations?"

She rolled her eyes. "You know I'm not. I hate being stuck in this bed. And the food's not the greatest, you know?" She'd never tell the people in the cafeteria. Many of the workers were friends.

Another chuckle from her favorite doctor. "It's not five-star cuisine, is it?"

"Not even close," she muttered. "Besides, my boyfriend is in town. I don't want to waste a minute of the time we have together. I don't know when he'll be deployed again." Despite his assurance that he was staying for a while, Grace knew Fortress resources were stretched thin these days. She also knew Trent's heart. If the mission was a rescue, especially one that involved children at risk, he wouldn't turn Maddox down. She loved that his job wasn't just collecting a paycheck for him. Trent St. Claire cared. A lot.

"I understand, my dear. It's a good thing I'd planned to discharge you this morning. When is your next shift?"

"Not for five glorious days." Grace didn't know how she'd been so lucky to have that many days off, but she'd take them just the same. The long stretch off work gave her more time with a certain drop-dead gorgeous Navy SEAL.

"Excellent. If the headache hasn't subsided by that time, let me know. Can't have you making mistakes on the job."

"Thanks, Doc."

"Where is your young man?"

"He went for coffee. He'll be back soon."

"I see. I suppose that explains the bodyguard outside your door."

Grace's cheeks burned. "Trent is worried about my safety."

"Perfectly understandable in light of the circumstances, my dear. Well, I won't repeat your discharge instructions. You know the signs for infection of your cuts. Keep an eye on them or let Rio check them."

"I'll pay attention, sir." The last thing she wanted to do was add to Rio's workload. He already worked at PSI, the bodyguard school outside of town, and went on Fortress missions with his teammates as well as volunteering for a shift or two each week as an EMT. She could monitor herself. The stitches were in places she could check.

"Good enough." Dr. Anderson patted her hand. "I'll let you dress. Charlene will be along with your discharge papers soon."

Rio's wife, Darcy, had stopped by the apartment to pick up a change of clothes for Grace before she opened her deli.

After a quick shower, she emerged from the bathroom, dressed and more than ready to leave. Grace loved her work but didn't love being a patient. Charlene was waiting for her. "Hi, Charlene."

"How are you feeling?"

She grimaced. "Truthfully, not that great, but don't tell Doc Anderson. My head is pounding and I'm sore all over."

"I bet. You're lucky you weren't injured worse, Grace." She had Grace sign, gave her a quick rundown of instructions, then told her to take it easy.

Right. Guess she wouldn't be jumping out of airplanes or rock climbing today. Not that she would do either on a normal day. She hated heights. And yet Trent did all those things plus more, like swimming with sharks. A shudder wracked her sore body. The man must have nerves of steel.

Would he be happy long term with someone like her, a small-town girl who had no yen to be a world traveler or live in a big city? Uneasiness swirled through her. Trent lived in Nashville, was based out of there with his team. He couldn't live in Otter Creek and stay with his teammates. They'd been together for years, had served together in the SEALs. He wouldn't leave them.

Grace sighed. What was she worried about? Trent hadn't indicated he was ready to move their relationship beyond dating.

Curious as to who her bodyguard was, she opened the door and peered to the side of the doorway. Rio's teammate, Alex Morgan, glanced her way with a quick smile. "Hi, Alex."

"How do you feel, sugar?"

"I'll live," she said, not about to complain to a Special Forces soldier who'd had much worse injuries than hers. "How is Ivy? I haven't seen her for a couple weeks."

The sniper's face lit up. "Fantastic."

"Is she feeling okay?"

"The morning sickness has subsided." He grinned. "Now she's eating everything in sight."

Grace laughed. "That's a good thing. It means the baby's growing. You're a lucky man, Alex."

A deep longing formed around Grace's heart. Though she was so happy for her friends, it didn't stop the wistfulness she felt. Grace dreamed of having a home filled with children. One day, she reminded herself, she would be the one carrying a precious baby, sharing love and laughter with the man of her dreams. Was that man Trent?

"I know," Alex said simply. "I never forget what a blessing she is and now we'll have a son or daughter to love."

Trent walked toward them, a to-go coffee in his hand. "What did the doctor say?"

"I'm free to leave."

"Excellent." He waggled the coffee cup gently. "We can stop somewhere and buy real coffee."

She smiled. "I warned you."

"I had hoped the rumors about the bad coffee were exaggerated. No such luck."

"You can stop by the bookstore or Darcy's deli," Alex said. "They both use Serena Blackhawk's coffee blends. Need me for anything else, Trent?"

"In a hurry?" Trent asked.

"I'm taking Ivy to her doctor's appointment. He's doing an ultrasound today."

"Go. We'll be fine." Trent held out his hand. "Thanks, Alex."

"Yep. Keep us posted. We want to help."

"Appreciate it."

With a nod at Grace, the sniper left.

"Ready, sweetheart?"

She nodded. "I need to grab my belongings." Trent followed her into the room. Grace picked up the bag with her clothes and her purse, glanced at his face, and froze. "Trent, what is it?"

He gave a huff of laughter. "You know, I'm supposed to be harder to read than this."

"Tell me," she whispered.

"About three o'clock this morning, a man tried to gain access to your room, claiming he was to take you for X-rays. Quinn wouldn't let him inside because he didn't have a hospital ID."

She blinked. That didn't make sense. She'd had X-rays when she was admitted to the ER and Dr. Anderson didn't mention wanting more when she talked to him earlier.

"He never returned."

Cold chills surged up her spine. "What does that mean?"

"He wasn't here for X-rays. He was here for you."

"You think it's the man who ran me off the road."

Trent curved his hand around the nape of her neck. "I do."

"The hospital has security cameras. Maybe you can identify him." If Trent could ID the man, all this madness would stop. Surely Stella could arrest him with the evidence she had collected.

"I checked with a friend who works in security here. None of the cameras caught his face."

"How can that be? Those cameras are everywhere." Just because she ignored them didn't mean she wasn't aware of them.

"He wore scrubs into the hospital with a baseball cap pulled low on his forehead until he entered a storage closet. When he came out, the baseball cap was gone, but he had a surgical mask over his face."

She sighed. "Great. We still don't know who this guy is or why he wants to hurt me."

"Doesn't matter. I'll find him, no matter how long it takes. He will never hurt you again."

A promise Trent meant but couldn't fulfill if he wasn't plastered to her side. Soon, he would return to work, leaving Grace to fend for herself. "I wish I knew what he wanted."

"We'll figure it out." He dropped a quick kiss on her lips. "In the meantime, are you hungry?"

She grimaced. Just the idea of eating made the nausea churning in her stomach worse. "Not really. I'm sure you are, though."

His stomach growled on cue. "Come on. Let's get out of here. Do you feel up to stopping by That's A Wrap?"

Darcy Kincaid, Rio's wife, owned the deli that was one of Grace's favorite places to go for a quick meal. "Sure."

"We won't stay long," he promised.

At the deli, Darcy hurried around the counter as soon as Grace walked in with Trent by her side. "How are you, Grace?" She hugged her.

"I'm fine," Grace said as she returned the hug. "Thanks for bringing clothes by the hospital for me."

"No problem. What can I get you? Are you hungry?"

Grace's stomach lurched. Definitely no food for her yet. "A soft drink to settle my stomach."

"I have something better." She stood on her tiptoes and kissed her brother's cheek. "What about you, Trent? What would you like?"

Once he'd given Darcy his order, Trent escorted Grace to a table at the side of the room. He seated her against the wall and dragged a chair around to sit beside her. Ever the Special Forces soldier, always on alert.

Minutes later, Darcy returned with Trent's wraps and a drink for Grace. "Iced chamomile mint tea. Should be just the thing for an upset stomach."

"Perfect. Thank you, Darcy."

By the time Trent finished eating, Grace's stomach was more settled. "Where did you learn about the tea?" she asked the next time Darcy stopped by the table to check on them.

"Rio, of course. He researches everything he thinks might help me and his patients."

Trent snorted. "Most Fortress employees would rather puke their guts out than drink herbal tea."

His sister rolled her eyes. "Thanks for the visual, bro. All I know is Serena Blackhawk, Del Cahill, and Ivy Morgan all swear by this tea's ability to conquer morning sickness." She ruffled her brother's hair and winked at Grace. "Later, guys."

Trent threw away their trash and helped Grace to her feet. "Let's get you home."

"I've been in bed for hours, Trent," she snapped. "I don't need to sleep more." Didn't know if she could with her head pounding.

He slid a surprised glance her way. "I won't make you do anything, Grace. I thought you might need to rest for a bit. You look tired."

Grace closed her eyes briefly, regretting her outburst. Trent had done nothing but take care of her. He'd raced directly from a mission to her side and then stayed awake most of the night, watching over her. "I'm sorry." She dropped her forehead against his chest, winced when she bumped one of her many bruises against his breastbone.

"Don't," he murmured, tucking her against his side as they walked to the SUV he'd borrowed from PSI. Trent opened the passenger door and tucked her inside. Before stepping back, he leaned down and claimed her mouth in a blistering kiss. "No need to apologize. I get it. Your head feels like a mad construction worker is whaling on it with a twenty-pound mallet and your body feels like you went a round in the ring with an MMA champion. Been there. Done that. Burned the t-shirt. Let me take you home so you can relax for a while. No pressure to sleep."

"That's your prescription for healing?"

"Dim apartment, hot boyfriend to snuggle with on the couch, and a favorite movie with a chaser of over-the-counter meds. Trust me. It'll work."

"Take me home, then. But I get to choose the movie."

The SEAL barely flinched. "Deal." He held her hand as he drove to the other side of town and parked in one of

Grace's two assigned parking spaces. Trent circled the SUV and helped her to the asphalt.

Grabbing her purse and clothes bag, Grace led the way to her second-floor apartment. She palmed her keys when Trent gripped her arm and moved her away from the door. She looked over, surprised to see Trent in full bodyguard mode.

He signaled her to be quiet and inclined his head toward her door.

Her eyes widened. The door she knew she'd locked before meeting Nicole now stood ajar with a shoe print near the knob.

CHAPTER FIVE

Palming his Sig, Trent pressed Grace against the wall. "Stay," he whispered. He doubted anyone was still inside. Grace hadn't been home in more than eighteen hours. Plenty of time for the creep to search her place if that's what he wanted to do.

On the off chance the guy had hung around waiting for Grace to return, Trent didn't want to tip him off that she wasn't alone and vulnerable this time.

He slipped into the darkened apartment. Enough light shone at the edges of the curtain for Trent to make his way through Grace's home without tripping over anything. He needed to talk to his girlfriend about safety measures. No need to announce to a potential thief you weren't home by leaving the place dark.

He waited for his eyes to adjust to the gloom, then began a silent search of her two-bedroom apartment. No one hiding in the bathroom or closets. He frowned. Also nothing out of place. Was it possible the door hadn't been pulled shut all the way?

Trent couldn't see that happening. Grace was too careful for that. She worked a varying schedule with odd shifts and was cautious about her safety. Not only that, the shoe print on the door hadn't been there last week. On a hunch, he returned to the guest bedroom where she kept her laptop. He touched the track pad and the computer came to life, showing Grace's calendar.

He slid the Sig into his holster as he returned to Grace. "It's clear," he said. "Come inside to check, but try not to touch anything."

Grace dropped her purse and bag on the couch and walked through her home with him trailing behind. She turned a troubled gaze to Trent. "I don't think anything is missing. Why would someone break in and not take anything?"

"Come here." He led her to the guest room. "Did you leave your calendar up on your computer?"

"I probably did," she admitted. "I was entering my work schedule for the next two weeks right before I left to meet Nicole. I don't remember closing out the program."

"The person who broke in knows your schedule, Grace. This guy was waiting for you to pass him on Highway 18."

She sighed. "I made it easy for him to find me. But why would he want to hurt me?"

He wrapped his arms around her. "We'll find out. In the meantime, we need to call the police."

She scowled. "What for? He didn't take anything."

"He may have left prints." Trent doubted it, but the police needed to check anyway.

Grace walked to the sofa and sat. "Do you want to call them or shall I?"

"I'll take care of it." He dropped a quick kiss on her lips, then grabbed his cell phone and called Nate Armstrong. "It's Trent. Is Stella working or is she off shift?"

"She goes in tonight at 10:00. Why?"

"Grace's apartment was broken into while she was in the hospital."

A soft whistle sounded in his ear. "I'll call her. She should be awake by now. You still at Grace's?"
"Yeah. Thanks, man."
"How's your girl?"
"She's fine."
"Glad to hear it. Stella should be at Grace's home soon."
Trent shoved his cell phone into his pocket. "Stella's coming."
"Good. Guess it's best for her to take care of this since she's looking into the accident."
"Where are your paid meds?"
"Basket over the refrigerator." Grace sank deeper into the cushions. "If you need to turn on the lights, let me grab my sunglasses."
His eyes narrowed. "Headache is worse?"
"Not really. I'm light sensitive right now."
While he was in the kitchen, he shot off a text message to Rio, asking him to stop by and check on Grace. Trent's girlfriend wouldn't like it. Tough. He wanted to be sure she was okay. He trusted Rio's judgment.
Grabbing the pain meds and a bottle of water from her refrigerator, he handed both to Grace, then draped a cold pack on the back of her neck. "See if this helps."
"Thank you, Trent."
He sat beside her and gathered her close. "Rest until Stella arrives," he murmured. By degrees, Grace relaxed against him until she fell asleep.
Trent savored the opportunity to hold her without worrying about deployment. He loved his job, but the constant missions were wearing on him.
Minutes later, a light knock sounded on the door.
Grace jerked and sat up, dislodging the cold pack.
"Stay here." Trent crossed the room, weapon in hand. A check through the peephole and he put away his Sig. "Stella, thanks for coming."

The dark-haired detective smiled. "I'm glad you contacted me." She walked into the apartment. "How are you, Grace?"

"Tired of answering that question. I'll be fine. Headache, a few stitches, cuts and bruises."

"I'm glad your injuries aren't serious. You were lucky." Stella put down her black bag. "Remember anything else about the accident, Grace?"

"Sorry, Stella. Most of it's a blur."

"Not surprising. Is anything missing?"

"Not that I could tell. The only reason I knew I'd had an unwanted visitor is because my door was ajar with a shoe print on it."

"I'm surprised none of your neighbors noticed."

"Stella, Grace's computer was open to her calendar."

The detective's gaze sharpened. "Do you use the calendar function frequently, Grace?"

"That's how I keep up with my odd work schedule."

"If someone broke in after you left for Knoxville, he'd know where you were yesterday?"

"That's right. I led him right to me." She sighed. "It's bad enough that he hurt me. This guy could have injured someone else in the process of running me off the road."

"I'm happy he didn't." Stella glanced around the apartment. "It will take me a while to process your home and I'll need to turn on the lights. You might be more comfortable somewhere else."

"How long should we stay away?"

"A couple hours."

"We'll be at Rio and Darcy's," Trent said. He had a key to the house since he used it as his home base when he was in Otter Creek.

"I'll let you know when I'm finished," Stella promised.

Trent helped Grace to her feet. "Let me put away the cold pack and we'll go." He paused. "I need to do several security upgrades before I'll be comfortable with you staying here on your own. If you insist on coming back here before I complete them, I'll be sleeping on your couch."

Grace's eyes widened. "Trent, you won't get any sleep if you stay here."

"You are my priority."

"And you are mine. I don't want you going back to work exhausted. It's not safe for you or your teammates."

"There's one way to fix that, Grace," Stella said. "Stay at Rio and Darcy's for a few days. She has a huge house with plenty of room."

Trent smiled. His sister had bought a Victorian monstrosity that had been a work in progress for months. Now that the renovations were complete, he had to admit the house was a real showplace. The whole town had been buzzing about it for months. "Darcy would love to have you stay, honey."

"Are you sure?"

"Positive."

"I'll go pack clothes for a few days, then. Why don't we stop by Delaney's Diner on the way? We can pick up dinner for the four of us."

"Great idea. I'll call Darce and let her know we'll be staying with them." Suited Trent very well. That way, Rio could keep an eye on Grace without being obvious.

As soon as she left the room, Stella got to work and Trent stepped into the kitchen to call Rio and Darcy. Just as he'd expected, Darcy was thrilled to have Grace stay for a few days.

He carried Grace's suitcase to the SUV and tucked her inside for the trip to Delaney's and then Darcy's.

When they reached the house, Rio walked onto the porch to greet them. "Welcome, Grace. Darcy said to put you in the room across from Trent's." His gaze dropped to the take-out bags in Trent's free hand. "Oh, man. Delaney's. You didn't have to do that, but it's much appreciated. I'm glad Darcy won't have to cook or eat my attempts at creating a meal. My cousin is supposed to come for dinner tonight. Show Grace around while I run out and pick up a meal for Mason."

"Not necessary. We brought a couple extras just in case."

"Mason loves the food from Delaney's." He opened the door and ushered them inside.

"Oh, Rio!" Grace's eyes widened. "This is beautiful. And look at the piano."

"Darcy still practices even though she's not touring anymore. I love to listen to her music."

"Same for me," Trent said. "Don't tell her I said so. Can't give her anything to hold over my head." He handed the takeout bags to Rio. "I'll put Grace's things in her room."

"Come with me, Grace," Rio said. "You can help me set the table. Darcy should be home soon."

When Trent walked into the kitchen, Grace was setting the table while Rio dumped ice into glasses. The doorbell rang, followed by the sound of a key in the lock of the front door. Mason.

Rio's cousin stopped short on entering the kitchen, his gaze taking in Trent and Grace. He nodded at Trent, smiled at Grace. "Good to see you out of the hospital, Grace."

She grinned. "Mason Kincaid, you are the first person I've run into since the accident that hasn't asked me how I feel. Thank you for that."

He chuckled. "I figured you felt lousy so why bother asking the obvious."

"Smart man."

"How bad is it?" Rio asked. He held up a hand before she groused at him. "I didn't ask if you felt bad, sugar. I know you do. You're living in my house for a few days. That makes your health a concern for me. Spill."

"The aches and pains will subside."

"And the headache?"

She blinked. "How did you know?"

"I see it on your face."

"I should wear a stocking mask for a while," she muttered. "The headache is pretty bad."

Rio walked over to the switch and dimmed the light. "Better?"

"Much. Thanks."

"Oh, boy. Mood lighting," Darcy said as she walked into the room. She made a beeline for her husband. "Thanks for taking care of dinner."

"Wish I could claim the credit. Trent and Grace brought dinner."

Darcy beamed at them. "Thanks, guys. Hi, Mason. How was work today?"

"We made a lot of progress on the PSI dorm. The trainees should be able to live there in another month."

"That's great news," Rio said. "Maddox will be glad to stop paying the motel fees. Let's eat. I'm starving. Josh had us running the obstacle course with the trainees today."

Trent grinned. Rio's unit leader, Josh Cahill, wouldn't let his team slack off. Couldn't since they could be deployed at any time. Now that Del, his wife, and Ivy, Alex's wife, were expecting babies, Trent wondered if the Delta team would be willing to go on as many missions.

He glanced at Grace. If she was his wife and expecting their child, he wouldn't be eager to deploy either.

By unspoken consent, the dinner conversation was neutral. Nothing upsetting to Grace or Darcy. At the conclusion of dinner, Rio said, "Sweetheart, do you want to play for a few minutes?"

Her eyes brightened. "If no one minds."

"I'd like that, Darcy," Mason said, his voice quiet.

"I might fall asleep," Grace said. "The nursing staff didn't let me sleep much last night."

Darcy laughed. "You won't be the only person I've put to sleep with my music. If you snore, I'll tease you unmercifully."

"Just don't record and upload it to the Internet."

Twenty minutes into Darcy's music, Grace was sound asleep, her arms wrapped around Trent and her head resting against his chest. Trent's lips curved. If she didn't wake up when the music stopped, he'd carry her to her room.

Darcy finished playing an hour later. "Beautiful," Rio murmured.

Mason stood, kissed Darcy's cheek. "Thank you," he said softly. "I needed that tonight."

Trent exchanged glances with Rio, got a slight head shake in return. Wonder what was up with Mason? He was a good man, one who'd been dealt a hard hand in life. He'd made something of himself despite the hardship.

Trent's cell phone buzzed as Mason left. He checked the screen. Zane. He'd call his friend after Grace was in bed.

"Anything wrong?" Rio murmured.

"Z wants me to call. Hope he has information for me."

Grace stirred and opened her eyes. "Guess I fell asleep after all."

"It's okay," Darcy said. "Rio thinks my music is good to sleep by as well."

Rio wrapped his arm around his wife. "Helps when I can't sleep because of PTSD. Now, though, I get live music instead of recordings. Grace, I want to check your stitches."

"They're fine," Grace insisted.

"I want to see them for myself. Besides, I have waterproof bandages that will make showering easier." He released Darcy. "Sit still while I get my mike bag."

"Let him help," Darcy said, a soft look on her face. "It makes him happy to help you."

"He did plenty at the accident scene. Your husband crawled into my wrecked car to render aid until the ambulance arrived."

"How do you know?" Trent asked. "I thought you were unconscious the whole time."

"One of my friends told me. She talked to Rio when they brought me to the ER."

Rio returned, mike bag in hand. "Go call Zane, Trent. I'll take care of your girl."

Trent grabbed his cell phone as he walked to the back door and out onto the deck. A breeze cooled his heated cheeks. Just the thought of Grace pinned in her car, helpless, made his blood run hot. He was looking forward to getting his hands on the clown who'd hurt his girlfriend.

"Murphy."

"It's Trent."

"Finally tracked down the truck that ran Grace off the road."

"And?"

"Nothing. Sorry, Trent. The truck was stolen yesterday morning. Whoever stole it dumped the truck in Knoxville at the West Mall. He took off on foot, climbed into another black truck two blocks over with false plates. The plates were registered to a minivan from North Carolina."

"Did you get a look at the guy?"

"Nope. He was very careful to avoid looking directly at the cameras."

Trent's grip on the phone tightened. Fantastic. This clown had the presence of mind to avoid giving them a visual. "Have the police processed the truck?"

"Not yet. The Knoxville police just got an anonymous tip about a stolen truck that might have been involved in an accident."

A tip Zane had called in, no doubt. "Keep an eye on their findings. Grace is staying at Rio and Darcy's for a few days. Her place was broken into while she was gone yesterday."

"Anything taken?"

"No. Someone probably accessed the calendar on her computer which had her schedule for yesterday."

"Supports the theory that someone targeted her. What did she see or hear that she shouldn't have?"

Good question. Another good question was how far would this guy go to shut Grace up?

CHAPTER SIX

Musical chimes woke Grace from a sound sleep. She felt around the nightstand for her cell phone, squinted at the screen, and sat up, propping her back against the headboard. "Kind of early for you to be calling, Nicole. Did you set your clock wrong?" she teased. Her friend believed four o'clock came once a day and it wasn't in the morning.

"You're never going to believe this, but someone broke into my apartment."

Chills swept over her body. "Are you okay? Did he hurt you?"

"I'm fine, Grace. I was too tired to drive home after shopping in Pigeon Forge, so I stayed over." She sighed. "Guess it's a good thing I did."

A soft tap sounded on her door. Trent came in and shut the door behind him. Grace scooted over and patted the mattress at her side, grateful she'd worn yoga pants and a shirt to bed. Knowing he'd want to hear the conversation, she switched the phone to speaker mode. "Nic, I'm staying with friends right now. Trent just walked in and I put you on speaker. Tell him what you just told me."

A pause, then, "Hello, Trent. Welcome home."

"Thanks. I'm glad to be with Grace for a while. Tell me what's going on, Nicole."

"Someone broke into my home."

Trent tugged Grace against his side. "You okay?"

"I haven't been home yet because I stayed in Pigeon Forge after Grace left. The cops called to tell me one of my neighbors reported hearing strange noises inside my apartment."

"Where are you now?"

"Getting ready to check out of my hotel. I had a series of work emergencies to clear up and couldn't leave when I wanted. Now I need to see what kind of damage I'm facing."

"You know what I do for a living?" he asked.

"Not really. Grace has been cagey about your job."

A squeeze from her boyfriend. "I'm in private security. I want you to listen to me. Grace was deliberately run off the road on the way home from Pigeon Forge and her apartment was broken into as well."

"Grace! Are you okay?"

"I'm fine. A few stitches and bruises."

"I don't understand this. What a strange coincidence."

"I doubt it's a coincidence, Nicole," Trent said. "No such thing in my line of work. The break-ins are connected. We need to find out why before either of you is seriously injured."

"Do you really think Nic is in danger, Trent?" Grace asked.

"I do."

Oh, dear. She didn't want Nic by herself and facing these people. "Can Maddox send someone to watch over Nic? What if someone tries to hurt her like they did me?"

"Don't worry," Nicole interrupted. "I won't be home for long. I have to go to a lawyer's office on Monday."

Goosebumps surged over Grace's body. "What lawyer?"

"Hang on a sec." Papers rustled, then, "Washington, Randall, and Satterfield. They're in Dumas, Tennessee."

Grace swallowed hard. "Oh, boy."

"What is it?" Trent asked.

"I received a letter from the same law firm, requesting me to show up in person on Monday."

Trent hugged Grace tighter. "Nicole, why don't you come to Otter Creek? That way I can drive you and Grace to Dumas."

"Is it safe for her to drive here?" Grace asked. She didn't want her best friend to experience the same horror she had.

"How could the guy who ran you off the road know Nicole would come here?"

"But what if he's waiting for her?"

"Not possible unless he's been staying in his car off Highway 18, waiting for Nicole to drive by. I can't see that happening."

A sigh from Nicole. "I guess it's probably best if I come to you. Give me an address."

Trent rattled off the address for Darcy's home. "You'll be staying here with us. My sister, Darcy, has plenty of room. She lives in a huge Victorian house."

"What should I do about my apartment? I still don't know how bad the damage is."

"Your home is the most logical place for this guy to wait for you to show up. Do you really want to be there without protection?"

"Good point. I'll be in Otter Creek in two hours."

"We'll have breakfast ready," Trent said and ended the call. He turned to Grace. "Did the letter say what the lawyer wanted?"

She shook her head. "Only that my presence was required at ten o'clock, that everything would be explained and any questions answered. This is really strange." And she didn't like it. Once glance at Trent told her he wasn't a fan either.

"Can you go back to sleep?" he murmured.

"Fat chance of that. I'm too keyed up after talking to Nic."

"Take a hot shower to loosen your stiff muscles. I'll put on a pot of coffee. Darcy's already left for work." He brushed a gentle kiss over her mouth and left the room.

A smile curved Grace's lips. Trent was one observant man. She thought she'd hidden the stiffness well. Should have known Trent St. Claire didn't miss anything.

She swung her legs over the side of the bed and made her way to the bathroom. After standing under the hot water for twenty minutes, she felt almost normal. Hopefully the loosened muscles would last long enough to swallow more over-the-counter meds. Today, she'd have to move around to help the soreness leave her body faster.

After dressing, she walked to the kitchen, stopped short at the sight of Trent through the French doors, leaning against the deck railing. Rio stood beside him, dressed in a black long-sleeved shirt and fatigues, combat boots on his feet. What interested Grace the most was Trent wore the same type of clothes. They were both alert, watchful.

Her heart squeezed. How did she get so lucky as to have Trent in her life? She didn't think he'd look twice at her so she'd been thrilled when he accepted a ride home from the hospital after he'd been injured. She believed that would be the last time she saw Trent. How wrong she'd been. Trent had called and asked her for a date the very next day. Grace didn't regret saying yes even with her boyfriend's erratic schedule. Her own work schedule wasn't set in stone either.

She found a mug, poured herself a cup of the steaming coffee. More awake after several sips, Grace walked onto the deck. Trent turned, smiled. Oh, wow. What she wouldn't give to see that face and that smile for the rest of her life.

"Good morning, Grace," Rio said. "How do you feel?"

"Headache's lessened, but I'm stiff and sore. In other words, on track to recover, Dr. Kincaid."

He chuckled. "Just looking out for you, sugar. Did you change the bandages?"

She rolled her eyes. "I did. The stitches are dry and there's no infection."

"Excellent. Trent tells me we have another guest for a couple days."

"It's all right, isn't it? I'm afraid for Nic's safety."

"Of course it is. Darcy will love having her here." He clapped Trent on the shoulder. "I have to go. Josh has us running five miles with the trainees in a few minutes." He grimaced. "If we're late, he tacks on another two miles."

"Go," Grace said. She didn't want to add more mileage to his morning. Good grief! She'd never be able to run that far even if her life depended on it. Her maximum distance was four miles.

"Darcy left breakfast wraps in the refrigerator. Should be enough for your friend as well." With a wave, he left.

"Come on," Trent said. "Time to eat."

"Do you need to run first?" Trent was as disciplined as the rest of the Fortress and PSI people. She knew he ran several miles first thing in the morning.

He slid an amused glance her direction. "I already ran this morning, babe."

"When?"

"I was awake at three."

He'd run and showered before Trent had heard her talking to Nicole. "Did you sleep at all?"

"I only need four hours, beautiful. Rio and I kept watch through the night in shifts. He woke up early to help Darcy get ready to leave this morning. That's when I ran."

"Black ops guys must be superheroes. I'd love to be fully awake with only four hours of sleep," she muttered.

A chuckle as he opened the door to the kitchen. "Military training will help you with that."

"I'll pass. Need help?" she said as she climbed on a barstool at the counter.

"Nope. The wraps will take less than a minute to reheat." He pulled a covered plate from the refrigerator. "Do you want juice with the wrap?"

The thought of drinking juice made her stomach churn. "I don't think so." Now that the caffeine had done its job, Grace needed something else. "Do you know if Darcy has more chamomile mint tea?"

Trent grabbed the pitcher from the fridge, poured her a glass, and set it in front of her.

After they finished their meal, Trent cleared their dishes, poured Grace more tea, and pulled out his phone. He dialed a number and placed the call on speaker.

"Maddox. Where are you and what do you need?"

"It's Trent. You're on speaker with Grace, boss. I'm in Otter Creek."

"How do you feel this morning, sugar?"

"Not bad, considering. Thanks for sending Trent in the company plane."

"It's little enough considering how much work he's done for me the past year. How can I help, Trent?"

"Called to give you an update. Grace's friend, Nicole, called. Her place was broken into soon after Grace was run off the road."

A soft whistle came through the speaker. "Interesting. Any idea why the two women were targeted?"

"Not yet. However, both women received a letter from Washington, Randall, and Satterfield, a law firm out of Dumas."

"I'm familiar with them. The firm has an excellent reputation. Grace, do you know what the law firm wants?"

"Not a clue. What kind of cases do they handle?"

"Unless they've expanded their practice, they specialize in family law."

Grace frowned. That didn't make any sense. Technically, she didn't have a family and neither did Nicole. They were both adopted. That was one of the reasons why they'd become fast friends in college.

"Grace was given up for adoption at birth," Trent said.

"Nicole is in the same situation," Grace added. "Her adoption was closed like mine."

A male voice called Maddox's name. Trent's boss growled. "I have to go. Call Zane if you need help with research. Trent, watch your six. Sounds like someone might be willing to kill to keep a secret under wraps."

Just hearing those words made Grace shudder. What could be so important? Certainly nothing that she knew of, and she suspected Nic would say the same.

"Come on." Trent held out his hand. "Let's sit in the living room. More comfortable for both of us while we research the law firm and hotels in Dumas."

"Why do we need a hotel room? Dumas is only a few hours from here."

"Got a feeling your business in Dumas won't be easily resolved."

CHAPTER SEVEN

When the doorbell rang, Trent rose, palmed his Sig, and checked the peephole. He froze. Nicole's resemblance to Grace was uncanny. After a glance over his shoulder at his girlfriend, he disarmed the alarm and undid the locks. "Welcome to Otter Creek, Nicole." After making sure no one was lurking nearby, Trent stepped back and allowed Nicole Copeland to enter the house. He shut and locked the door behind her, then reset the alarm.

"Nic!" Grace hurried to her friend and swept her into a hug. "I'm so glad you're here."

"I like your town, Grace. It's charming."

Trent blinked. Charming? Not how he'd describe the place. It was...nice. Guess no one could accuse him of talking too much. Went along with the rapid-fire reports operatives gave their commanders whether in black ops work or in the military.

"It is, isn't it? I love living here. Nic, this is Trent St. Claire."

"Nice to meet you, Nicole." He took the handle of her rolling suitcase from her hand. "Did you have any problems?"

"No. You were right about me coming here unannounced." She flashed him a smile that reminded him of Grace. Did she and Grace not see the resemblance? Maybe he was seeing things. "I'm still not convinced I'm a target, though."

"Come sit down." Grace led her friend to the couch. "Tell me what you did after I left Pigeon Forge."

She laughed. "Nothing exciting. I found a hotel with an available room and went to sleep. I've been putting in too many hours at work for months."

Trent left them to take Nicole's suitcase to the room beside Grace. He figured they would like being close to each other. When he returned to the living room, he stopped at the archway and watched the two women sitting side by side.

If the lighting was low, someone might not be able to tell them apart. Same build, same hair and eye color. Their voices were different. Nicole's voice was more husky than Grace's. Was it possible they were related?

Trent's lips curved. That would make both of them happy, he suspected. Grace glanced over and smiled at him, making his heart skip a beat. Grace Rutledge had one potent smile, one he saw in his dreams every night. "Are you hungry, Nicole?" he asked.

"Starving. It was too early for me to eat when I talked to Grace. We can go out for breakfast. My treat for putting everybody out this way."

"Having you here is not a bother. My sister left a breakfast wrap in the refrigerator for you. If you prefer something else, we have a great diner in town." And listen to him claiming Otter Creek as his town when he lived in Nashville. The only reason he spent so much time in town was because of Grace.

"You'll love the wrap," Grace said. "Come on. I'll heat it up for you. Want some coffee?"

"That sounds great. I'd kill for a cup right now."

"I'll brew a fresh pot," Trent said. Once Nicole was seated at the breakfast bar with the heated wrap and a steaming mug of coffee, he leaned back against the counter by the sink, arms folded across his chest, studying the newcomer. "Know anything about the law firm?"

Nicole's blond hair brushed across her shoulders as she shook her head. "I haven't had time to do any research." She tilted her head, speculation in her gaze. "I take it you've looked into the firm."

"They handle family law."

She exchanged a glance with Grace before turning back to him. "What would they want with me? The people I consider my family adopted me when I was a baby."

"Grace told me." He looked at his girlfriend, considered whether or not to say anything. "Look, I don't know if it means anything, but have you two noticed that you look an awful lot alike? Same hair color, eyes, build, smile."

Nicole frowned. "Funny you should say that. People in college asked if we were related. You think there's a chance we're from the same family?"

He shrugged. "It's an interesting question. I suppose there's no way for us to know until Monday." Maybe Zane could look into things for him. Wouldn't be the first time the Fortress tech guru had skirted the law to dig up necessary information.

"I wish I knew what the lawyers wanted," Grace said. "This waiting is going to drive me crazy, especially now."

"Me, too." Nicole took her first bite of the wrap, froze. She closed her eyes and sighed as she consumed that bite. "Oh, man. This is amazing. Your sister should sell these, Trent. She'd make a bundle."

Trent chuckled. "She does sell them. Darcy owns That's A Wrap." Her deli was so busy she'd had to hire another worker to help with the sheer volume of orders.

"After you finish eating, we'll take you to town and introduce you to Otter Creek's bustling town square."

"Deal. I'm looking forward to it."

Minutes later, Nicole had polished off the wrap and coffee, and they were on their way to the square. Trent lucked out and found a parking space in front of Darcy's deli, a rare event in the daytime. On the sidewalk, he said, "Come on. I'll introduce you to my sister."

Inside the deli, the tables were full and the room buzzing with conversation. Several people called out to Grace and Trent as they approached the counter.

Darcy glanced up, grinned. "Hi, guys. Glad you stopped by." Her gaze shifted to Grace's friend. "You must be Nicole. I'm Darcy, Trent's sister. I'm so glad you'll be staying with me for a couple days."

"Thanks for extending the invitation. Your home is gorgeous."

Darcy laughed. "It's a work in progress. With a home that old, something is always breaking down. Makes me glad my brother-in-law is in the construction business."

"Got a minute?" Trent asked.

"We just hit the lull between breakfast and lunch. Come on back to my office." She met them at the hall. "Mason is fixing my wall in there. We can go somewhere else if that's a problem."

"It's fine, Darce. What happened to your wall?"

His sister grimaced. "The pipe under the bathroom sink burst overnight. Apparently, I need some major repairs. This building is starting to show its age, too. It seems I invested in two old buildings."

"Ouch. Sounds expensive," Grace said.

"I'm hoping Mason will give me a family discount. I'm certainly keeping Elliott Construction busy these days."

They walked into the office, Trent's hand on Grace's lower back. "How is it going, Mase?"

Rio's cousin glanced over his shoulder. "Slower than I'd like. I'll need to replace some of the flooring in the bathroom. How do you feel today, Grace?"

"Better. Mason, this is my best friend from college, Nicole Copeland. Nic, Mason Kincaid, fix-it man extraordinaire."

To Trent's amusement, Mason's attention shifted to Nicole and stayed there. Looked as though Rio's cousin was thunderstruck and from Nicole's expression, she seemed as fascinated with him. This could be fun to watch. If Trent was around long enough to see if anything developed from the obvious attraction between the two. Then again, Nicole was from out of town and leaving in 36 hours. Unlike Trent, Mason wasn't as free to travel which made a long-distance relationship difficult if not impossible.

"Nice to meet you, Mason." Nicole crossed the room and set aside her handbag. "What are you doing?" She knelt on the floor by his side as he gave her an explanation in a soft tone.

A small smile curved Darcy's mouth as she watched the two converse. "Where does she live?" she whispered to Grace.

"About an hour from Nashville."

"Too bad. Maybe you can convince her to relocate. That's the most animated I've seen him in weeks." Darcy turned to Trent. "What did you want to talk to me about?"

"I'm leaving town for a few days."

"You just got here," his sister protested. "Can't you take a few days off work?"

"It's my fault this time," Grace said. "He's driving me and Nicole to Dumas."

"What's in Dumas?"

"The offices of Washington, Randall, and Satterfield. We have an appointment Monday at ten o'clock to see one of the partners, but we don't know why. The letter didn't give any details."

"Hmm. I'll be very curious to hear about your meeting. I'm glad Trent is home to go with you, especially after your accident."

So was Trent. He felt a lot better about taking her that distance in a reinforced vehicle. He also needed to call Bear and get the process started on replacing Grace's wheels. Hopefully, his friend had something currently available. Bear always had loaners and was constantly retrofitting vehicles for Fortress.

He wanted his girlfriend safe no matter how much it cost him. Maddox paid all his employees well. Trent would gladly part with some of his savings to protect Grace. A few lessons in combat driving techniques might be in order as well. Couldn't hurt.

Would she be willing to learn to handle a weapon? Something he needed to find out. If not, he'd use some of his time off to teach her self-defense tricks guaranteed to work.

Again, he thought about his crazy work schedule and was grateful Maddox had insisted he take a vacation. Pure luck that he'd been in the country when Grace was injured. He could have called on Durango to watch over her, confident they would do whatever was necessary to keep her safe. As much as he trusted those men, though, Trent wanted to be the one to protect his girlfriend.

"Thank you for breakfast, Darcy," Grace said. "The wraps were wonderful."

"Happy to do it. Trent, since you're off work, are you interested in grilling hamburgers for dinner? I'm sure Rio would help."

"Sure. We'll stop by the grocery store on the way home. Rio and I will take care of everything."

"Fantastic. Hey, Mason."

The construction worker paused in his conversation and glanced over. "Yes?"

"Trent is grilling hamburgers for dinner. Want to join us?"

His face flushed. "I'd like that. Thanks for the invitation."

Darcy glanced at her watch. "I've got to get back. The lunch rush will start soon." She kissed Trent's cheek. "Thanks for taking care of dinner."

"Yep." He tapped her nose. "See you later, kiddo."

They filed out behind Darcy, with Nicole glancing one last time over her shoulder at Mason. Oh, yeah. This would be fun if Nicole lived in Otter Creek.

They spent the next few hours touring the town's stores. Trent breathed a sigh of relief when they walked into Otter Creek Books, the store Del Cahill owned. The wife of Durango's leader greeted them with a smile.

"Trent, you're back!" She came around the counter and walked into his open arms. "I'm so happy to see you."

"I'm glad to be here." He released her and moved her back a few steps. "You're looking great, Del."

A rosy color flooded her cheeks. Her hand dropped to her slightly distended stomach. "Thanks."

"I guess Cahill is keeping a close eye on you these days."

"No more than Alex does with Ivy. Honestly, you'd think we were experiencing high risk pregnancies or something the way they treat us."

"Josh and Alex adore you and Ivy. I don't blame them for being protective." He felt exactly the same way about Grace, not something he was comfortable discussing with Del or anyone else aside from Grace. His lips twitched. If he ever had the chance. He hadn't been able to spend much time alone with her since he'd been here.

"We aren't telling them it's okay, so don't spill our secret. Josh and Alex will become overbearing if they learn we don't mind as much as we claim."

He chuckled. "Nice. Don't worry. I won't tell on you."

Del turned to Grace, gave her a quick hug. "I'm so glad you weren't hurt too much in that accident."

"Thanks. This is Nicole Copeland, a friend from college. Nic, Del Cahill. Her husband is a teammate of Rio's."

"What can I show you?" Del asked. "We had some new books arrive today."

Grace glanced at him.

"Go take a look," he said. "I'm going to sit here with Annie and make a couple calls." A red-haired grandmother of four rambunctious boys, Del's part-time sales associate smiled and poured a cup of coffee for him.

"We won't be long," Grace said.

"Take your time." He waited until she followed Del and Nicole down an aisle, then turned to Annie. "Thanks, sweet thing."

The lady laughed. "You save that charm for your lady, Trent St. Claire. My heart belongs to my grandsons."

"My loss."

Another laugh from the lady as a customer entered the store. She greeted the man and walked with him up the stairs to the bookstore's second level.

Trent pulled out his phone and called Bear. "It's Trent."

"What do you need, St. Claire?"

"A ride."

"What did you do to my work?"

"Nothing. It's not for me," he assured the other man. "My girlfriend was forced off the road. The accident totaled her car."

"Hold." Keys clicked in the background. "Got an SUV that will be ready the first of next week."

"I'll take it. Thanks, Bear."

"Your lady all right?"
"She'll recover."
"Good. Catch the clown who caused the wreck?"
"Not yet. Vehicle was stolen."
"Sounds like the wreck wasn't an accident."
"You're right, Bear. Someone deliberately targeted my girlfriend." No matter what it took, he was going to find out who and why, and make them pay.

CHAPTER EIGHT

Monday morning, the alarm went off way too early for Grace. She groaned, felt around on the nightstand until she found her cell phone and turned off the infernal alarm that woke her from an awesome dream featuring a heated kiss from Trent.

She rolled out of bed, pleased to note much of the soreness was gone. Thank goodness. In a few days, the stitches would be gone, and she'd be left with an unpleasant memory and a couple small scars to show for her experience on Highway 18.

After a quick shower, she dressed and packed her belongings. Trent had taken her home for a few minutes the day before, giving her a chance to pack more clothes. The length of their stay in Dumas depended on what the lawyer told them later this morning. Hopefully, they would return to Otter Creek in a day or two. Grace didn't want to waste whatever time she had with Trent before he was deployed again.

She still couldn't figure out what the lawyer wanted with her and Nicole. Besides, she was scheduled to return to work on Wednesday. She couldn't stay more than a couple days.

A light tap sounded on the door. She smiled at Trent. "Hi."

"Good morning, baby." He leaned down, kissed her long and deep.

Oh, man. She could so get used to having this every day, though now wasn't the time to tell him as much. She wouldn't ask him to change his life for her. Trent loved his work and was at the top of his field. The Navy SEAL saved lives. If she wanted to be a part of his world, Grace would have to adjust to him being gone so often. Military wives dealt with it all the time. So could she.

Grace wrapped her arms around his waist, squeezed. "Have I thanked you for going with me today?"

"Last night." A quick grin curved his mouth. "You gave me a blistering-hot kiss I won't soon forget." His expression sobered. "I wouldn't have it any other way, Grace. I'm really glad I was home to do this with you."

She caught the undertone in his voice. "You're worried."

"I will be until we figure out what's going on and stop the danger dogging your steps."

"Maybe it will be good to get away from Otter Creek. Stella might figure this out while we're gone and we can enjoy being together before you have to leave again."

"I won't be leaving for a while, sweetheart. Even if I wanted to go back to work, Maddox won't let me."

Grace frowned, considering his words and the emphasis he'd given them. "Why won't he deploy you?" Was Trent's boss worried about him? Did her boyfriend not want to go on more missions?

He was silent a moment. "When operatives work nonstop missions, they don't have time to decompress and process everything they saw and did in completing their job. Sometimes it leads to repercussions."

"PTSD?"

"It's a fact of life in my profession." He stared intently at her. "Is that going to be a problem for you?"

His soft words kicked up her heart rate. Did he realize what he'd insinuated? "Trent, anyone can have PTSD. I care about you." A lot more than she could tell him standing in the hallway where any number of people might interrupt them. "On our first date, you were up front with me about your job. I knew then what kind of repercussions might come with the Trent St. Claire package. I told you a year ago I was willing to take the risk. I haven't changed my mind."

If anything, she was even more convinced he was the right man for her. Now if the man in question thought the same about her, they might have a chance at a lifetime of happiness.

His expression softened. "I'm glad. The last thing I want to do is cause you pain."

"Are you having second thoughts about us?" Please say no, she begged silently. It would kill her to lose him. Her heart would mend, but it would take a very long time.

"No. The opposite, in fact."

What did that mean? Before she could ask, Nicole's door opened and she stumbled into the hallway, bleary-eyed and pulling her rolling suitcase behind her. "Morning," she muttered. "Please tell me there's coffee in my near future."

Trent chuckled. "There's a pot already made in the kitchen."

"Thank goodness." Nic yawned, then turned toward the living room. "I'll set this by the door while you kiss the handsome prince, Grace."

He shook his head, amusement in his gaze. "A prince?"

"Don't forget the description of said prince, one I happen to agree with." Although to Grace's mind, calling Trent handsome was an understated description. Her boyfriend was drop-dead gorgeous.

"If your suitcase is ready, I'll take it to the door."

"Thanks."

Trent glanced at Grace. "Go get some coffee, babe. I'll be there in a minute."

She brushed his mouth with a soft kiss and made her way to the kitchen. To her surprise, Mason Kincaid was sitting at the breakfast bar beside his cousin. "Good morning, Rio, Mason." She eyed the construction worker. "What are you doing here so early?" Had he come to see Nic?

"I'm going with you to Dumas."

Nicole's head whipped around, her eyes wide.

Trent walked into the room, stopped. "Mase. What's going on?"

Rio circled the breakfast bar, headed to the coffee pot. "Mase is going with you, Trent."

"Why?"

The medic glanced at him. "You need someone to spell you on night watch. We have a new class of bodyguard trainees starting today or I'd go with you."

Trent shook his head. "No way. Darcy doesn't sleep well when you're out of town. I'm not going to be the reason my sister looks like she's sleepwalking."

"Then take Mason. He's helped Durango keep watch a few times over the last year. He'll provide enough security for you to sleep a few hours. He'll alert you if there's a problem. He knows what to look for and you can trust him to have your back."

The SEAL stared at Mason a moment. "You can work things out to be out of town?"

The cheeks of the construction worker darkened. "I got clearance, Trent. I'll need to check in every day and keep to the same guidelines."

Grace's brow furrowed. What was going on? There was enough subtext in the conversation to choke a horse. Nicole glanced at her, unasked questions in her gaze.

She shook her head. Grace poured coffee into a mug and took a sip. Perfect. Hopefully, the caffeine would wake up her brain cells.

"I don't know, Mase," Trent said. "I'm not sure if this visit to Dumas is related to Grace's accident and Nicole's break in. If it is, things could escalate."

"You need another pair of eyes." His gaze shifted to Nicole. "I want to help."

Another few seconds of silence, then Trent said, "I appreciate the backup, Mase."

Mason's shoulders relaxed. "My bag is in my truck."

Grace had to admit having Mason come along made her feel better. Oh, she trusted Trent, knew he was very well trained for whatever emergency might arise. She'd been around him and his friends enough to know he'd be on constant alert unless someone he trusted helped protect her and Nicole. Plus, based on the way Nicole's face lit up when she realized Mason was going along, her friend was in favor of the plan. If they had more time, maybe a romance would bloom.

"It's settled, then." Rio placed his empty mug in the dishwasher. "Now I can report to the love of my life that you have someone she trusts watching your back. I have to go. Call if you need us, Trent."

Trent saluted.

Rio chuckled. "Darcy left breakfast for you in the refrigerator. See you in a few days." He strode out the back door.

Trent opened the refrigerator. "We need to leave soon. I already have the route mapped including places to stop and let Grace walk."

"I feel pretty good today," Grace said. In fact, today was the first time she didn't have a headache since the accident.

"You won't feel good if we drive straight through. You'll be sore if we don't stop."

"Don't argue with the man." Nicole refilled her coffee cup. "His mind is already made up."

Grace held up her hand. "I'm not arguing. He's right."

Her boyfriend's coffee cup paused halfway to his mouth. "What did you say?"

She wrinkled her nose. "You're right. I will be stiff if I sit for three hours without getting out to walk. Don't let it go to your head, St. Claire."

"Of course not." The SEAL grabbed a large platter of pancakes from the refrigerator and placed it on the table along with a bottle of maple syrup.

While consuming the pancakes, she couldn't help but wonder what lay ahead in Dumas. Did the summons by the law firm have something to do with the trouble trailing her and Nicole? If so, Trent and Mason would be in the center of a firestorm.

CHAPTER NINE

Trent opened the passenger door and held out his hand to Grace. "We made good time. We have a few minutes to walk around."

Grace shook her head. "I'm too anxious."

"Me, too," Nicole said. "Maybe the lawyer will see us early. The wait is driving me crazy."

Trent and Mason exchanged glances. His friend's lips twitched. Yeah, Trent agreed. Any time he dealt with a lawyer, he waited beyond his appointment time.

They escorted the women into a brick two-story building. In the lobby, a receptionist directed them to the second floor to the offices of Washington, Randall, and Satterfield where an administrative assistant indicated for them to sit in the waiting area. Ten o'clock came and went.

Thirty minutes beyond the appointment time, an outer door opened and a tall, slender man with a scowl on his face stalked inside. He glanced their direction, then turned his back on them. Following a low-voiced conversation with the assistant, he dropped into a seat on the opposite side of the room from Trent and the others.

Five minutes later, an office door swung open to reveal a man around sixty, dressed in a dark gray pinstriped suit. "If you all will come with me, please."

Interesting. The other man was also involved in whatever was going on. Inside the room, the lawyer had chairs ready for each of them.

"Please, be seated. I'm Simon Randall. Ladies, thank you for coming to Dumas to meet with me."

"What's this about, Randall?" the blond man asked. "Who are these people?"

"All in good time, Mr. Bowen." Randall held out his hand to Trent. "Simon Randall."

"Trent St. Claire. This is Grace Rutledge. Beside her is Nicole Copeland and Mason Kincaid."

"Get on with it, Randall," the other man snapped. "I have an appointment with my tailor. I don't want to be late. He's booked solid for two months."

His tailor? Trent's lip curled. He visited a tailor to have a jacket fitted so his weapon wouldn't show. Other than that, he didn't spend time with men who wielded sharp needles and scissors like he handled his Ka-bar and Sig. Though he had stitched himself up on the battlefield when necessary, he preferred to avoid needles when possible.

Randall's smile didn't reach his eyes. "Of course." To the others, he said, "This is Devin Bowen."

"Fine. Now you've fulfilled your obligation to society by displaying good manners," Bowen said. "Why am I here?"

"Be patient, Mr. Bowen, and you'll find out why you're present." Randall turned his attention to Grace and Nicole. "I suppose I'd better start from the beginning."

He turned his gaze toward Bowen. "Hold your questions until I finish my explanation. I'll answer what I can."

Bowen motioned for him to continue.

"Twenty-nine years ago, a woman named Gayle Bowen was the victim of rape."

Bowen surged to his feet. "What are you doing, Randall? These people are strangers. You have no business discussing my mother's past with them."

"Sit down, Mr. Bowen. All will be clear in a moment."

Gayle Bowen? Trent frowned. She founded G & N Chemicals, a billion dollar company. What did she have to do with Grace and Nicole?

Once Devin sat, a scowl on his face, Randall continued. "Understandably, Mrs. Bowen, known as Gayle West at the time, wanted her assault kept quiet. She didn't want to be the center of attention any more than she already was. Her father was a wealthy and powerful man in this city."

"Did the police find the rapist?" Trent asked.

"Unfortunately, they did not."

"What does this have to do with us?" Grace asked.

"Mrs. Bowen became pregnant as a result of the rape."

Oh, man. Trent glanced at his girlfriend. He could guess where this was headed. Nothing else explained why Grace and Nicole were here. He reached over and gripped Grace's hand. Her skin was cold.

"What are you talking about?" Bowen frowned. "Mother never mentioned having a child before me. Did she terminate the pregnancy?"

Randall shook his head. "She carried to term. However, she didn't want to be reminded of the rape when she saw their faces every day so she gave the babies up for adoption."

And there it was. Trent's grip tightened around Grace's hand. "Mrs. Bowen had more than one child?"

"Twin girls. Fraternal twins."

Explained why Grace and Nicole looked similar but not carbon copies of each other. They were sisters.

"But why are we here?" Nicole asked.

"You and Ms. Rutledge are Mrs. Bowen's daughters."

"No way!" Bowen's hands fisted. "You can't be serious. How do we know these are the same girls? I demand a DNA test to confirm their claim."

"Mr. Bowen, I assure you these young ladies are your half-sisters. Though she didn't want to be part of their lives, your mother kept track of the girls, making sure they were adopted into good homes."

"Nicole and Grace's birth mother watched over them from a distance?" Mason sounded skeptical. "Why do that if she didn't want anything to do with them?"

"Although Mrs. Bowen didn't want to be reminded about the assault, that didn't mean she wasn't concerned about their wellbeing. She also didn't want the knowledge of the circumstances of their conception to damage them."

"I'm sorry for the trauma Mrs. Bowen suffered," Grace said. "Why are we here, Mr. Randall?"

"Mrs. Bowen passed away three months ago. She set aside provisions for you and your sister in her will."

Grace and Nicole exchanged glances as Bowen once again leaped to his feet.

Trent watched him as did Mason.

"This is insane." Bowen stabbed a finger in the lawyer's direction. "Why didn't you mention this when you read the will after she died?"

"I'm bound by your mother's wishes. She wanted you to have ninety days to deal with the emotional and financial turmoil in the aftermath of her death before I contacted Ms. Rutledge and Ms. Copeland."

"What did she leave them?"

"Five million dollars each."

CHAPTER TEN

Grace snuggled deeper into the leather of the SUV's passenger seat as she tried to process the announcement from the lawyer. Slim chance of that happening. She still couldn't wrap her mind around the staggering amount of money her birth mother had left for her and Nicole. The woman had given them up for adoption yet set aside a chunk of money to be delivered to them upon her death. Why bother making provisions if she turned her back on them?

Faced with the same circumstances, Grace wasn't sure what she would have done. If nothing else, she was grateful her birth mother decided to have her and Nicole. They both had good lives and, in a twist of fate, had met and become friends.

One bright spot in this bizarre situation? Learning Nicole was her sister. Maybe that's why she and Nic bonded so fast in college. So strange that both of them attended the same college and ended up best friends.

They had both been scholarship recipients. The current circumstances made her wonder if the scholarships were simply the result of their hard work in high school after all. Was is possible Mrs. Bowen provided the money for college for her daughters? Something to ask Mr. Randall tomorrow.

"You okay?" Trent threaded his fingers through hers.

"I suppose."

"You don't sound convincing."

"I understand," Nicole said. "I'm not sure how I feel about all this. Discovering Grace and I are related is amazing, but I wish I didn't know the rest of the information."

No kidding. Knowing their conception was caused by a physical assault was difficult. Grace had worked with sexual assault victims at the hospital. Their devastation and sorrow had always affected her deeply. She'd never again see another rape victim without thinking of her birth mother.

"Did you two know each other before college?" Mason asked.

Nicole shook her head. "Grace and I met in general education classes and became fast friends. We thought our birthdays being on the same day was a coincidence."

Grace gave a soft laugh. "Now we understand why people thought we were related."

"I noticed the resemblance the minute I saw you together at the house," Trent said.

"Same here. What will you do with the money, Nicole?" Mason asked.

"I don't really want it."

"According to the lawyer, you have to take the money. What you do with it is up to you."

Grace glanced over her shoulder, noted that Nic looked as uncomfortable as she felt. "The money seems tainted to me."

"Blood money," Nicole said.

"Exactly. Devin certainly wasn't happy about his mother's gift to us, either."

"Can't blame him. He thought he was the sole heir to his family's fortune and we just lightened his bank account by a cool $10 million."

Trent snorted. "I doubt he'll miss the money. My guess is his mother set aside the funds soon after you were born."

"Out of sight, out of mind?" Grace asked.

He inclined his head, sympathy in his gaze.

"Just like us." Nicole sighed.

Feelings of rejection and being unloved resurfaced. No, Grace told herself. She'd put those feelings to rest a long time ago. She couldn't let them have a foothold now. Those feelings colored everything she said, did, or thought if she didn't squash them like a bug.

Besides, Susan and Greg Rutledge couldn't have loved her any more even if she'd been their biological daughter. Grace had been doted on and treated like a princess.

She sighed. Oh, goodness. She needed to tell her parents about Gayle Bowen and the money. If the news media got wind of this before she told them, her parents would be hurt. She couldn't allow that to happen.

"Devin won't miss what was never in the main account." Trent glanced at Grace. "Do you recognize the Bowen name, babe?"

"Not really." Though she'd heard the name mentioned in the news, she didn't remember the connection.

"Mrs. Bowen founded G & N Chemicals."

"Are you sure?" Nicole whispered.

"Positive. I'll have a friend verify the information if you want."

"Zane?" This from Grace.

"He can unearth anything although an Internet search of G & N's website would confirm the founder's name."

Grace glanced over her shoulder at her sister, received a nod. "Call him. I think learning as much as we can about the Bowen family might be wise."

"People can be intense when it comes to money, especially that much." Mason sat forward. "Do you still believe Nicole's break-in and Grace's accident are related to their Dumas visit?"

Trent lifted one shoulder. "Not sure, but I don't believe in coincidences."

"How could the incidents be related?" Grace stared at him. "No one knew about the bequest."

"The lawyer knew and so did his staff. As much as secrecy is part of their work, I wouldn't be surprised if word leaked."

"What about Devin?"

"He has more to lose than anyone else. People have killed for much less than $10 million."

His theory didn't make Grace feel better. In fact, Trent's words made her wonder how good an actor Devin Bowen was.

Trent squeezed her hand, then called Zane.

A moment later, the tech guru answered his phone. "Murphy."

"It's Trent. You're on speaker. I need a favor."

"Perfect timing. I was going to call you. What do you need?"

"All the information you can dig up on Gayle Bowen of G & N Chemicals as well as her family. I need to know everything, Z. Finances, enemies, friends, future plans, the works."

"This have anything to do with Grace?"

"Oh, yeah. Grace and her friend Nicole Copeland are Mrs. Bowen's biological daughters. They were given up at birth."

A soft whistle from Zane. "I'll let you know what I find out."

"You said you were going to call me. What's up?"

"The Knoxville police have processed the truck."

Grace twisted in her seat to look at Trent. Could this be the break they needed? If the police found fingerprints, they could identify the person who forced her off the road.

"And?" Trent prompted.

"The vehicle was wiped clean. No prints inside the truck and nothing on the driver's door or handle. They found paint transfer that probably came from Grace's car so they can prove the truck was involved in the hit-and-run, but that's all."

Her boyfriend blew out a breath, frustration evident on his face. "So the cops have nothing."

"Sorry, man."

Disappointment spiraled through Grace. She'd wanted a quick end to the danger. Looked like that wasn't happening anytime soon.

"Did you have a chance to check hotels in the area?" Trent asked.

"You have a suite reserved at the Westbridge Hotel. Need an address?"

"I saw it on the way through town. Thanks, Z."

"Yep. Is Grace with you?"

"I'm here, Zane," she said.

"Are you all right, sugar?"

Was she? Grace didn't know how to answer the mysterious Zane Murphy. Physically, she was healing. Her heart, however, was bruised. Thinking of Gayle Bowen made her heart hurt. "It's a lot to process." Though the words didn't really answer his question, she spoke the truth. "I'm glad Trent is home."

"So am I. I'm here if you need me. Trent, make sure Grace has my cell number."

Trent's eyebrows rose. "I'll take care of it." He ended the call and looked at her. "Zane must like you."

"Why do you say that?"

"He doesn't hand out his cell phone number to just anybody, babe."

"How long will we stay in Dumas?" Nicole asked.

"As long as the lawyer takes to prepare your paperwork. I hope to leave tomorrow sometime."

"We have to leave tomorrow." Grace looked at Nicole. "I'm scheduled for a shift at the hospital Wednesday."

"My boss won't be happy if I take more time off. He's already griping about letting me off for the marketing conference and two extra days. I'm not sure what he'll do if I take another day or two."

"We'll get you home," Trent promised Grace. "If the paperwork is delayed, we'll come back on your day off to sign the forms. Nicole, perhaps the lawyer will send you the forms electronically."

Fifteen minutes later, they parked in front of the Westbridge Hotel, its white facade gleaming in the noon sun. When the bellhop showed them to the suite, Grace breathed a sigh of relief. Finally, the crawling sensation of someone watching them was gone.

"Is this room all right?" Trent set her suitcase on one of the double beds in the bedroom on the right.

"It's perfect. Thank you for arranging this."

"All I did was call Zane." He captured her lips with his. When he eased back, his eyes twinkled. "I've been wanting to do that for hours."

She smiled. "Me, too." They were a well-matched pair. Grace had also been wanting to kiss him all day. She missed him so much when he was gone.

"Don't tell anybody, but I'm addicted to your kisses." He sobered. "You've been feeling the eyes on us, haven't you?"

"It's not my imagination?" Thank goodness. She'd thought she was paranoid.

"Imaginary spiders have been crawling on my neck since we arrived in Dumas."

"Did you see who was watching us?"

He shook his head. "Didn't want to be too obvious about checking our surroundings and let on I was aware of their presence." He smiled. "I'd prefer to catch them off guard."

"Why is someone determined to hurt me and Nic?"

"We'll figure it out." He glanced at his watch. "Time for lunch. Order in or eat out?"

"Eat out," Nicole said as she walked into the bedroom with Mason at her heels, dragging her suitcase. "I'd love to walk around town a bit. If I don't expend some energy, I'm afraid I'll explode." She grinned. "Or worse, become cranky."

"We'll walk, then, as long as we don't walk far." Trent circled Grace's waist with his arm. "Grace is still recovering from the accident. I don't want to push her too hard, especially with that cut on her leg."

Grace sent an amused glance toward Trent. "I'll be fine as long as we don't run a marathon."

"I saw an Italian place a couple blocks from here." Mason placed Nicole's suitcase on the second double bed. "How does that sound?"

"Perfect." Nicole rubbed her hands. "I love Italian."

"Me, too." Grace sat on the edge of the bed. "However, I should walk in different shoes." She and Nicole had chosen dress pants, sweaters, and low heels for the morning's appointment. Although she didn't want to admit as much to Trent, Grace's leg was aching already. If he knew, he'd insist on driving to the restaurant. She wanted a chance to breathe fresh air and take in the feel of Dumas as well.

"Mason and I will wait in the other room. Take your time. I have a call to make."

After the men left, Nicole dropped on the bed next to Grace. She leaned close. "Tell me what you know about Mason."

She smiled. Guess her instincts were right on target. "Not much. I know he's Rio's cousin, works with Elliott Construction, and is friends with several PSI employees, and Darcy dotes on him."

Nicole frowned. "That's it? What about his background?"

"What have you heard?"

"A rumor about trouble with the law."

How did she hear that much? Nic had been in town for two days. "I don't know the details, Nic. He doesn't talk about it because he came to Otter Creek for a fresh start. I know the incident was a long time ago and he served his time. Mason is a good, kind man. If you're interested, give him a chance. If I wasn't crazy about Trent, I'd be tempted to go after him myself."

Nicole was silent a moment. "You like him that much?"

"I do. I trust him, Nic. I also know Mason was injured a few months ago protecting Darcy from a murderer. That's when I met Trent."

Her sister's gaze shifted to the closed door to the living room. "I'm impressed. No one bothered to mention that."

"There are people in Otter Creek who hold Mason's past against him." Grace nudged Nicole's shoulder. "Don't be one of them. I'm not."

Minutes later, she and Nic left the suite with Trent and Mason. Outside, the bright sun made the walk more comfortable in the cool breeze. The lunch crowd bustled along the street. Grace smiled to see Mason and Nicole walking close together.

Trent squeezed her hand. "What's up with that smile, beautiful?"

"Enjoying the scenery." She stared pointedly at the couple ahead of them.

"Should be fun to watch," he murmured. "I hope I'm around for most of it."

"A relationship may take a while to develop since Nic lives in a different town."

"True. Mason can't move without jumping through several hoops. He's still reporting in to Ethan Blackhawk every week."

The Otter Creek police chief was a tough, but fair man. No wonder he frequently dropped in on the jobs where Mason was working. She'd seen it herself a few times, heard of several other visits from her friends and patients. Mason galvanized people on both sides of the line. Some were rooting for him to succeed while others wanted to run him out of town.

The one thing she noticed for the past several months was no one said an unkind word about or to Mason when Rio, his teammates, or their wives were present, all of them staunch defenders of Rio's cousin.

When they took their seats in the restaurant around a four-top, Grace's stomach started to growl. Nice. This was the first time she'd been hungry since the accident, a sign her body was healing.

The waitress had just brought their meals when a strikingly beautiful woman stopped at their table. She stared at Grace, then Nicole before saying, "You're Grace Rutledge and Nicole Copeland, aren't you?"

"We are," Nicole said. "Have we met?"

"You've met my husband."

Grace's blood ran cold at the woman's clipped words. "Who are you?"

"Clarice Bowen. Devin is my husband." She planted her hands flat on the table. "You think you're going to cut into his inheritance? Not if I have anything to say about it. We'll fight you in court. You're gold diggers. There's no proof you're related to Devin. For all we know, you're lying to gain control of what's rightfully his." She leaned closer. "My husband and I pandered to that old bat. We deserve the money. If you think you'll get away with this, you're dead wrong."

CHAPTER ELEVEN

"Does your husband know you're here?" Trent asked the woman. Bowen's wife was a piece of work. She was allowed to behave that way as long as she didn't impose her attitude on Grace or Nicole.

"I have a mind of my own," Mrs. Bowen snapped.

"I'll take that as a no. Mrs. Bowen, you should go to your table or leave the restaurant. You're making a scene."

"What do you care?" Her tone was snide.

"I don't. But I don't live here. You do. You're the one providing a show for these interested folks."

Clarice glanced around, finally noticing the restaurant had gone silent, the patrons watching her with avid curiosity. Color flooded her face. "We're not finished with you, not by a long shot." She whirled and stormed from the restaurant, head held high.

As soon as the door closed behind her, the chatter picked up. People sent speculative looks toward their table.

"That was awkward," Nicole said. "I think Devin whined to his wife the minute he stomped out of Randall's office, breathing fire and cursing a blue streak."

Trent reached for Grace's free hand under cover of the table.

"How did she know where we were eating lunch?" Grace asked. "We didn't know we were coming here until a few minutes ago."

Had Clarice been following them? He wouldn't have missed her trailing behind them. Clarice wasn't subtle and Trent wasn't that distracted.

"I think I know how she found us." Regret filled Mason's gaze. "I asked the hotel's desk clerk if the restaurant required reservations while we were waiting for you to finish your phone call with Maddox. The clerk must have shared our destination with Mrs. Bowen. I'm sorry, Trent. I should have been more careful."

He waved off Mase's apology. "I would have asked about the reservations as well if I'd thought about it. You didn't know someone would go to the trouble of tracking down our hotel, then track us here." But Trent should have thought of that and warned the others. If anyone was at fault, it was Trent. "Mrs. Bowen might have seen us through the window from the street and come in to confront us. She intended to fire a warning shot."

"If that was her goal, mission accomplished," Grace said. She picked up her fork, poked at her lasagna. "What does she expect us to do? Give the money back?"

"My guess is she wouldn't turn it down." Trent squeezed her hand. "You can find something better to do with the money."

"Good point." Nicole forked up a bite of her lasagna. "To be honest, I'd hate to hand off the money to Devin and his wife. I know of many charities that could use donations."

A cell phone signaled an incoming call. Grace startled, dug into her pocket for her phone. She frowned. "It's the law office. I'd better take this. I'll be back in a minute." She walked quickly to the door and slipped outside, phone to her ear.

Trent kept an eye on her, pleased she stood near the windows where he could see her and intervene if a problem developed.

Within a couple minutes, Grace returned, a puzzled look on her face.

"A problem, babe?" Trent asked as he seated her at the table again.

"Mr. Randall invited us to dinner at his home tonight. He's hoping to have the paperwork ready for us to sign. I guess we will be able to go home tomorrow."

Trent blinked. Dinner at Randall's? He'd never heard of a lawyer hosting a dinner party for total strangers that he most likely would never see again after tomorrow. "What time?"

"Seven."

He shrugged off the uneasiness he felt. "That gives you a chance to take a nap." He smiled. "Both you and Nicole. You ladies were up late last night."

They looked at each other, laughed. "Hope we didn't keep Darcy awake," Nicole said.

Trent shook his head. "She didn't mention it this morning. The insulation is good between floors."

At the hotel, Nicole and Grace did opt for a nap. Mason watched a college basketball game while Trent read his emails from Fortress. Zane had sent the preliminary results of his search on the Bowen family.

Gayle's parents were Arthur and Adele Kingsly, both employed in the medical field. Grace's birth mother had married Harry Bowen and been happy with him for more than thirty years, a love match by all accounts.

Trent calculated the timeline in his head. Grace and Nicole had been born after Gayle and Harry were married. Must have been hard on both Gayle and her husband. They couldn't have been married for long before the rape occurred.

According to Zane, Devin was born two years after Grace and Nicole. Both parents and grandparents had doted on the boy. Gayle didn't attempt to have another baby after her son was born.

Devin had been in and out of trouble with the law from the time he was thirteen although he never spent an hour behind bars. The Bowen money was put to good use by keeping him out of the gray bar motel.

Based on the attitude the man exhibited, Devin might have been better served having to reap the consequences of his actions. Right now, he acted as though he was entitled to every penny of his family's fortune despite Randall's assurance that the girls were legitimate heirs. Grace and Nicole could challenge the will in court to petition for two-thirds of the Bowen estate. Maybe that's what Devin feared more than losing the $10 million.

Trent didn't see that happening, though. If anything, he thought they might bank part of the money and give away the rest.

He frowned. When people found out they were heirs, friends and strangers alike would ask for handouts. He'd have to warn Grace to be prepared. She needed to come up with a plan for the money and stick with it.

Mason turned the game down and turned to Trent. "I figure you didn't sleep much last night. You were probably awake as long as Grace. Do you want to sleep? I'll keep watch."

"You don't mind?"

A shoulder shrug. "I don't have your skill set, but Rio and the rest of Durango have given me pointers so I can relieve them on night watches in cases of emergency. I'll stay alert and let you know the minute something looks or feels off."

"I trust you, Mason. More importantly, I trust Grace with you."

With those words, Mason's shoulders relaxed. He thought Trent didn't trust him enough to watch over him or Grace? Mase should know better. He'd earned Trent's respect when he put his life on the line to protect Darcy from a killer. Trent would never forget the debt they all owed the quiet construction worker.

Trent shut down his computer. "I'll be up in an hour. Don't let the ladies leave the suite."

As soon as his head hit the pillow, Trent fell asleep. At the one hour mark, his internal clock woke him. He swung his legs over the side of the bed, fully awake. His lips quirked. Military training was good for many things, including waking on command from a combat nap, refreshed and ready to roll. When you were in war zones as often as he was, you learned to sleep every chance you got because there were long stretches where sleep wasn't possible without risking life and limb.

After tying his shoes on, he returned to the living room and focused immediately on Grace who was stretched out on the couch. Trent glanced at Mason, his eyebrows raised.

Mason left the French doors where he kept watch and crossed the room to Trent's side. "She came in a few minutes after you went to sleep. Bad dream shook her up." He cast a troubled glance her direction. "I think she was looking for you. If she'd been hysterical or something, I would have woken you."

Grace didn't do hysteria. Trent rubbed the back of his neck. He'd have to talk to her about seeing a counselor if the nightmares didn't stop soon. She needed rest to fully recover and she wouldn't take a sleep aid.

"I can hear you, you know," Grace murmured. She turned her head, smiled. "You look rested, Trent."

"You don't." He crouched beside the couch and trailed his fingers down one cheek. "You're worrying me, sweetheart."

"A few bad dreams won't kill me."

He was silent a moment. "Would you tell me that if I was having trouble dealing with a trauma?"

She remained silent.

"I'll find you a good counselor." When she scowled and opened her mouth, Trent pressed a finger against her soft lips. "Do it for me if you won't do it for yourself. How effective will I be if I'm worried about you while I'm on the next mission?"

"Dirty pool, babe."

A small smile curved his lips at her bad-tempered endearment. "I'm not apologizing for my tactic if it will get you the help you need."

"But I see the aftermath of violence every day at work."

"You don't experience the violence yourself. Seeing a counselor doesn't make you weak, love. It makes you smart enough to know when you need help processing an event. I'm not ashamed to admit I've seen counselors off and on through the years. Some missions are worse than others." Especially those that involved women and children. "I do what's necessary to stay healthy emotionally and physically."

He leaned down and placed a gentle kiss on her lips. "Will you see the counselor if I set up the appointment, Grace?"

"Only for you, Trent. I want you safe. I'd never forgive myself if you ended up injured or worse on a mission because you were distracted."

An hour later, Trent parked in the driveway of Randall's home. The four of them climbed from the SUV and walked to the front door. Trent glanced at the expensive sports car parked in front of his vehicle, including the license plate.

He sighed. Great. Just what he didn't want to see. The sweet car belonged to Devin Bowen. That uneasy feeling in his gut had turned into a ball of ice.

CHAPTER TWELVE

Grace noticed Trent stiffen beside her, his gaze locked on the pretty, sleek car in the driveway in front of Mr. Randall's house. "What's wrong, Trent?"

"That car belongs to Devin."

She paused, swung around to stare at him. "How do you know?" Grace held up a hand. "Wait. Zane, of course. I think he knows almost everything. What are the chances Clarice is with Devin?

"What do you think?"

"Near one hundred percent, unfortunately for us. I don't relish another run-in with the lady."

"I'll protect you, Grace." Nicole smiled. "I can take her in a fair fight."

The men chuckled.

Grace didn't. She knew Nic. "Hope it doesn't come to that since I have to replace my car. I don't have bail money."

"Clarice seems the type to have lawyers on speed dial," Mason said.

"Don't worry about the money." Trent's hand squeezed hers. "You're a newly-minted millionaire, as is Nicole. She can pay for her own bail."

"I'll believe the money is mine when my bank balance looks healthier."

"Same here," Nicole said. "If the Bowens can find a way to divert the payout, they will."

Mason pressed his finger against the doorbell. A moment later, a red-haired woman opened the door, smiled. "Hello. I'm Judy Randall, Simon's wife. Please, come in." She stepped back. "Simon, Devin, and Clarice are in the living room to your right."

Judy closed the door. "This way." She preceded them into a large room with leather furniture, and wooden coffee and accent tables. The Bowens sat on one of the couches while Mr. Randall occupied a recliner.

The lawyer stood. "I'm glad you could make it this evening."

Clarice's lip curled though she remained silent.

Maybe they'd survive the evening without another scene. "Thank you for inviting us," Grace said.

"Is there anything we can help you with, Mrs. Randall?" Nicole asked.

"Judy, please. Everything is ready although I'd appreciate help carrying food and drinks to the table."

"We'll be happy to pitch in. I'm Grace. This is Trent, Nicole, and Mason."

"Nice to meet all of you. Ladies, the kitchen is this way." Judy led them to the other room. She stacked china plates and the three of them plated the food. Judy shrugged. "I thought serving the food this way was easier than passing dishes around the table."

"Good idea." Grace eyed the glasses. "What about the drinks? Do you want to handle them the same way?"

"I do. I made unsweetened iced tea and placed sweetener on the table."

When the glasses were filled, the three of them carried food and drinks into the dining room to the gleaming cherry table. Judy lit the candles and stepped back with a smile.

"The table is gorgeous," Nicole said.

"Thank you, dear. I'll tell the others we're ready. I appreciate your help." She hurried to the living room.

"She and Simon are so hospitable," Grace said. "I'm glad we came."

Nicole studied the table a moment. "There are too many places set. Do you think Judy miscounted?"

Before Grace replied, the doorbell pealed. "Guess the final person has arrived."

"Wonder if this one will be more pleasant than Devin's wife?" Nicole whispered.

They didn't need more antagonism around the table. Grace was positive Clarice would make her and Nicole as uncomfortable as possible without causing strife with Judy and Simon. Not a wise idea to antagonize the lawyer handling the Bowen estate.

She followed her sister into the living room. A tall, dark-haired man spoke in animated tones to Clarice. The lady smiled and laughed, laying her hand on top of his arm. Wow. Who knew Devin's wife had a charming side to her.

Simon clapped the other guest on the shoulder. "Ron, I'd like you to meet Grace Rutledge and Nicole Copeland. These ladies are Gayle Bowen's biological daughters."

"That's not been established," Clarice said.

Grace's lips curved. Hmm. Guess Mrs. Bowen's charming side was reserved for Ron.

"Enough, honey," Devin said. "This isn't the place."

"I'm sorry you feel that way, my dear." Simon patted Clarice's shoulder. "Gayle had DNA tests run to prove as much before the girls were adopted."

Ron Satterfield crossed the room to shake Grace's hand. He pressed her hand between both of his. "I'm so pleased to make your acquaintance, Ms. Rutledge. How long will you be in town?"

"If our paperwork is finished, we'll leave tomorrow morning. I have to work Wednesday."

"I hope you'll stay over another day at least. I'd love a chance to show you around Dumas. It's a great city with many things we can do together."

Amusement swirled through Grace when she felt Trent's hand pressed against her lower back, staking his claim. "I appreciate the offer, Mr. Satterfield, but we need to return to Otter Creek."

"Please, call me Ron." He shook hands with Trent and Mason, then turned his attention on Nicole. "Welcome to Dumas, Ms. Copeland."

"Time to eat, everyone," Judy announced. "The food is growing cold."

At the table, Trent sat beside Grace with Nicole and Mason on her other side. Grace had to give Clarice credit. She was a charming guest with everyone at the table except her and Nic. She ignored them, a much better alternative than they'd faced at the restaurant. Besides, where Clarice ignored them, Ron Satterfield made an extra effort to draw them into the conversation. Judy, on the other hand, cast puzzled looks at Clarice.

"Would anyone like refills?" Judy smiled. "Save room for dessert. I made strawberry shortcake."

Grace rose when several people indicated they needed more tea and waved Judy to her seat. "I'll do refills. You've been on your feet making this fantastic meal."

"Thank you, dear. I'll keep the conversation going until you return."

"I'll help you,." Trent gathered glasses with Grace and followed her to the kitchen. "Interesting party," he murmured.

"Understatement."

He replenished ice and passed glasses to Grace. "Ron seemed interested in showing you around."

Grace shrugged. "I'd rather spend time with you."

Trent leaned down and kissed her. "I feel the same," he said against her lips.

Judy walked in followed by Ron. "Everyone is ready for shortcake."

"Sounds great, but I'm not sure I have room."

"Try a bite or two, Grace. The recipe is new and I'd love your opinion."

"I'll have to jog a few extra miles." She wrinkled her nose. "What I can run."

"Why can't you run?" Ron asked. "You injured?"

"Grace was in an accident a few days ago." Trent poured tea into the glasses. "She has stitches in her leg."

"What happened, Grace?"

Grace loaded one tray with refilled glasses. "A truck forced me off the highway and into a ditch."

"Oh, Grace." Judy's eyes widened. "Are you all right?"

"I will be. The stitches come out next week and the bruises are fading."

"What about your car?" Ron leaned back against the counter. "How did it fare?"

"Totaled."

He grimaced. "Sounds like you were lucky."

She shook her head. "Not luck. Good friends on speed dial."

Ron captured her hand and kissed her knuckles. "I'll take care of the tea. Judy told us how you and your sister helped her. You should be resting." He sent a pointed glare Trent's direction.

The implied insult to her boyfriend sparked her temper. "I'm not an invalid and Trent takes great care of me."

"No offense intended, Grace. I simply meant you did your part before I arrived. Now it's my turn to earn my meal."

"The glasses are arranged in order of the seating arrangements."

"Got it." Ron finished the task. "Go sit down with your friend. I'll bring the tea with the shortcake."

Moments later, Ron distributed the tea and resumed his seat across from Grace. Judy brought in a large tray loaded with strawberry shortcake. By the time everyone finished devouring the dessert and visited a few minutes, Grace noticed Devin looked pale. "Devin, are you all right?" she asked.

He swallowed hard. "I...don't know. I'm not feeling well."

"Dev?" Clarice looked worried. "Should I take you home?"

Devin folded his arms around his middle and groaned. "I don't think I'll make it home before..." His face lost all trace of color.

Grace glanced at Judy. "Restroom?"

"I'll show you."

Trent and Mason hustled Devin from the room in their hostess's wake with Grace close behind. By the time they reached the bathroom, Devin was already heaving.

"I need a couple washcloths," Grace said to Judy. The woman hurried off.

"What do you want me to do, baby?" Trent asked as he kept Devin upright while he vomited repeatedly.

"Exactly what you're doing right now."

"Do you need me for anything?" Mason eyed Grace's half brother with sympathy. "I'm afraid I'll be in your way."

The bathroom was only a half bath and, although beautiful, too small to handle Trent, Mason, Devin, and her. "Check the kitchen for a carbonated drink."

He left as Judy returned with two washcloths, and a wrapped toothbrush and toothpaste. "I thought Devin might need these." She handed everything to Grace, worry in her gaze. "I hope it's not food poisoning or an allergic reaction to something I served."

"Wrong symptoms for a food allergy. I doubt it's food poisoning because all of us ate the same thing and no one else is sick." She dampened the cloths with cold water and, after wringing them out, placed one against the back of Devin's neck. The other cloth she held to his forehead.

He sagged against Trent and moaned. "I'm going to die."

"Were you feeling bad before you came?" Grace asked.

Devin shook his head.

"Did you eat anything new at dinner tonight, something you haven't had before?"

"No." His teeth chattered. "So cold." He shuddered as Trent closed the commode lid and helped Devin sit.

Grace glanced at Judy who stood in the doorway. "We need a blanket."

Mason returned with a bottle of Coke. "Will this work?"

"Perfect. Thanks, Mason."

"What should I tell his wife? Clarice is upset."

"Everything upsets her." Devin leaned his head against the wall, eyes closed. "I'd love that drink."

"Only a couple sips." Grace broke the seal and held out the bottle. It took Devin a few tries to grip the bottle.

Grace frowned. "How is your vision?"

"Blurred."

Judy hurried in, carrying a blanket. Trent wrapped the cover around Devin.

Within a couple minutes, Devin's breathing became labored. Alarmed, Grace knelt beside him. "Devin, look at me."

He frowned, blinked. "What's wrong with me?"

"Grace?" Trent laid his hand on her shoulder.

"We need to take him to the hospital."

Judy gasped. "Oh, no."

Trent dug his keys from his pocket and tossed them to Mason. "Crank up the heat in the SUV."

The construction worker raced from the room. A minute later, Clarice pushed her way into the bathroom. "What's going on?"

"He needs to go to the hospital." Trent's tone brooked no argument. "Mason is warming up the SUV."

"I'm not letting you take him. I don't know any of you. Besides, it's a virus or something. He'll be fine."

"Grace is a nurse. She's the best qualified of any of us to judge how much danger he's in. If she says he needs to go to the hospital, you'd be wise to listen to her."

The woman glared at Grace. "I can take him myself."

"No, you can't." Devin's voice was faint. "You'd kill us both."

"My driving is not that bad."

"The cops don't agree. You're not driving my car, Cee."

"Clarice, I'll drive you in Dev's car," Ron said from the hall. "You're too upset to drive safely. Come on, you know I'm right."

Trent lifted Devin to his feet. "We need to get moving."

"Need help with him?" Ron asked.

"I've got him. You just take care of Mrs. Bowen."

Ron clasped Clarice's arm and urged her from the house.

"What else can I do?" Judy asked.

"A plastic bag would be handy." Grace grabbed the soda and left the bathroom to give Trent room. Judy and Nicole met Grace at the front door. Judy pressed a bag into her hand and a cold pack. Nicole had the jackets for the four of them and the purses.

"We'll be a few minutes behind you," Simon Randall said.

"What's the closest hospital?" Grace asked.

"There's only one. Dumas Medical Center. Take a right at the end of the block. Go straight for five miles. The hospital will be on the right. You can't miss it."

Grace hurried to the SUV and climbed in the back seat with Devin and Trent. As soon as she shut her door, Mason put the vehicle in gear. "Right at the end of the block, Mason. Straight ahead for five miles. Hospital is on the right."

She shook the chemical cold pack to activate it, then pressed the pack to the back of Devin's neck. He moaned, shivering. "I'm sorry. The cold helps with nausea." If they were lucky, they'd get her half-brother to the hospital before he threw up again.

"Any idea what's wrong with him?" Trent asked.

"I'm not sure." It was possible he'd come down with a virus, but she had a feeling someone poisoned Devin Bowen.

CHAPTER THIRTEEN

Trent and Mason practically carried Devin Bowen into the emergency room entrance of the Dumas Medical Center. Medical personnel hurried to assist Devin into an examination room.

Grace stopped one of the nurses and spoke to her for a moment. After a nod, the woman walked in behind the doctor. A moment later, the nurse opened the door and motioned for Grace.

"Why is she allowed in there?" Anger filled Clarice's eyes. "It should be me, not her."

"Grace is a medical professional," Ron said. "If we were allowed in the room, we'd be in the doctor's way. You want Dev treated as soon as possible."

"It's a virus and I don't want her in there. She and her sister don't want my Dev to get well."

Trent eyed the woman, disgusted at her attitude. "Grace will be in there long enough to tell the doctor Devin's symptoms. It's important he has the information as soon as possible."

Grace hadn't said anything in front of Devin. She didn't have to. Trent knew her well enough to realize she suspected something besides a virus. This was more serious. A couple minutes passed and she still hadn't returned. "We should sit down. All we can do now is wait."

"She's not telling them anything I couldn't," Clarice said. "I want her out of there."

"We'll be in the way if we stand outside his room, waiting for word that might not come for a long while."

"He's right." Ron turned Clarice and nudged her forward. "It will take time to figure out what's wrong with Dev. Would you like some coffee, hon? I'm sure I can find some for you." He flashed her a quick smile. "It might even be drinkable."

Devin's wife beamed at the lawyer. "That's so thoughtful. Thank you, Ron. I'd love coffee."

In the waiting room, Mason and Nicole were seated along the far wall. Perfect. Trent didn't want his back to the room, especially considering the animosity from Clarice. Truthfully, he didn't trust any of the players in this drama except Grace, Mason, and Nicole. He dropped into a seat beside Mason.

"Where's Grace?" Nicole asked.

"With the doctor. She'll be here soon."

Ron seated Clarice a couple seats away.

Trent's lips twitched. The lawyer couldn't seat her too far because the waiting room was nearly full. Within a few minutes, Grace returned.

"What did the doctor say?" Clarice demanded.

"Dr. Prescott doesn't know anything yet. He's still evaluating Devin."

"What does that mean?"

"I reported his symptoms. The doctor makes a diagnosis."

"If you've cost us hundreds of dollars for a simple stomach bug, I'm sending you the bill."

"Clarice, don't be unkind." Ron sat next to her and handed Clarice a cup of coffee. "Two sugars and one cream, just as you like it."

"Sit down, babe." Trent clasped Grace's hand and gently tugged. As she had crossed the waiting room, she'd been limping. "You hurting?"

"A little."

Trent frowned. Grace never complained. If she admitted that much, his girlfriend needed some pain meds. "Do you have anything to take for it?" When she shook her head, Trent turned to Grace's sister. "Nicole, do you have ibuprofen?"

Nicole unzipped her purse and pulled out a small white bottle. "Here."

Trent shook out a couple of pills and handed them to his girlfriend. "I'll be back in a minute with a drink." He looked at Mason, got a slight nod in return. Satisfied Mase would keep an eye on Grace, he searched for a vending machine. Though she would prefer water, Trent bought her a bottle of soda, figuring the carbonation would dissolve the pills and send relief into her system sooner. He wasn't a doctor, but he'd dealt with his share of pain. Black ops wasn't exactly a safe, comfortable job.

He popped the tab on the can before handing it to Grace. Trent smiled at her grimace. "Drink it anyway, sweetheart."

She downed the pills and chased them with several sips of the fizzy drink.

Thirty minutes later, Judy and Simon arrived. "Any news?" he asked.

"The doc's with Devin now," Ron said. "We've been waiting for almost an hour."

"What's taking so long?" Clarice stood. "I'm going to the desk and demanding an update."

"The nurse won't know anything," Grace said.

"She better go ask someone for information."

"She can't leave the desk, Mrs. Bowen."

Devin's wife scowled. "What kind of hospital is this?"

"A busy one." Trent's phone chirped, signaling a text. "Excuse me." He left the waiting room and walked outside. Seconds later, Zane answered his call. "Working late again, Z? You're still a newlywed, my friend."

"I'm at home. Claire fell asleep while we were watching a movie. She's using my shoulder as a pillow."

"So you decided to work." Trent chuckled. "Your wife must be exhausted. She loves to watch movies."

"Tell me about it." Zane's tone was wry. "Can you talk?"

Glancing around to make sure he was still alone, he said, "Yeah. What do you have?"

"I've been checking into the Bowens' financial situation."

"And?"

"Devin tells anyone who listens how strong G & N's financial position is. He's blowing smoke. The company needs an infusion of cash, fast. G & N has burned through a ton of cash in research and development, cash that was earmarked for dividends."

Trent frowned. "Dividends aren't required, are they?"

"No, they're not. However, the company has paid out dividends since the first year of operation. If Devin doesn't authorize a payout, the market will wonder if the company's in trouble. They've already lost stock value because of the death of his mother. If the market believes G & N is in trouble, the stock value will plummet and compound their financial issues."

"He can't borrow the funds?"

"Not if outside investors think the company's in trouble."

Trent gave a soft whistle. "When are the dividends to be paid?"

"Two weeks."

"Guess $10 million would help Devin's bottom line."

"It would definitely give him some breathing room. Why?"

"That's the amount of money Gayle Bowen left Grace and Nicole."

"Oh, man. Yeah, that would qualify as a lifeline. Won't be enough cash, but with that much on hand, Devin could borrow the rest easily. The money might be the reason Grace and Nicole were targeted."

Not something Trent wanted to hear. "Great. They will stay targets until we stop the threat."

"Do you have backup, Trent?"

"Mason Kincaid is with me. I'll be fine."

"Mason's a good guy, but he isn't trained."

"If I need more help, I'll see if one of my teammates is free. Z, I'm at Dumas Medical Center."

"Why?"

"The four of us were eating dinner with Simon and Judy Randall, Devin and his wife, Clarice, and another partner in the law firm, Ron Satterfield. After dinner, Devin became violently ill. Grace insisted we bring him to the emergency room." Trent glanced up at the light footsteps heading his direction. Grace. "I don't think this was a stomach bug or the flu. Came on too fast. Grace said it wasn't food poisoning or an allergic reaction, either."

"Poison?"

"We're waiting on information from the doctor." He held out his arm for Grace to snuggle against his side as he rattled off the symptoms.

"Hmm. All of you ate and drank the same thing?"

"Only Devin became sick."

When Grace shivered and pressed closer to his side, Trent shifted to hold her against his chest to share his body heat.

"I don't like that, Trent."

Trent heard the sounds of Zane typing over the cell phone. "Neither do I."

"Were any of you alone with the food or drinks?"

He stiffened. Trent's gaze dropped to Grace's puzzled one. "Yeah."

A sigh from his friend. "I was afraid of that. Watch your back, buddy."

"Keep digging, Z. I need to figure out who's doing this and stop it before someone dies." Trent slid the phone into his pocket. He wrapped his free arm around Grace. "You okay?"

"Got tired of dealing with Clarice's drama. How does Devin live with her?"

"I wouldn't be able to. Any news on Devin?"

"Not yet."

"Are you going to tell me?"

"You are an observant man."

He lifted one shoulder. "I've made it a point to study a beautiful woman named Grace Rutledge. Every one of her facial expressions fascinates me. Quit stalling, love. What do you suspect is wrong with your half brother?"

"I'm not a doctor."

Trent squeezed her tighter against his chest and waited her out in silence.

"I think he was poisoned."

"Any idea what the poison might be?"

She shook her head, a few strands of hair catching on his beard shadow. "Any number of things could cause the symptoms, many available to the public."

"Were you alone with the food or tea, Grace?"

Her head popped up from his chest. "What?"

"Don't look at me that way. I don't think you're guilty of trying to knock off Devin. I do think someone might try to frame you or Nicole, maybe both, for doing just that."

"What's our motive?"

"Money."

"We have money, more than we've ever had in our lives. Although our parents weren't wealthy, no one could have loved us more than they have. Despite Gayle Bowen giving birth to us, the Rutledges and Copelands are our real parents, Trent. They taught us that family, love, loyalty, and honor are more important than money."

"I know, baby." Trent trailed one hand up and down her back while the other cupped the nape of her neck, urging her to relax against his chest again. "An outsider might think you and Nicole have millions of reasons to be Gayle Bowen's only heirs."

"That's crazy," Grace protested. "Nic and I didn't know we were Mrs. Bowen's offspring until this morning. Even if we had figured out who our birth mother was, how would that tie in with my car accident and Nic's break-in? We didn't attack ourselves."

"You could have hired someone to make it look as though you were victims, just as Devin appears to be a victim."

Again, Grace's head popped up from his chest. "Devin's behind this?"

"It's possible. He might have acted shocked by the news of your inheritance this morning."

Grace was shaking her head before he finished his thought. "If that's true, Devin deserves an academy award." She shivered and pressed closer to Trent.

"Come on. Let's go back inside. Maybe there's been word about Devin by now."

They returned to the waiting room. "Any news?" Trent asked Mason.

Rio's cousin shook his head. "Think Grace might be able to learn something?"

"I can try, but the nursing staff may not tell me anything." She squeezed Trent's hand and walked from the waiting room.

Ten minutes later, Grace accompanied the doctor to the corner where Trent and the rest stood, waiting.

"Mrs. Bowen?"

"I'm Clarice Bowen." Devin's wife stepped forward. "Is my husband going to be all right?"

"Too soon to tell."

Clarice's mouth gaped. "What are you talking about? He has a stomach bug."

"Mr. Bowen doesn't have a virus, ma'am. He was poisoned."

Clarice pressed a hand to her mouth. "What about the rest of us? Have we been poisoned, too?"

"You would have exhibited symptoms by now."

"I don't understand." Judy Randall clutched Simon's arm with a white-knuckled grip. "We all ate and drank the same things. How could Devin have been poisoned?"

"That's a matter for the police to investigate. My concern now is helping Mr. Bowen survive the next twenty-four hours."

"He's that sick?" Clarice whispered.

"Your husband is lucky Ms. Rutledge was with him. If she hadn't been there, he'd probably be dead."

CHAPTER FOURTEEN

Grace's stomach tightened into a knot despite the gratification of knowing she was right. Who wanted to hurt Devin and why? Was it the same person who caused her wreck and broke into Nic's place? "Dr. Prescott, do you know what poison Devin ingested?" she asked. She ignored the venomous looks Devin's wife threw her direction.

"Tetrahydrozoline."

She swallowed hard. Easy to obtain and deadly if the person wasn't treated in time. Unfortunately for Grace, her medical knowledge might work against her in this case. She could guess what Mrs. Bowen would have to say. Then again, that information was at the fingertips of anyone with a computer and an Internet connection.

"What is that?" Clarice snapped.

"It's the active ingredient in eye drops."

"Which one of you has prescription eye drops?" Clarice's accusatory glance shifted from one to the other of the four people from Otter Creek. "I'll find out and make you pay for hurting my husband. I swear it."

"That ingredient is also used in over-the-counter eye drops as well," the doctor pointed out.

"So it's easy to buy," Simon said.

A nod. "You'll find eye drops with that ingredient at any drugstore."

"What are you doing to treat Devin?" Clarice asked.

"We've given him activated charcoal to neutralize any poison left in his stomach and we're administering fluids through an IV."

"Is that all?" She frowned. "Doesn't sound as if he's all that critical to me. I think you're trying to make Grace Rutledge appear to be a good person when I know the truth. She's a money-grabbing, horrible excuse for a human being."

"I don't know what you're talking about, Mrs. Bowen. I've never met Ms. Rutledge before today. Even if I had, I would never help camouflage the truth about anyone."

Grace winced. Clarice was rubbing the doctor the wrong way, not a smart thing to do to the man who was laboring to save your husband's life. "Are you doing anything else to help Devin?" Maybe Devin's breathing had improved.

"Mr. Bowen is also being given airway support."

"What does that mean?" Ron asked.

"He's on a ventilator. If he survives the next twenty-four hours, Mr. Bowen has a good chance of survival." He inclined his head toward Grace. "You should consider going to medical school, Ms. Rutledge. You have good instincts."

She smiled, shook her head. "I've had my fill of school for a while." Still had nightmares about waking up late, being locked out of a critical exam, and failing a class. No thanks.

"Think about it. We always need good physicians. I think you would be an excellent candidate."

Grace didn't commit one way or the other. In truth, she couldn't afford to go on for more schooling. She was still paying off her nursing degree. Maybe later, though.

If she enrolled in school, her schedule would be much less flexible. Her gaze locked with Trent's. Her available time to spend with her boyfriend would shrink dramatically. Grace protected their time together, ruthlessly rescheduling dinners and outings with friends when Trent was in town. After a year, her co-workers and friends weren't surprised when she canceled plans at the last minute. Classes and exams couldn't be rescheduled and professors wouldn't be nearly as understanding as her friends.

She hadn't talked to Trent or anyone else except Nic about this, but Grace wanted to have a family of her own in the not-too-distant future. Going to medical school would take another five years or more to complete. Plus, where would she go to school? Otter Creek didn't have a university with a medical program and she didn't want to move. She loved the town and people in her life.

Dr. Prescott returned his attention to Clarice. "Mr. Bowen is being admitted to the critical care unit where we'll keep a close watch on him. One of the nursing staff will let you know when he's settled. Only family is allowed in the room and only two at a time."

"I'm the only family he has left," Clarice insisted.

"That's not accurate, my dear," Simon said. "Like it or not, Grace and Nicole are his sisters."

"I don't want them in there with my Dev. One of them might have tried to kill him."

The doctor's eyebrows rose. He cleared his throat. "I've notified the police of the poisoning. They should be here soon. I'll let them sort this out. In the meantime, I have patients to see."

"Are you seriously accusing us of attempted murder?" Nicole asked, incredulous. "If we wanted Devin dead, all we had to do was keep quiet about the necessity of taking him to the hospital. He would have died."

"Maybe you had an attack of conscience or something. But I know someone is responsible and I won't rest until that person is behind bars or dead." Clarice stalked out of the waiting room with Ron close behind, an uneasy expression on his face.

"Nasty woman," Mason said.

"You don't know the half of it." Simon sighed. "I don't suppose you ladies have lawyers on retainer?"

Trent spoke up. "They have a lawyer."

Grace's head whipped around to stare at her boyfriend. "We do?"

He winked at her. "Trish Phillips."

Simon's shoulders relaxed. "Excellent. Ms. Phillips is well known in legal circles. She's a shark in the courtroom. I didn't realize she was taking new clients."

"She isn't. Trish is a friend and owes me a favor. She'll represent them if there's need."

Eyes narrowing, Grace recognized the ugly emotion swelling in her gut. Plain, old-fashioned jealousy. Great. She was jealous of a woman she had never met. With Trent's personality and looks, Grace suspected he had many female friends in his background.

Might as well come to grips with the fact that either he belonged with Grace or he didn't. Either way, she wasn't wasting her time and energy worrying about something she couldn't control. With his job, Trent ran across beautiful women all over the globe. Grace trusted him with everything, including her heart.

At that thought, her chest tightened. She loved Trent St. Claire. Fine time to realize the truth. She didn't know how deep his feelings ran. What if he didn't feel the same? Not a comfortable question to face.

Trent's arm wrapped around her shoulders, squeezed. When she focused on his face again, his eyebrow soared upward in silent inquiry. She shook her head. This wasn't the time to discuss her revelation. It might never be, although she didn't think that would be the case. Not considering the scorching kisses that had been increasing in frequency and urgency each time he returned from a mission, and the habit he'd developed of touching her hand, her back, her neck or hair all the time. Grace loved the touches. They reminded her of his care for her, a feeling she reciprocated.

"I'm glad you have someone to call upon for legal counsel. I'm not comfortable advising anyone about criminal defense. I focus on corporate and family law." Simon paused. "Trent, you should notify Ms. Phillips about the circumstances and that you might be needing representation for Grace and Nicole. I can almost guarantee that's where this is heading."

"I'll take care of it now." His lips curved. "Before the police arrive."

Satisfaction gleamed in his eyes. "Very wise, young man."

Trent glanced around the still crowded waiting room. "I'll be back in a minute." He kissed Grace's temple. "Stay with Mason and Nicole. I won't be long."

When he finished talking to the lawyer and returned, two Dumas police detectives arrived.

"Let me speak to them first," Simon said. "I'm sure they'll want statements from us all. You should prepare yourselves. Clarice will do her best to convince the officers that Grace and Nicole are responsible for Devin's illness and that you two young men are guilty of covering for your girlfriends."

Despite the serious warning from the lawyer, Grace thought the fact neither Mason nor Nicole corrected Simon about their relationship was interesting. Maybe it was simpler not to try and clarify the situation. When Simon walked away to intercept the policemen, she glanced at Trent. "I've never been questioned by the police about a crime. Any words of advice?"

"Answer their questions truthfully, but don't volunteer information they haven't asked. They will separate the four of us to compare our stories."

Mason grimaced. "I need to call Ethan before the detectives contact him."

"You're positive they will?" Grace asked.

"Without question. I want Ethan to hear about this from me. If the cops contact him first, he will not be happy."

"Do it now, Mase," Trent said. "Be casual as you leave the waiting room. Go outside. If they can eavesdrop on you, they will. No need to arm them with more ammunition. We'll have enough trouble convincing them we're innocent as it is without fueling their suspicions further."

The construction worker squared his shoulders and walked past Simon and the policemen. In the hall, he turned left toward the ER entrance, phone in his hand. Minutes later, he returned, his expression tense.

"What's up?" Trent asked, his voice soft.

"Ethan said the cops will take a hard look at me, might even detain me until I'm cleared of all suspicion. He'll do what he can from his end, but it might not be enough to keep me free." He looked sick at the thought. "Thinking about spending even one more minute in jail makes me want to hurl." While he spoke, Mason avoided looking at Nicole.

Grace felt for Rio's cousin. He'd paid his debt, still felt guilty for his part in the accident which sent him to prison, and yet the police might automatically consider him guilty of yet another crime? Hardly fair.

Instead of asking the obvious questions of Mason, Nic clasped his hand. "You'll be cleared. Let them do their job. If they won't, we'll prove you had nothing to do with Devin's poisoning."

If anything, Mason's face paled further. "You know about my past."

"I do."

"I'm supposed to help Trent protect you and Grace, especially at night. I can't do that if I'm behind bars."

"Nic's right." Grace moved closer to Trent's side as the detectives turned in their direction, their expressions ones of stunned disbelief. "We're friends. We have your back, Mason."

"This place is too noisy to ask questions," Nic said. "Too many people around to discuss the things they want to cover. Do you think the cops will try to find a quiet room here?"

Trent snorted. "They'll take us down to the station so we're on their turf for the interrogation. Don't let them rattle you. Expect the questioning to last for a long while and for them to repeat questions in several different ways. They'll also ask you to repeat your story more than once, hoping to trip you up and catch you in a lie."

"You aren't helping," Mason whispered. "The memories might drown me."

"Mason," Nicole said, her voice soft. "You can do this. You've done nothing wrong."

"You don't understand." He lifted his chin, faced her head on. "You don't have a record, Nicole."

"You're right. I don't. I still believe everything is going to work out."

"I hope you're right. However, I won't breathe easy until Dumas is in our rearview mirror."

Simon moved their direction with the two detectives following behind. When he reached the group, he said, "This is Detective Clint Barton and Detective Grady Weston. Detectives, Grace Rutledge, her boyfriend Trent St. Claire, Nicole Copeland, and her boyfriend Mason Kincaid. These folks are here from Otter Creek at my request. As I mentioned a moment ago, Grace and Nicole are the half sisters of Devin Bowen. His mother, Gayle, gave the girls up for adoption at their birth."

"I bet that frosted your cookies, didn't it?" muttered Barton. "Missing out on the swanky mansion, pots of money to spend on whatever your heart desired, power, and prestige. Your brother got it all while you got nothing."

Nicole scowled. "Excuse me?"

"Nic." Grace shook her head. They didn't need Nic to lose her cool with these detectives. Trent was right. These men were going to rattle their cages hard, hoping for a confession, a confession they wouldn't get since none of them tried to kill Devin. Barring that, the men meant to be as antagonistic as they could because the four of them were strangers suspected of attempting to murder one of Dumas's leading citizens.

"We need you to come with us," Weston said. "We have questions that need answering."

"Of course," Simon said. "You're working out of the Mid-Town station, correct?"

"Yes, sir."

"You'll need to speak to Devin's wife, Clarice, and another partner of my firm, Ron Satterfield. They ate dinner with the rest of us." He glanced around. "I'm not sure where they got off to. They're here in the hospital somewhere. Mrs. Bowen was understandably upset when she heard about her husband's poisoning. She won't go far when he's so ill."

Barton frowned. "How sick is Bowen?"

"The next twenty-four hours are critical," Grace said.

"In other words, he could die," the detective said flatly.

"That's correct."

"We'll find Mrs. Bowen and Mr. Satterfield," Weston said. "In the meantime, we'll start questioning the six of you, the four from out of town first."

Implying they were flight risks. Grace's lip curled. Nice. She wallowed in guilt when she received a traffic citation and these guys suspected her of attempted murder. Unbelievable. She understood how they reached their conclusions. Still didn't make her happy.

"What's the station's address?" Trent programmed it into his phone. "We'll meet you there."

"We'll follow you," Barton snapped.

"Afraid we'll skip town? Why should we? We don't have anything to hide."

"That remains to be seen." The detective motioned them forward. "After you."

Trent tightened his hold on Grace, holding her back when she would have started toward the door. Warmth spread through her when she realized he was giving Mason and Nic the chance to leave first, then put himself and Grace at their backs. In his own way, Trent was protecting Mason, giving him some distance from the cops trailing them.

The gesture seemed futile. If Mason was correct, he'd spend a lot of time in the company of the detectives or behind bars. She so hoped that didn't happen. Mason had come a long way in the year he'd been in Otter Creek. These policemen might destroy whatever confidence the construction worker had managed to cobble together.

Inside the SUV, Trent said to Mason and Nicole, "You two didn't correct Simon when he introduced you as boyfriend and girlfriend."

"I'll set them straight," Mason said, his voice tight.

"No." Nic shook her head. "We let it stand. We don't give them an excuse to hammer you on that omission."

"Nicole, I appreciate the thought, but I've known you for three days, not long enough to carry this off. If they find out I'm lying to them, the detectives will assume I have something to hide and push that much harder. I don't want to deal with that and I don't want you to, either. I'm not letting them pressure you that way."

"Listen, buddy. I'm not a pushover. I can handle them. The detectives don't need to know we omitted the truth. Tell them we haven't known each other long." A smile. "It's the truth."

Mason stared. "Truth, but not. I like it. How should I tell them we met?"

"Exactly like it happened. I met you when I came to Otter Creek to visit Grace and we haven't been dating long." Another smile. "We don't have to tell them I met you three days ago. In any case, it gives us an excuse for not knowing as much about each other as Grace and Trent."

At the police station, Weston looked at Nicole. "Come with me, Ms. Copeland. Mr. Kincaid, wait here with Mr. St. Claire. Sit against the wall." He inclined his head toward a row of hard, plastic chairs lined up like soldiers against a wall with a dull paint job.

"You're with me," Barton said to Grace, disdain in his gaze. "Let's go."

Trent kissed her. "I'll be waiting, love."

The detective led Grace down a long, narrow hall to a wooden door with a window in it. He opened the door and motioned for her to go inside. A scarred wooden table and three chairs were in the small room. The walls were plain except for a large mirror on one wall and a camera near the ceiling, its lens pointed downward toward the lone chair where she assumed a prisoner or person of interest would sit.

Barton had brought her to an interrogation room. Grace was innocent yet her heart was thumping madly in her chest. Just being in this room made her want to run and hide far away from this place. She wondered if someone would watch the question-and-answer session from the other side of the two-way mirror or watch the recording. Either possibility made her skin crawl.

She didn't want to do this. How had Mason stood being in prison for years, knowing he was being watched by prison officials, living with too many inmates, constantly on guard for an attack? No wonder he didn't want to spend even one more minute behind bars. The memories must be eating at him right now. Her respect for Mason's inner strength ratcheted up several notches.

"Sit down, Ms. Rutledge." Barton gestured to the far side of the table, the seat which faced the mirror. When she complied, he said, "State your full name and date of birth for the record." That done, he leaned back in his chair. "So, Ms. Rutledge, tell me why you tried to kill your brother."

CHAPTER FIFTEEN

"What do you do for a living, St. Claire?" Barton propped his back against the wall beside the two-way mirror, looking bored and disinterested.

Trent didn't like the detective much. The man had a chip on his shoulder the SEAL would love to knock off. Worse, this clown upset Grace. When she returned to Trent's side, she'd been shaking, skin pale, eyes damp. He ignored Barton's demand that Trent follow him for several minutes while he held Grace until the shaking stopped.

Much as he'd enjoy decking the surly cop, Trent didn't want to make things worse for his girlfriend. The detectives believed the sisters were guilty of trying to murder Devin and claim the Bowen fortune for themselves.

Trent knew better. Grace would never hurt anyone intentionally and, with her medical knowledge, if she planned to harm Devin, he'd be dead now. Grace had never shown much interest in wealth, perhaps because the Rutledges didn't focus their priorities on wealth. They taught her the value of people and integrity, lessons she learned well. In the past year, Grace didn't ask how much money he made, a question posed by previous dates early in the relationship. None were happy when he refused to answer.

That Grace resisted the temptation to ask about his salary said something to him about her character and her priorities. She was interested in him rather than his bank account.

He studied the detective a moment before answering. "I work for Fortress Security."

Contempt filled Barton's gaze. "A rent-a-cop."

"We track missing persons and rescue HVTs around the globe." Along with other things he couldn't discuss with the detective.

"HVTs? What's that?"

The detective didn't have a military or SWAT background. "High-value targets."

"Never heard of your outfit."

"We don't advertise."

"Why not? How do you find clients?"

"We don't have to advertise. Our clients find us through referrals."

"Who are your clients?"

"People who value their privacy."

Barton watched him in silence. Hoping to intimidate him? Trent bit back a laugh. Intimidating Trent would take someone tougher than the detective. The Navy had trained him well beyond tactics Barton learned at the police academy. The government had poured millions of dollars into training him and his fellow SEALs. Trent and his Team had excelled in their training.

"Fortress any good?" The cop's tone insinuated he believed the answer was a resounding no.

"The best." Other operatives clamored for Maddox to hire them. Unfortunately for them, his boss was selective in hiring.

"What did you do before you started working for Fortress?"

"Military."

"Yeah? My old man was an Army grunt. What branch were you with?"

"Navy."

Again, Barton waited. Got nothing. Frustration sparked in his eyes. "You on a submarine or something?" he finally asked.

Figuring the detective wouldn't let his terse comment rest without an explanation, Trent said, "SEALs."

The detective straightened from the wall, his gaze sharp. "You were a Navy SEAL?"

Trent lifted one shoulder. He still was. Once a SEAL, always a SEAL.

"You know I'll run your name through the system."

"You won't learn anything. My missions are classified and the military has safeguards in place to protect them."

"You could have killed Bowen."

He didn't bother to confirm the obvious. Hopefully, Barton knew enough about SEALs to realize Trent could have killed Devin in dozens of ways, including from a distance. The one method he hadn't used on the enemy was poison, a woman's weapon, something he refused to mention as Grace and Nicole wouldn't benefit from his attention to that detail.

"Why did you come to Dumas, St. Claire?"

"Grace had an appointment this morning with the lawyer, Simon Randall. I wanted to spend time with her." Leaving Grace became more difficult each time he left Otter Creek to train with his team and deploy on yet another mission. He worried when he returned from every deployment, he'd discover Grace was tired of his extended absences and intended to move on.

He'd suffered wounds from knives and bullets in the military and working for Fortress. The injuries were painful, but he'd survived. Trent wasn't sure he'd survive intact if Grace rejected him.

He stilled. Stuck in this rank interrogation room with a police detective who longed to toss him behind bars, he admitted the truth to himself. Trent St. Claire was crazy in love with Grace Rutledge. Question was, what would he do with the knowledge?

His jaw clenched. At the first opportunity, he planned to buy the woman who owned his heart an engagement ring, one large enough to warn off any potential suitors like those young pups at PSI. Then he'd convince a certain sexy nurse to marry him as soon as possible. They'd dated a year already. Trent wanted a lifetime with Grace. Maybe, if they were blessed, he'd be a father one day, a daughter who looked like Grace and a son to play catch with in the yard.

What did that mean for his career? Something to consider. Trent loved his job. He loved Grace more and didn't want to be a part-time husband and father.

"You're in love with her?"

His gut clenched. "Not your business, Detective."

"On the contrary. In a murder investigation, everything is my business. If you're in love with Blondie, you have motive to cover or kill for her." A cold smile stretched across Barton's face. "And now I know you have the skill to neutralize a threat to your woman."

"If Grace's life was in danger, I would use every skill in my arsenal to protect her without an ounce of remorse. But to kill for money?" Trent shook his head. "Never happen."

"Oh, come on, St. Claire. You're a high-priced assassin. I bet if Blondie batted her pretty lashes at you and promised you pots full of money to spend, you'd do just about anything."

"I'm not hearing any questions, Barton. Start asking or I'm walking out of here with my friends."

"Tell me what happened at the Randall house tonight. Walk me through the evening from the time you arrived there until you brought the vic to the hospital."

Trent recounted the events of the evening in rapid-fire fashion. Years of giving situation reports for his SEAL commanders and then for Maddox made his recitation of events a condensed version. If Barton wanted details, he would have to ask for them.

"How long was Blondie alone with the food and drinks?"

"Her name is Grace." Trent's soft tone elicited a slight flinch from the cop. "To my knowledge, she was never alone in the kitchen or dining room."

"Same for her sister?"

"That's right."

"What about the sister's boyfriend?"

"Mason was never in the kitchen." His lip curled on one side. "You going to ask if I was in the kitchen, Detective?"

Another scowl came at his words. "Were you?"

"I helped Grace with tea refills and stole a kiss."

More frustration on the cop's face. "You realize we've sent a crime scene team to the Randall home."

"I'd be surprised if you hadn't."

"We will find out who did this. I don't care which of the four of you is guilty or if all of you are guilty. I'll throw you in jail and toss away the keys."

"I guess your mind is made up." Trent wasn't surprised although he was disappointed the detective wouldn't consider a different alternative. Didn't bode well for Mason with his record. "Are we finished, Barton?"

"Not even close. Let's go through the night's events again."

By the time Barton reluctantly allowed Trent to leave the interrogation room with a stern warning to stay available for further questions, Trent was as frustrated as the detective and hungry enough to eat a side of beef.

When he walked into the bullpen, his gaze tracked automatically to Grace. His heart turned over in his chest.

He longed to be alone with her even if only for a few minutes. Relief filled her gaze at the sight of him. Yeah, he was crazy about that beautiful woman and wanted to marry her, soon. He'd waited long enough to make Grace Rutledge his.

That's when he noticed Mason was still being interviewed. Not good. He felt for the guy. Weston would push harder with Mason because of his record. Even people in Otter Creek who didn't know Mase assumed he hadn't changed his ways. How quickly would Weston call Ethan Blackhawk and would he shove Rio's cousin behind bars while he made the contact? The way things were trending, Trent wouldn't be surprised if Weston tossed Mase in jail and neglected to call Blackhawk for a day or two.

His suspicion was confirmed when Mason walked into the bullpen, hands cuffed behind his back. Weston's hand clenched his arm, guiding Mase toward the double doors. Crap. Not what Trent wanted to see.

Nicole jumped to her feet and intercepted them. "What's going on, Weston? Why is my boyfriend in handcuffs?"

"He's spending a little time as our guest while I check with his parole officer."

"Nicole, it's all right." Resignation filled Mason's face.

"No, it's not. You didn't do anything wrong. You're a free man and Weston can't throw you in jail because he feels like it."

The detective scowled. "He's a flight risk."

She snorted. "None of us live here. You tossing all of us in jail, too?"

"Don't tempt me."

Amusement wound through Trent. Seemed Grace's sister had butted heads with the cop. Very nice. Trent found himself liking his future sister-in-law more and more.

"You have thirty minutes to call his parole officer, Detective." Nicole wrapped her arms around Mason's waist.

"If you haven't released him by that time, you'll be hearing from his lawyer. Mason better be in a holding cell by himself. If he comes back to me with so much as one hair out of place, the Dumas Police Department will be looking at a lawsuit."

"Baby, stop." Mason pressed a kiss to her temple. "I'll be fine. I promise."

"You better be." After a fierce glare at the detective watching their every move, Nicole stood on her tiptoes and touched her lips to his. She stepped back. "Clock's ticking, Detective."

Weston muttered under his breath about mule-headed women and nudged Mason toward the door.

As soon as the door closed behind the men, Nicole sat in the nearest seat and covered her face with her hands.

"Are you okay, Nic?" Grace sat beside her sister and wrapped an arm around her shoulder.

"I don't know. Will Mason be mad that I kissed him?"

Trent crouched beside her chair. "Didn't look like he objected to me. In fact, I'd say he wouldn't mind a real kiss when you don't have an audience."

Her face lit up. "I'd like more kisses from Mason. I've been in a kissing drought for months."

Grace frowned. "What happened to Ivan?"

"We broke up."

"I'm sorry, Nic."

"I'm not." Her gaze shifted to the door through which Mason had walked. "Especially now."

Trent stood. "Do either of you want a soft drink? I saw a vending machine as we walked into the station."

"That sounds perfect." Nicole's lips curved as she looked at her sister. "I know your answer. A bottle of water."

Grace's cheeks flushed. "So I like water."

"Your water consumption resembles that of a camel."

"Did you know a farmer who lives outside Otter Creek has a couple camels?" Trent figured his girlfriend would appreciate a change of subject.

Nicole's mouth gaped. "You're serious?"

"Grace can tell you about them. I'll be back in a minute with the drinks."

The outer hallway and lobby were quiet at this time of morning. Glancing out the front windows, he noted the Randall vehicle was gone. He snorted. Simon and Judy must not have been considered serious suspects. No doubt Randall had power in this city. From what Trent read, the law firm represented the most powerful people and companies in Dumas and the surrounding counties.

He located the vending machine, made his selections, and returned to the bullpen. By the time they had finished their drinks, the time limit Nicole set for Weston to call Blackhawk expired.

She sent a dark look toward the detective's empty chair. "Where is that man?"

"If he's smart, hiding from you." Grace nudged her sister's shoulder. "You probably scared him off."

Trent glanced up as the double doors opened again. Weston led a still cuffed Mason into the large room.

Nicole jumped to her feet and hurried across the floor. "Well?" she demanded of the detective.

"His parole officer vouched for him. I'm still not convinced Kincaid isn't guilty of this crime."

"But you don't have any proof."

"I'll find it."

"Good luck with that, Detective, because he didn't poison Devin and neither did the rest of us." She stared pointedly at Mason's restrained hands. "Get the cuffs off of him. Now." Once Rio's cousin was freed of the restraints, she asked, "Is Mason free to go?"

"Yeah. For now."

Nicole circled Mason's waist with her arm and turned him toward the doors to the lobby.

"You'll be seeing me again, Kincaid," Weston said.

Neither Nicole nor Mason bothered to respond to the detective's warning. Weston eyed Trent and Grace. "Where are you staying? We will have more questions for you."

Trent gave the name of their hotel.

"Phone number?"

He smiled. No way was he giving the cop his private cell phone number. Very few people had that number, Grace being one of them. He gave Weston the main number at Fortress. "I can't always answer my phone, Detective. I might be deployed for another mission at any time." He doubted the latter as his boss insisted he take a break from work, but the possibility existed if hot spots popped up around the globe and Maddox didn't have enough available teams. "Tell whoever answers the phone you want me to call. They'll see I get the message. Don't bother asking for Grace's number. You won't get it." The bullpen went silent.

When it had become obvious that he and Grace were in a long-term relationship, Trent bought her a secured cell phone through Fortress so they could talk or text when he was deployed. That way her safety and his weren't compromised should someone try listening to their conversations electronically.

Fury burned in Weston's eyes. "I ought to arrest you for obstruction of justice, St. Claire."

"But you won't because it'd be a waste of your time and would bring a lawsuit. I'm not hindering your investigation, merely delaying contact by minutes if I'm still in the country. If I'm not, a phone call at the wrong time could cost my life and those of my team. You don't want that on your conscience."

"Get out of here, St. Claire."

Trent pressed his hand against Grace's lower back and nudged her forward. Once the double doors closed again, the noise the in bullpen resumed. The lobby was empty.

"Where are Mason and Nic?" Grace whispered.

He shook his head. "Maybe outside." He hoped Rio's cousin remembered Nicole was still a target. Now that he and Trent were known to be involved with the women, both of them were also under scrutiny. The desk sergeant watched them with suspicion.

Outside the glass doors, Mason stood with his arms wrapped around Nicole. Or maybe she was the one holding him. Hard to tell from this angle. The one thing Trent knew without a doubt? Mase was holding on by a thread. He needed a safe place to decompress, fast.

"Let's get out of here, babe." He escorted her from the building. "Ready?" he asked the other couple.

"More than." Nicole wrapped her hand around Mason's. "I'm starving. Is there any chance the hotel kitchen is still open?"

"Doubtful. We'll look a drive-thru still open on the way to the hotel. If we're not successful, I'll go back out after I drop off you three."

The ride back to the hotel was silent. Trent kept an eye on the mirrors and his passengers. Since he hadn't located a fast-food place still open, he stopped in front of the hotel. "I'll be back as soon as I can." He kissed Grace. "Don't leave the suite or open the door for anyone but me."

"Be careful, sweetheart."

His heart skipped a beat. Man, he could so get used to hearing that from her sweet lips for the rest of his life. Once the three of them were safely inside the hotel lobby, Trent drove the opposite direction from which they'd come.

He found a fast-food place with an open drive-thru window. Minutes later, he left the restaurant's lot. As he made the turn into the hotel's parking lot, a loud crack sounded and the driver's side window spiderwebbed.

CHAPTER SIXTEEN

Trent stomped on the gas pedal and shot into the hotel's parking garage. He parked away from the entrance and grabbed his Sig, alert to the possibility the shooter might have slipped into the garage and waited in the shadows. No one stepped from the shadows with a weapon pointed his direction.

At the entrance, Trent hugged the deepest pockets of darkness and found what he expected to find. Nothing. The shooter had left when he failed in his objective. Trent holstered his weapon. He scanned the area where his SUV had been hit and estimated the angle of the shot.

He considered hunting for a shell casing. Trent opted to retrieve the food growing colder by the minute. His better option was to wait for daylight. The area he wanted to explore was dark and he would draw less attention if he wasn't pacing back and forth with a flashlight. If the shooter was a professional, he would have policed his brass, leaving Trent nothing to find. If he was an amateur, he likely panicked and fled the area. Chances were good the shell casing would still be there at dawn.

As he rode the elevator, Trent thought about calling the cops to report the incident, rejected it almost before the idea was fully formed. He was out the price of a window and wasn't injured. He could just imagine the response from Barton and Weston. A mixture of disdain and disbelief that a Navy SEAL was calling them about an alleged shooting. They already believed Grace and Nicole attempted to murder Devin, and suspected he and Mase might be involved as well. Trent doubted the detectives would put themselves out. There were no witnesses and he could have shot his own window once he was parked to throw suspicion off himself.

No, he'd take care of this himself. If he scored a shell casing, Trent would send it to one of the labs Fortress used. He didn't have the same constraints as law enforcement. All he needed was a direction to go looking for a motive to murder Devin Bowen and possibly his half sisters. Once he had the motive, Trent would find the necessary proof to hand over to the police after he neutralized the threat to his girlfriend and her sister.

He unlocked the door to the suite. Mason and Nicole weren't in sight. A ball of ice formed in his stomach. They weren't supposed to leave. In light of the shooting incident, Trent worried they might run into more trouble than they could handle. Maybe the shooter had gone after easier prey. Where could they be?

Grace got up from the couch, took one look at Trent's face, and said, "What happened?"

"Where are Mase and your sister?"

Her eyes narrowed. "On the balcony. Mason took a shower as soon as we arrived in the suite, but was still feeling claustrophobic when he returned to the living room. Nic is keeping him company." She took the bags of food and set them on the breakfast bar that separated the kitchenette from the living room. "Trent, what's wrong?"

He wrapped her in a tight embrace. "When I turned into the entrance of the garage, someone shot at the SUV." When she jerked, Trent tugged her closer. "I'm fine. I'll need a window replaced, but that's the only damage." Hopefully, Bear would have the window in stock. The damaged window was vulnerable to shattering with its integrity compromised. He'd send Bear a text after they ate, tell the car guru Trent's SUV needed repairs completed as soon as possible. He couldn't afford to leave the window as it was. Grace's life was at stake as well as the lives of the others.

"I want to see the damage."

Trent pulled back enough to see her face. What little color she'd regained since they left the police station was gone, leaving behind an icy pallor. "Can you wait until morning?"

"I don't want to wait. Show me your vehicle." A stubborn light gleamed in her eyes. What bothered him the most was the hint of dampness gathering there.

Trent studied her expression, considering his options. In the end he only had one he could live with since he wanted Grace as his partner for life. Should be safe enough to take her to the garage since the shooter was probably long gone. If the shooter had sneaked into the enclosure, he would have shot at Trent as he approached the entrance.

A further plus? By giving in now, Trent and the others would be able to eat sooner and get some sleep afterward. "Let me tell Mase where we're going." Despite the trauma from being behind bars even for a short while, Mason wouldn't allow anything to happen to Nicole. Knowing Trent was away from the suite would galvanize him into careful vigilance.

After a quick conversation with Mason and Nicole, Trent escorted Grace to the elevator and down to the garage where his SUV was parked. He was silent while she examined the window, saw the exact moment when she realized how close he'd come to being shot and possibly killed. If the SUV wasn't equipped for safety, he wouldn't be alive right now.

"Trent." Grace's voice broke. "I could have lost you."

He cupped her beautiful face between the palms of his hands. "You didn't. I don't have a scratch on me."

She said nothing for a moment. "If the killer had succeeded, I wouldn't have been able to tell you something I've been holding back."

Trent stilled. Holding back? What secret had Grace been keeping? Uneasiness coiled in his gut, he prayed Grace hadn't decided the risks he took on the job and off were too great for her to tolerate. "Tell me now."

"I love you, Trent St. Claire. I'm sorry if it's too soon or if the knowledge sends you into a panic, but I want you to know how I feel. I couldn't live with myself if something happened to you and you didn't know what joy you bring to my life. I hope if you're ever seriously injured, you take strength and comfort from my words and my love, and fight with everything you have to come back to me."

He closed his eyes, pressed his forehead to hers as relief swept over him in a tidal wave. "Thank God," he murmured. "It's not too soon to tell me you love me."

"It's not?"

"I've been holding back a secret as well. I'm head-over-heels in love with you, Grace Rutledge. I think I have been for months. I'm grateful you didn't give up on me or find someone who is home more while I was in a cesspool attempting a rescue and protecting my teammates."

"Never. I would never give up on you, love." She wrapped her arms around his neck and drew his head down to hers. A long, hot, deep kiss later, Grace said, "Come on. Let's return to the suite. You must be hungry."

The way she said that and the words she chose made him pause. "Aren't you?"

She shook her head. "The prospect of eating makes me feel a little sick." A grin appeared. "I wouldn't be opposed to another kiss or two or perhaps a dozen."

Trent chuckled. "Want more kisses from me, do you?"

"Oh, I definitely want a lot more. They might even stoke my appetite for food."

Using a bribe since he was concerned about her calorie intake? He grinned. "I'll see what I can do." Definitely not a hardship on his part. When he'd been keeping watch deep in the night on many missions, Trent remembered kisses Grace shared with him and longed for more. Yeah, he wouldn't mind sharing a lifetime more of those addicting kisses with Grace.

Back in the suite, Nicole was pulling hamburgers and French fries from the bags and dividing the food on the breakfast bar. "Drinks?" she asked Trent.

"Vending machine. I'll be back in a minute."

"I'll go with you." Mason shoved his hands through his hair, displacing the neatly combed strands.

Trent didn't need another pair of hands for this job. So what was up? "Sure. Why don't you bring the ice bucket."

Mason didn't say anything as they walked to the opposite side of their floor to the alcove with vending machines containing snacks, soft drinks, and water as well as the ice dispenser. Trent pulled out his wallet and fed dollar bills into the drink machine.

He glanced at the construction worker who stood staring into the bowels of the ice machine without using the scoop to gather cubes. "What's up, Mase?"

"The memories are too close."

"Figured. You can handle them."

Mason's gaze locked on his. "I spent every minute in that godforsaken police station praying I didn't hurl in front of Nicole." He swallowed hard. "I still might."

"You won't. I know you, Mason. You're a strong man with an iron constitution and a titanium spine. If you hadn't been, you never would have made it out of prison in one piece and with your sanity intact."

Rio's cousin said nothing for a minute, then sighed, discouragement evident. "I should stay away from Nicole."

"Why?"

A snort. "As evidenced by what happened with the detectives, I'll never be free of suspicion. I don't want my lousy history to affect her. No woman deserves to be tainted by my past."

"Don't sell yourself short."

Mason grabbed the scoop and jabbed at the mound of ice. "I suppose it doesn't matter. We don't live in the same town."

Trent didn't bother to tell the other man his reasoning might not matter soon. He had a feeling Nicole wasn't happy with her job. Plus, now that she knew Grace was her biological sister, she had a good reason to move closer to her blood relative.

He doubted either of the women would ever consider Devin anything more than an acquaintance. Besides, Devin had made it clear he didn't want a relationship with them and neither did his wife. They were both too worried the sisters wanted two-thirds of the Bowen estate for themselves.

"I'm not an expert on relationships, but if you're interested in Nicole, go for it and start courting that woman." He held up his hand when Mason looked as though he would protest. "Just think about it. You don't want to throw away the best thing that ever happened to you because you were being noble. She wouldn't appreciate you protecting her from you." Trent's lips curved. "Grace's sister will make up her own mind."

They carried the drinks and ice bucket back to the room.

"Perfect timing," Nicole said with a smile. "Grace and I warmed the hamburgers and fries."

Within minutes, the food was gone. Guess Grace's appetite had resurfaced without his kisses. Too bad. He'd been looking forward to them. Trent checked the time. "We should try to sleep."

"I'm afraid it's a waste of time for me." Grace gathered trash. "I still have enough adrenaline running through my veins to keep me awake for hours."

Nicole looked at Mason. "Since you're my new boyfriend, why don't you walk me home."

He blinked, glanced at the door on the other side of the suite. "Sure." Mason held out his hand to Grace's sister and escorted her to the bedroom door. After a whispered conversation, he kissed her cheek and nudged her inside the room before returning to the balcony and pulling the door closed behind him. He sat with his back to the glass, looking as though he was settling in for a while.

Trent suspected Nicole and Mason had contrived to give him and Grace time alone. He helped his girlfriend with the cleanup. "Come on. Let's see if we can find a movie to watch for a few minutes." Once she was down for the night, Trent planned to call Bear.

He led Grace to the couch and gathered her close to his side. Grabbing the remote, Trent hunted for an old movie. The pace on those was slow. He hoped his body heat and a slow-developing plot would be the perfect antidote to a difficult evening. Once her adrenaline dropped, Grace would crash, hard. He knew she was exhausted even though she didn't feel it at the moment. Trent felt the drain on his energy as well.

He found one of his favorite movies with Humphrey Bogart. Perfect. Black and white with a slow plot, mystery, and romance all wrapped in one package. Trent eased her head against his shoulder. "Relax. Let me hold you for a while. I can't tell you how much I miss this."

"Me, too," she murmured. "Sometimes when you were gone for weeks, I would ache to feel your arms around me."

Was it any wonder he loved this woman? Trent pressed a kiss to the top of her head. "Those late night phone conversations and texts kept me sane when all I wanted to do was jump on the nearest plane and come home to you."

"Do you consider Otter Creek home?"

"Home is wherever you are, my love."

Grace tilted her head back and smiled. "That's the second-best thing you've ever said to me."

"It's the truth." He pressed a soft kiss to her lips and turned up the volume on the television. "Have you seen this movie before?"

She shook her head. "I've heard of it, though."

"You're in for a treat." Although he'd have to watch the flick again with her at another time. Grace's eyes were already growing heavy. She might last another fifteen minutes.

At the ten-minute mark, Trent glanced down at the woman he needed more than his next breath and discovered she was sound asleep. Excellent. Hopefully, she would sleep through what remained of the night.

He waited another thirty minutes before sliding one arm beneath Grace's knees, the other braced against her back. He carried her into the bedroom she and Nicole shared. Nicole had poked her head out of the room just after Grace had fallen asleep and motioned for him to bring Grace to the room whenever he was ready, that she was going to sleep herself.

Nicole had left the bathroom light on with the door partially closed, allowing Trent to see she had pulled back the covers of Grace's bed. He lowered Grace to the mattress, pulled the sheet and comforter up to her chin, and left.

Three hours later, a heavy pounding on the suite door woke him.

CHAPTER SEVENTEEN

Grace paused while tying her tennis shoes. Who was knocking on their door at five in the morning? She winced. Horrible hour. The overnight shift at the hospital was her least favorite though she'd pulled her share of them.

Tomorrow's shift at the hospital would be rough. If she was allowed to return home. The way things were going, Grace wasn't sure Barton and Weston would let them go home. But they couldn't hold her and the others in Dumas indefinitely. The detectives might not solve the crime at all. What would happen then?

Grace didn't want a cloud of suspicion following her the rest of her life. Worse, Mason didn't deserve another black mark on his record with an unfounded accusation.

And Trent? Nausea swirled in the pit of her stomach. Surely Brent Maddox wouldn't believe his operative guilty of murder. Trent was a protector to his bones.

A rumble of male voices drifted through the closed bedroom door. Grace recognized Trent's voice. Who was the other man? His voice was too muffled to figure out his identity.

She finished tying her shoes and sat up as Nic opened the bathroom door, fully dressed, brushing her hair. "Did I hear someone knock?"

"Someone is talking to Trent, but I can't make out who it is."

Her sister tossed her hairbrush into her bag. "We should find out what's going on. Anybody beating on the door this early in the morning isn't bringing good news."

That's what Grace was afraid of. She hoped the bad news wasn't about Devin. "Let's go. Whoever is here sounds like he's making Trent angry." Difficult to do and unwise. It took a lot to make her boyfriend angry. This guy had managed to accomplish that feat in less than a minute.

The sisters walked into the living room and pulled up short when they saw Barton and Weston glaring at Trent who scowled back at them. At their entrance, the men turned to face Grace and Nicole.

"Good morning, baby." Trent left the two cops standing in the entranceway and wrapped Grace in a strong embrace. "How are you this morning, Nicole?"

"Grumpy, thank you. What's going on?" Nicole asked. "Kind of early for the Dynamic Duo to knock on our door."

"Mrs. Bowen is missing," Detective Weston said.

Grace frowned. Did she leave Devin at the hospital alone? The woman had acted so concerned for her husband's welfare. Why would she leave knowing his life hung in the balance? Maybe Ron convinced her to go home to rest and something happened to her en route.

If the patient was Trent, Grace wouldn't leave his bedside. "Maybe Clarice needed to rest."

"She went to her car to retrieve her cell phone and never came back," Barton said. "The car's still there. You wouldn't know anything about that, would you, Blondie?"

She blinked. Blondie?

Trent growled. "I told you to knock that off. Her name is Grace."

"I'd think a murderer would have thick skin."

Her boyfriend's body hardened as his muscles tightened. Grace hugged him tighter. He couldn't lose his temper. They were pushing, hoping for a reason to toss Trent in jail. Assaulting an officer would definitely accomplish that. But that action would also leave her and Nic vulnerable to attack. Mason would protect them with every skill he had, but he wasn't combat trained like Trent.

Whoever was after them had proved himself willing to harm them. Grace and Nicole needed Trent out of jail. The detectives didn't have the right to sling mud at the SEAL. "Trent isn't a murderer."

Barton gave a short bark of laughter. "You're an idiot if you believe that. Your man is a stone-cold killer, sweetheart. However, I was referring to you being a murderer. Got to have no heart to poison a man for a few lousy bucks."

Someone believed the Bowen estate was worth killing for, but it wasn't her. This time, Grace was the one fighting her temper. "How many times do I have to tell you I had nothing to do with Devin being ill?"

"You can tell me the same lies until you're blue in the face, lady. You're guilty and we'll find evidence to put you away. If we're lucky enough, we'll build a strong enough case for the death penalty."

"Enough," Trent snapped. "Why are you here besides being the bearers of bad news?"

"You don't care that Mrs. Bowen is missing?" Weston's keen gaze focused on the SEAL. "Or maybe you're not surprised. Where have you been since you left the police station earlier, St. Claire?"

"In this suite except for a short trip to a fast food place two miles from here." He told the detectives the name of the restaurant and the approximate time he'd left the hotel and returned.

"Any of your friends ride with you?" Weston asked.

He shook his head. "The drive-thru had surveillance cameras. The hotel has cameras pointed at the passenger drop-off and in the hotel lobby and elevators. You'll be able to confirm my whereabouts. I would have to imitate a race car driver to pull off kidnapping Mrs. Bowen, hiding her somewhere or dumping her body, buying food, and coming back here in the time frame I gave you." A cold smile curved his lips. "I'm good, Detective, but not that good."

The cop grunted. "What about the rest of you? I want a detailed account of your movements in the past four hours."

Grace and Nicole reported their movements. By the time they finished their statements, Mason walked from the second bedroom. He stopped at the sight of the detectives.

"What's going on?" he asked. "Is Devin all right?"

Nicole greeted him with a quick kiss and wrapped one arm around his waist. "Clarice is missing and the Keystone Cops think we might be to blame."

"Where did you go after leaving the police station, Kincaid?" Barton folded his arms across his chest.

"Here. I didn't leave the suite except to buy drinks from the vending machine on this floor. Trent was with me."

"Got any proof of that?"

A bitter smile curved Mason's lips. "Just my word and that of my friends."

"We all know what your word is worth."

"A lot more than yours, Barton," Nicole snapped.

"That's enough." Weston stared hard at the four of them. "If you had anything to do with Mrs. Bowen's disappearance, we'll find the proof and nail you to the wall."

Trent shrugged. "You won't find evidence because there isn't any. Now, if that's all, Detectives, we have plans today."

Grace fought to keep her expression neutral. She didn't remember any plans in the works unless he meant seeing

Simon Randall about the paperwork to sign. With Devin's illness and the interrogation, they had forgotten about the signatures.

The detectives exchanged skeptical glances. "At this hour?" Weston asked.

"You're the ones who barged in here before the sun rose."

"Don't leave town until we give you permission." With that parting shot, the two men strode out, slamming the door behind them.

"I don't like those two," Nicole said with a scowl.

"They don't like us, either." Grace turned to Trent. "What plans do we have?"

"Bear should be here in the next few minutes to replace my window."

"Wait a minute." Mason looked puzzled. "Your windows were fine a few hours ago. What happened?"

Trent summarized the sequence of events after he purchased the early morning meal.

"Did you see who it was?" He held up his hand. "Never mind. If you had seen the shooter, he'd be occupying a jail cell or a metal slab in the morgue. Someone has made a run at the three of you. I guess I should assume I might be next."

"Not if we find him first." Trent pressed a kiss to Grace's forehead. "Hopefully, Randall has your paperwork finished so you can take care of that today."

"But the detectives said for us not to leave town." Nicole didn't look happy about that prospect.

Grace noted the worry in her sister's eyes. "Nic, is everything all right?"

"Not even close. My boss hates me and is looking for an excuse to fire me. This might give him the opportunity he's been waiting for. If I don't return to work tomorrow, I don't think I'll have a job to go back to."

"I need to call the hospital and tell my supervisor I can't work my shift tomorrow night." Grace scowled. "I hate to call her. We've had several nurses out with the flu recently."

At least she wouldn't lose her job, Nicole thought. Unlike her, Grace's job was secure. Nurses were in short supply while marketing people were plentiful, the job market competitive. She hadn't been exaggerating. Chances were high Sullivan would use this as an excuse to hire someone who agreed that his every thought and marketing idea was a golden moneymaker. Nicole wasn't that person, much to her boss's displeasure. If the idea was lame, she didn't hesitate to voice her opinion.

"I should do the same." She flashed a weak smile. "Wish me luck." Not wanting the others to hear her boss lay into her, Nicole unlocked the French doors and walked onto the balcony.

Shivering in the cold morning air, she called Sullivan. She felt bad about calling him this time of morning. Well, she felt bad for about one second. He'd called her often enough over the past two years before five. Time to return the favor.

"Do you know what time it is?" Sullivan's growl greeted her.

"Sorry to call so early." Not really, but if she was civil, Nicole might keep her job a little longer. Thoughts of the money from her birth mother surfaced. She shoved them aside. Until the money was in her account, she wouldn't count on it. Things happened. "I can't return to work tomorrow."

"Why not?"

Not eager to admit she was suspected of murder, she said, "It's complicated."

An exasperated sigh came through the speaker. "Copeland, it's always complicated with you. I'm tired of your drama. You've got one more day. The only excuse for not showing up then is you're dead or dying. Got that?"

Her cheeks burned. Seriously? She wasn't the dramatic sort and only missed work for scheduled vacations. Last fall, she'd come down with a virus, but stumbled into work anyway because they had a high-dollar campaign due that morning. "Yes, sir." The jerk ended the call without replying.

Shoving the phone into her pocket, Nicole leaned against the balcony rail, the cold air feeling good against her burning cheeks. She was tired of Braxton Marketing and Sullivan, the worst boss on the planet.

She faced the fact it was time to start searching for another job. She didn't have enough savings to last for long. Hopefully, it would be enough to land something else.

The door opened behind her, closed again. "Everything okay?"

Mason's deep voice soothed her raw emotions. Why that was she didn't know. He was a virtual stranger. A hot one, she admitted to herself. Nicole shook her head in answer to his question.

"What happened?"

"What I expected. If I don't return to work the day after tomorrow, I won't have a job." Her stomach lurched at the thought.

"I'm sorry, Nicole." His hard hand brushed against her lower back.

"My friends call me Nic."

Mason shook his head. "Your name is as beautiful as you are."

Nicole found herself charmed by his soft, heartfelt words. "Thank you." The detectives and their ugly suspicions doused the feelings Mason engendered. "Since we're supposed to be a couple, we should at least know the basics about each other. You start."

He remained silent for a couple minutes.

"Mason?"

Finally, he sighed. "Tell the cops I'm a jerk and you dumped me. You should stay away from me." Mason's gaze remained fixed on the city vista in front of him.

Nicole's heart sank. Did he not like her personality? Was she not pretty enough for him? "Why?"

"I'm tainted, Nicole. People will always look at me and see ex-convict flashing in LED lights over my head." His grip on the railing was so tight Nicole could see the whites of his knuckles.

"Knock it off, Mason."

A narrow-eyed glance her direction. "It's the truth. The cops would love to hang this on me. If you're associated with me, they'll assume you're part of the crime. Trust me when I say you don't want them looking at you like that."

"Let them look." She stepped closer, moving into his personal space. "They won't find anything. I won't turn away from you or run because I'm uncomfortable. What kind of woman would that make me if I did?"

"A smart one."

"A weak one," she countered. "I'm not walking away, Mason." Nicole shifted so closer her mouth brushed his as she spoke her next words. "Deal with it." Then she kissed him.

CHAPTER EIGHTEEN

Trent clapped Bear on the shoulder. "I appreciate the curbside service." His voice echoed in the concrete and steel garage. This early, none of the hotel guests were stirring, giving him the opportunity to talk to the car tech without an audience.

The six foot eight Army grunt eyed him, his expression sober. "Your woman's safety is at risk. I hope someone does the same for mine if I can't take care of her."

He stilled. "You have a special lady in your life?"

A scowl from the mountain-sized man. "Why wouldn't I?"

Right. "You never talk about her."

Bear grunted. "Security. The less common knowledge about Nina is out there, the better I like it. We have enemies. I take safety precautions wherever my wife and my kids might be. No one is going to hurt my family." His gaze frosted at the prospect of an attempt.

He'd hate to be on Bear's bad side. The Fortress tech had the thousand-yard stare down to a science. "The bunker?"

A nod.

So it was true. Trent heard from other operatives the car guru had a bunker beneath his warehouse completely stocked with food, water, and weapons to hold off a siege for a month, a haven for his family, his employees, and their families. That included multiple escape tunnels leading away from the structure once it was safe to evacuate.

Bear's place didn't look like much from the outside, a run-down warehouse just this side of falling apart from appearance. Inside housed top-flight equipment and the best weapons and ammunition cache outside of Fortress headquarters. With Bear's ingenuity, Trent figured the man had surprises ready for anyone who attempted to breach the bunker's security, none of them pleasant.

"What do I owe you?"

Bear waved his hand. "Maddox took care of it." A smile curved his lips. "You met his little girl yet?"

Should have figured Maddox would sign off on the repairs. The boss had his hands on every part of his company. "Alexa is a little charmer." And she had her adoptive father wrapped around her finger. Of course, no one dared share that opinion with Maddox. The man was a Navy SEAL, after all.

"The boss will have his hands full when she is a teenager."

Trent chuckled. "I can't wait until her first date shows up."

"I bet Maddox answers the door in full combat gear, complete with his MP-5 in hand." Laughter from the two men filled the cavernous space of the garage. "Tell your Grace her SUV is ready. Text me when you're arriving so I can have it detailed. I look forward to meeting the woman who tamed the frog boy."

His eyebrow rose. Bear was detailing Grace's SUV? "Why don't I get that service from your shop?"

A snort. "Detail your own ride. Women appreciate the service and they don't treat my vehicles as though they are rolling garbage cans, unlike some of the operatives."

"Hey, don't look at me. My mother trained me well." She hated trash left in their family vehicles. The bittersweet memory made Trent wish she was still alive to tease with a wrapper or two in the floorboard. He and Darcy had been on their own for several years. The ache left by their parents' passing still caught him by surprise some days.

Bear stepped back. "I need to go. Got another window to replace two hours from here. Watch your back, St. Claire. Something ugly is circling your woman."

He waited until the burly car tech with arms as thick as steel beams left before he turned toward the elevator. Bear was right. A snake hid in the grass, waiting to strike when Trent least expected the blow. He couldn't afford to mess up. Too many lives were at stake, not the least of which was Grace's.

Once again, he considered calling in reinforcements. Mason was a good man to have at his back, but he couldn't have a weapon on him because he was a convicted felon. On the other hand, he didn't want Mason to think Trent didn't trust him.

The sun was peeking over the horizon when he stepped off the elevator and let himself into the suite. Grace twisted on the couch where she'd been watching the sky lighten. The silhouettes of Mason and Nicole indicated the two were once again on the balcony. Unless he was mistaken, the two were sharing a heated kiss. Guess Mase had taken his advice to heart.

Grace walked to his side. "Is Bear finished?"

"Just left. Your SUV is ready."

Satisfaction lit her gaze. "As soon as we're home, I want to pick it up."

Trent hugged her. "Tired of my company already?"

"Of course not. You might be deployed any time. I need transportation while you're gone. PSI doesn't mind you borrowing an SUV from them. I doubt they'd be so accepting of me doing the same. I'm not part of Fortress or PSI."

"You're mine. Fortress and PSI look after their own and that includes the families of their operatives. No one would say anything if you used the vehicle. They'd be happy to know you're safe."

"I'm still glad I don't have to. I hate driving someone else's vehicle. How should I pay for the SUV? Do I need a loan from the bank or pay Fortress in installments?"

Would he start this long day by fighting with his girlfriend? Man, he hoped not. Trent had many things he wanted to do in the next few hours, starting with kissing Grace Rutledge. "You don't pay anything."

She stared. "How can that be? Bear worked hard to retrofit the SUV. He probably has a family to feed and needs money to do that."

Funny how she assumed Bear had a family while Trent always believed the man was single. "The SUV is my gift to you. Your safety matters to me, Grace. Remember, you agreed to the SUV as a safety measure for me."

"I didn't expect you to pay for it."

"I love you. I want to do this. It's for your peace of mind and mine. Please, let me give this gift to you and myself."

Grace threw her arms around his neck and drew his head down to hers. Long kisses later, she pulled back enough to whisper, "Thank you, Trent."

"The first of many gifts I want to give you over our lifetime."

"The first of many gifts we'll give each other," she corrected. "We're a team."

He lowered his head and captured her lips. When he came up for air, he said, "A team for life, my love."

Nothing would make his life more complete. Unless they added a child or two or more to their home. But he was getting ahead of himself. Trent hadn't asked Grace to marry him yet. He wanted an engagement ring before he popped the question.

"Are you hungry?"

Grace wrinkled her nose. "Not really."

"What about something light? Maybe yogurt, granola, and fruit."

"That sounds good as long as it comes with a large coffee. Does the hotel restaurant serve yogurt?"

"If it doesn't, we'll find one that does. I need to check for evidence of the shooting before the sun rises much higher. Do you still want to come with me?"

She nodded.

"She's not the only one," Nicole said. She and Mason walked in from the balcony, hands clasped. "We want to go as well. You might need backup."

Trent's eyebrow rose. Backup from two untrained people?

Mason squared his shoulders. "At least you can use two more pairs of eyes to look for clues or keep watch for trouble."

He smiled. "Can breakfast wait until we finish searching the area? We don't want to attract attention. I wouldn't be surprised if Barton and Weston have posted a watch on us."

"Will you spot them?" Grace asked.

"Depends on how good the surveillance is."

"We can provide cover for you." Nicole grabbed her purse and slipped the thin strap crosswise over her body.

The hotel lobby was deserted except for the sleepy desk clerk who barely acknowledged them with a glance before returning his attention to a thick textbook laid open on the desk.

Trent was grateful his school days were long behind him. He'd never been a fan of tests or homework. He wished the kid a silent good luck with his studies.

"What do we do now?" Grace asked.

"We're going to look for a restaurant that serves breakfast, including yogurt. On the way, I want you to stop at the entrance to the alley on your right. There are several flags from different countries hanging on the balconies of the apartments. Point them out to me and the others. You and Nicole get your cell phones out and take pictures. Mase, keep your attention on the street. I'll search for a brass casing from the shooter's weapon."

Nicole grinned. "We're supposed to distract anyone watching us."

"Exactly. Mase, if something grabs your attention, sing out."

"You got it."

They walked the hundred plus feet between where Trent suspected the shooter stood and where his SUV had been struck by a bullet. "Get ready." They walked a few more feet. "Now."

Grace glanced up at the apartment balconies. "Hey, Nic. Look." She stopped and pointed at the flags fluttering in the cool breeze.

"That is a gorgeous sight. I want pictures of that."

Trent let go of Grace's hand for her to take pictures as well. Mason casually moved behind him and turned his back on the girls snapping pictures with their phones.

Easing into the alley's shadows, Trent scanned the ground. Light glinted off a small piece of metal. Satisfaction swirled in his gut. Behind the cover of his friends and girlfriend, he crouched and scooped up the brass casing with a cloth and shoved it into his pocket. "Got what I needed," he said. "Let's get out of here." His skin was crawling, a bad sign. Were the police watching them or the enemy? Urgency to hustle Grace out of the line of fire led Trent to clasp her hand and urge her to walk.

"Great." Nicole shoved her phone into her purse. "I'm hungry. We're heading for a restaurant for real, right?"

"Yes, ma'am. Grace wants something light."

"Perfect. I saw a place across the street." Nicole headed for the corner to cross with the light.

"Wait, Nicole." Mason hurried to catch up with her, his attention focused to his left.

Trent's instincts kicked into high gear. "Stay here," he said to Grace and began to run.

At that moment, tires squealed on the asphalt. A black Silverado raced up the street and angled straight for Nicole. No cars or pedestrians were in the way of the driver.

"Nic, look out!" Grace screamed.

Mason sprinted toward Nicole, grabbed her, and shoved her out of the path of the truck. The vehicle leaped the curb, fender clipping Mason before the driver steered back to the street.

The construction worker flew through the air, hit the ground and rolled to a stop.

Nicole scrambled to Mason's side. "Mason!"

Trent aimed his Sig at the fleeing truck, pulled the trigger twice, shattering the rear window. He caught a glimpse of a dark baseball hat on the head of the driver before the vehicle careened around the corner and disappeared from sight.

He turned to see Grace on her knees beside Rio's cousin. Trent crouched by her side as he scanned the area for more threats. "How bad is he?" Sliding his Sig into his holster, Trent grabbed his cell phone to call for an ambulance.

"I'm fine," Mason said, struggling to a sitting position. He winced and clamped a hand to his side.

"Mason, you could have internal injuries." Nicole wrapped her arm around his shoulders to lend her assistance. "You need to go to the hospital."

"I'll pass. We just left there. I don't want to spend any more time in that place."

"You were hit by a truck," Grace said. "A doctor needs to examine you."

"I told you, I'm okay."

"Mason, please," Nicole whispered.

"I'm fine, baby. I promise."

Grace scowled at Mason. "If Rio were here, he'd simply haul you up and force you to do what's best. Don't make me play the bad guy, Mason. You won't like it if I do."

A frown. "How did I miss the fact that you're stubborn?"

"Look at it this way. If you're just bruised, you'll be out of the ER in a couple hours. Do it for Rio. He loves you and I owe him for saving my life."

Mason sighed. "You play hardball, Grace."

"Only with people she cares about." Trent waggled his phone. "Do we need an ambulance or can you make it to the SUV?" He'd bring the vehicle around if he had to. The possibility of another assailant in the area concerned him. If someone else targeted the women, Trent want to be on hand.

"I'll make it." Mason's tone was grim. "Let's go. I don't want to create a spectacle on the street."

Trent helped him to his feet. When Mason swayed, he draped the man's arm over his shoulder and started him toward the garage.

"Hold it!" a deep voice ordered. "You can't leave."

CHAPTER NINETEEN

Trent's eyes narrowed at the stocky man jogging their direction. The guy had authority almost oozing from his pores. The cop sent by Barton and Weston to keep watch on them. He looked the part, including the bulge under his ill-fitting jacket from a shoulder holster.

"This man needs to go to the hospital," Grace insisted as soon as he was close enough.

"He looks fine to me."

"You're a cop, not a doctor." Trent glared at the man. "Grace is a nurse. She says Mason needs a doctor so we're taking him to the hospital. Tell the detectives if they have questions, they can talk to us while my friend is being checked out."

He maneuvered Mason around the cop blocking their path and continued walking to the garage. By the time they reached the SUV, Mason was pale. Trent unlocked the vehicle and assisted him into the back seat where he slumped against the cushion with a hiss. Nicole climbed in after him.

Reaching into the cargo area, Trent grabbed his mylar blanket and thrust it into Nicole's hands. While the trip to the hospital wouldn't take long, the blanket would help him retain heat and prevent shock.

Minutes later, Trent pulled up to the emergency room entrance for the second time in twenty-four hours. He helped Mason from the vehicle and into the hospital with Grace and Nicole trailing close behind. Once his friend was in an exam room, Trent moved his ride to the parking area and called Rio as he walked back to the ER. His gaze scanned the area.

"Kincaid."

"It's Trent. Mason's been injured. He's mobile, so I don't think his injuries are bad. He's in the ER being examined by a doctor."

"What happened?"

Trent filled the medic in. "The truck clipped him, tossed him into the air. I don't know if Nicole realizes it yet, but your cousin saved her life. That truck was aiming for her. Mason shoved her out of the way, but didn't get clear fast enough to spare himself."

"I'll contact Josh and tell him I'm heading to Dumas. I'll be there in two hours."

"Look, I know he's family, but let's wait and see what the doctor says. I'll let you know as soon as I hear anything."

"You need backup, Trent."

"If Mason is out of action, I'll request help. Deal?"

The medic was silent a moment. "Yeah, okay. As soon as you hear from the doctor, I better be the first phone call. I'll have to contact his father if Mase's condition is serious." A sigh came through the speaker. "I should call Ethan, too. He'll want to know the latest."

"Copy that."

He strode into the hospital waiting room in time to see Barton get into Grace's face, crowding her into a corner where she couldn't get away from him. Fury roared through Trent. "Back off, Barton," he snapped.

"The detective swung around. "You left the scene of an accident. I ought to run you in for failing to report it."

"You're here. Obviously your own man reported the accident. My priority was getting our friend to medical help." He eased in front of Grace and folded his arms across his chest. "You have questions, Detective? Ask them instead of browbeating my girlfriend."

Barton scowled. "I want a rundown of everything that happened, starting from the time Weston and I left the hotel. You leave anything out, I'll slap the cuffs on you for obstruction of justice."

Trent's eyebrows soared. "You want a detailed accounting of the number of kisses I scored from my girlfriend, too? Because that was the most important time I spent."

"Don't, sweetheart," Grace whispered. Her hand pressed against his mid-back.

"Recount your movements, St. Claire." Barton yanked a ratty notebook and pen from his pocket.

Trent reached behind him and threaded his fingers through Grace's. He hated she was in the limelight again because of their unknown assailant.

He summarized what happened, leaving out the detail that he needed a window replaced in his SUV because of a bullet. Shouldn't make it too easy for the irritating detective. That would raise his suspicions since Trent hadn't made his dislike a secret. Besides, Trent had to remain out of jail to protect Grace and her sister. If Barton and Weston discovered he hadn't reported the shot at his SUV, that's exactly where he would end up.

"Go through your story again, St. Claire. You say you went to the garage after we left. Why?" A smirk appeared. "Making out in the backseat with Blondie?"

That weasel. He'd go to any lengths to show Grace in a bad light. Trent's free hand clenched. "I needed a window replaced. Road hazard cracked the glass." Not a lie. The shooter was a hazard on the road in front of the hotel.

"Uh huh." The cop's tone indicated he didn't believe Trent's claim for a minute. "Any way to verify your story?"

"Call Fortress headquarters. They'll pass a message to the car tech who replaced the glass." Trent made a mental note to send Bear a text, explaining the situation, and to call Fortress. He didn't want Bear to hold back too much information. If Barton and Weston detected the deception, they'd wonder why it was necessary.

"Give me his direct number."

"He works for Fortress. Maddox protects his employees. The car tech will call you."

"And how long will that take?" the detective spat out.

"About five minutes after you leave the message, depending on what he's involved in." Trent grinned. "Once Maddox determines you're a legitimate detective with the Dumas PD, of course."

"The beat cop said you took a couple shots at the truck racing from the scene. You could have hit an innocent civilian. You're a prime candidate for reckless endangerment charges."

"I hit what I aimed at, Barton. I wasn't reckless."

"I need your weapon. Now." The detective held out his hand.

Trent blew out a breath. That Sig was a particular favorite of his. "I want this weapon back, Detective." Fat chance of that happening any time soon. Barton would delay the return as long as possible.

"Might be a while, though. A long while. We have to run ballistics tests and match the slugs to what's found in the truck. If we find the truck."

Jerk. Good thing he had another Sig in his Go bag plus a backup weapon.

"Why did you shoot at a moving target?"

Seriously? "This clown jumped the curb and tried to mow down Nicole. Grace and her sister are my principals. My job is to protect them."

Disbelief crossed Barton's face. "How do you know he aimed for her? Maybe this guy is a bad driver. Plenty of them out there on the road."

"This one aimed the truck at Nicole and never corrected his course, even when he jumped the curb," Trent said as he handed over his Sig, grip first. "No other vehicles on the road or pedestrians or stray animals, and no reason to swerve toward Nicole. This was not an accident."

Barton grunted and shifted his attention to Grace. "You're next, Blondie. If you can quit hiding behind your boyfriend." He sneered.

Grace shifted to Trent's side. He tucked her under the shelter of his arm. "My name is Grace, not Blondie, and my story is the same as his." She recited a detailed account of what happened since the detectives left their suite, including the number of kisses she exchanged with Trent. "In case you wanted to know, he's an exceptional kisser, Detective."

Trent pressed a gentle kiss to her temple to hide his smile. Grace Rutledge had spunk and he couldn't wait to marry her.

A flinch from the cop. "I'll take your word for that. What about the other broad? Where is she?"

"I imagine my sister is in the hallway, waiting for word on Mason's condition."

Muttering under his breath, Barton strode from the waiting area.

Grace sagged against Trent's side. "He's convinced we made up the whole incident."

"His own man will dispute that."

"We could have hired someone to attack, making us look innocent."

Trent eased her into his arms. "Complicated. There would be a money trail."

"Your teammates or another operative could have pulled it off."

"If the attack were part of an operation, absolutely. Otherwise, no. We're mission oriented, love. Because we're well trained, we are careful to confine our skills to operations, not personal vendettas."

Raised voices in the hall drew Trent's attention from Grace. Nicole. "Come on." He led his girlfriend from the waiting room.

In the hall, Nicole glared at Barton who loomed over her. "I told you what I know, which isn't much. The only thing I'm concerned about is my boyfriend's condition. And no, you're not barging in there to question him until the doctor is finished. Buzz off, Detective Barton."

"Listen, lady, I'll run you in for interrogation if you don't cooperate. I can question you for several hours."

"Try it, buddy. I answered every question you asked me. You'll have to dig up rest of the answers for yourself."

"You don't have any idea why someone wants to kill you?"

Nicole was silent a moment, leading Trent to believe she hid something. Barton came to the same conclusion because his eyes narrowed and he leaned in so close his nose practically touched hers.

"You're holding back on me, Ms. Copeland. Why?"

"I don't have an enemy who hates me enough to kill me, Detective. Sorry. No easy answers for you today."

Hmm. Definitely a story there, but Trent didn't think the tale related to the accident. The least he could do was deflect the detective's questions. "Any news on Mason?" he asked Nicole as he and Grace covered the last few yards to her side.

At that moment, the doctor opened the door to the exam room and walked into the hall. "You here for Mr. Kincaid?"

Nicole turned. "I'm his girlfriend. How is he?"

"A lucky man from where I'm standing. You must be Nicole. He's asking for you. He's more concerned about you than himself."

"How is Mason?"

"He has multiple contusions, some bone deep, a few scrapes. He'll be sore, but he's lucky. I've given him a prescription for a mild pain killer, but I suspect he won't take them. If over-the-counter pain relievers don't work, you may have to insist so he can rest. He should be fine in a few days."

"May I see him?"

"Of course. He's wrestling with his shirt." A smile from the doctor. "I'm sure he'd appreciate the help."

Nicole brushed past him.

"Thanks, Doc," Trent said.

"I hope I don't see you folks again any time soon." He smiled. "Might be wise to drive wherever you're going from now on."

After he left, Grace glanced at Trent. "I'm going to the nurses' station to check on Devin."

Trent lowered his head and brushed a soft kiss over her mouth. "Stay where I can see you," he whispered against her lips. He didn't want to leave the area near the exam room, concerned the detective might push his way inside and demand answers from Mason before his friend was ready to deal with the cop.

"Where's your partner, Barton?"

"At the site of the accident, where you should be."

Too bad. Neither of the men were going on his Christmas card list, but he preferred Weston over Barton.

From the corner of his eye, Trent saw Nicole hugging Mason before he had a chance to pull on his shirt.

Interesting. The hug was followed by a kiss that was more than a polite peck on the lips. Maybe something real was brewing between them. In spite of his encouragement for Mase to go after what he wanted, Trent didn't want his friend hurt, either. He'd been dealt enough hard blows in the past thirteen years.

"I need to question the ex-con." Barton made a move toward the door of the exam room which Trent blocked. "Out of the way, St. Claire."

"You can wait five minutes for Mase to finish dressing. He's not going anywhere. Only one exit from the room."

"Don't you want to capture the driver who allegedly tried to run down your friend?"

"Two minutes won't make a difference. You'll learn more detail from your own man and the traffic cameras than Mason."

"What do you know about traffic cameras?" The detective's voice registered suspicion.

Trent smiled. Zane routinely hacked into traffic cams to track perps. He obtained results faster than the police with the added benefit of not having to wait for a warrant.

"Move." Barton shoulder-checked Trent as he shoved past the SEAL. Since Nicole was helping Mason with his shirt, Trent didn't bother trying to stop him again. If his friend needed help, he'd step in. From what he had observed the past year, the construction worker could handle himself.

Trent stood in the doorway, back to the room, so he could watch Grace and hear the conversation behind him.

To Barton's frustration, Mason told the same story as the other three. "Why did you notice the truck while St. Claire missed it?"

Mase flashed him a glance. "He was looking at the flags on the apartment balconies."

The detective snorted. "It's a bunch of stupid flags, St. Claire. What's the big deal?"

Trent glanced over his shoulder. "I've been in many of the countries represented by those flags, Detective." True enough. "Sometimes seeing those flags brings flashbacks." Also true, but not a problem today. Too much was at stake. Getting lost in the memories would have endangered Grace and the others.

Barton stilled. "PTSD?"

"Hazard of the job."

"Isn't that the truth." The cop sighed and shoved his notebook and pen in a pocket. "I'll be in touch if I have more questions. Stay available."

Trent moved aside for the detective. Maybe Barton had a human side after all. Made him wonder if the detective suffered from flashbacks or knew someone who did. The condition was common in law enforcement circles, an unfortunate byproduct of dangerous, sometimes deadly situations. Trent saw ugly things in his line of work, as did the police.

Grace returned from the nurses' station. "Devin is improving. He's still weak and out of it most of the time, but the doctor thinks he'll recover."

"Good to hear."

"Trent," Nicole called.

He swiveled to face the exam room. "Looking rough around the edges, Mase."

"You try tangling with a truck and see how you feel," he said, but his lips curved at the corners.

"You ready to go, man? I'm starving."

"More than ready." He slid from the exam table gingerly, flinched. "I don't think I'm up to running from another truck anytime soon."

"I'll drive us to the hotel. We can order room service, then Grace and I will go to the law office and pick up the papers. We'll return them later."

Mason shook his head. "I'll take a pain reliever and be fine for a while. No need to have Nicole and Grace exposed to danger for my sake." He flashed a grin. "I hurt worse after football practices in high school and college."

His opinion might change after a few more hours passed. "Let's go. I'll find a restaurant with padded seats."

The construction worker huffed out a laugh. "Oh, man. Don't make me laugh. It hurts too much."

Trent found a restaurant with cushioned seats. Between him and Mason, they coaxed Grace and Nicole to eat a decent meal. Once they finished, Trent drove the group to the offices of Washington, Randall, and Satterfield.

The receptionist waved them through to the law office. Randall's assistant smiled when they walked in. "Welcome back. How may I help you?"

"We need to see Mr. Randall," Trent said. "He has papers for Grace and Nicole to sign."

The smile faded. "I'm sorry, Mr. St. Claire. Mr. Randall hasn't come in today."

"Do you know if our papers are ready to sign?" Grace asked.

"Mr. Randall didn't leave anything."

"Can you tell us when he's expected in?" Nicole asked.

"I have no idea. He's missed three meetings this morning, and he's not answering his phone."

CHAPTER TWENTY

Grace twisted in her seat as Trent drove from the law firm's parking garage. "I hope nothing is wrong with the Randalls."

"Maybe they overslept. We were at the hospital and police station late into the night." Despite her words, Nic's voice indicated her doubt.

"Let me drop everyone at the hotel," Trent said. "I'll try to locate Simon and Judy."

"You think there's a problem?"

"Lawyers don't make money by skipping meetings and not answering their phones. The way things have gone the last two days, I think we should be prepared for the worst." He sent Grace a pointed glance. "You and Nicole don't need to be on site if there's a problem."

"We might be overreacting," Nic pointed out. "If we're with you, we can sign the papers and be done with this part of the program. Then we can convince the detectives to let us leave Dumas."

"If there is a problem, you'll be the first ones on the scene of another crime," Mason said. "Trent's right. You and Grace shouldn't be near the Randall house."

Nic scowled. "We're not hothouse flowers needing protection against the harsh environment."

Mason held up his hand to forestall more of Nic's tirade. "Not protected, Nicole. I want to keep you out of jail. If your name continues to be connected to crimes around Dumas, you'll see the inside of a jail cell up close and personal. Trust me, it's not a pleasant experience." His eyes darkened with memories.

"If the Randalls are in trouble, I might be able to help." The likelihood of that was almost nil. Didn't stop Grace from wanting to help the gracious couple.

The rest of the ride to the Randall home was finished in silence. Trent could be wrong. Her gut disagreed.

Her boyfriend parked on the street in front of the house. "Are you sure you want to do this?"

Instead of replying, Grace shoved open the door and slid to the curb. She loved his protective streak most of the time. This wasn't one of them. The others followed suit.

Trent caught up with her in three strides and positioned himself in front of her in case trouble waited for them. The thought of him hurt on her account made her stomach lurch in protest.

He lifted his hand to knock, stopped with his hand raised. Between one heartbeat and the next, Grace found herself swept behind Trent, a big black gun in his hand.

"What's wrong?" she whispered.

Trent held up his hand in a signal he'd taught her meant to be silent. He pointed to the front door which was ajar. Goosebumps surged over her body.

He mouthed for her to wait. Using his elbow, Trent pushed the door open further and slipped inside. Grace longed to follow on his heels, but made herself do as he asked.

He returned, a grim look in his eyes. "Grace, come with me."

"Trent?" Nicole's voice rose. When the SEAL shook his head, she blanched. "Oh, no," she whispered, and turned into Mason's embrace.

"Want me to call the cops?" Mason asked.

"I already called." Trent led Grace toward the kitchen, his pace fast. "Simon is gone, but Judy is still alive."

Grace spared Simon a quick glance before dropping to her knees beside his wife. "Find some towels, honey." Judy had been shot once in the chest. She had a head wound as well, perhaps from striking her head on something. The wound didn't appear to be from a bullet, but it had bled profusely, as most head wounds do.

Trent thrust a handful of towels toward her. "I'll find more if you need them."

She wadded up the cloth and pressed hard on the still-bleeding chest wound. Judy had lost so much blood. "Trent, what's the ETA on that ambulance?"

He snatched up the handset of the house line and spoke to the dispatcher softly. "Two minutes."

They needed to hurry. Grace checked for a pulse while holding the pressure steady on the chest wound. The weak beats stopped. "Trent!"

He tossed the handset on the counter and knelt beside her. "What do you need?"

"Do you know CPR?"

"Yes."

Thank goodness. "Start chest compressions." Together, they worked to keep Judy alive. When the EMTs arrived, they took over. As they wheeled the woman to the waiting ambulance, Grace and Trent washed their hands in the bathroom. Nothing could be done about the blood on their clothes.

"What are her chances?" Trent handed her a clean towel.

"Not good." She tugged her shirt away from her skin. Maybe the hotel laundry could salvage it.

"I have extra shirts in my Go bag. I'll bring you one." He returned in under a minute and handed her a black long-sleeved t-shirt, then returned to the hall and closed the door behind him.

When she walked from the bathroom minutes later, he'd changed his own shirt and was now talking to Detective Weston at the end of the hall.

"You and your friends are bad news, St. Claire," Weston said. "You're like a four-man crime wave." He sighed. "You know the drill by now. I want a rundown on your activities since you left the hospital."

Grace slipped her hand into Trent's as he summarized their movements.

Weston shot her a glance before turning back to Trent. "Why bring Ms. Rutledge inside? You further contaminated the crime scene."

"Judy was alive. Grace is a nurse."

"You have witnesses to corroborate your whereabouts?"

Trent smiled. "Surveillance cameras at the restaurant, a parking stub for the law firm's garage. The receptionist will vouch for us. Check traffic cams."

"Right. Ms. Rutledge, tell me what happened from the time you left the hospital."

Once she finished her summary, Weston sent them outside to wait until Barton finished with Nicole and Mason. She wasn't surprised to find Nic still in the circle of Mason's arms. Her sister's face was pale. But was the embrace for the detective's benefit?

She so wanted things to work out with Mason and her sister. Nic deserved some happiness and her friend deserved a break. Wonder if Nic would be willing to move to Otter Creek?

Barton closed his notebook with a snap. "Stay out of trouble for a few hours." He pushed past all of them and strode into the house.

"Like we want to keep company with that toad," Nic muttered. "Do you think the hospital will give us an update on Judy?" she asked Grace.

"If we're at the hospital to see Devin, I might be able to learn something from one of the nurses." She took in the deepening lines at the corners of Mason's eyes. He didn't complain, but it was obvious he was hurting. "If we're free to leave, I want to return to the hotel for a shower." Although she'd washed Judy's blood off, she still felt sticky.

Trent dropped them off in front of the hotel and parked the SUV. In the suite, he also took a shower, then returned to the living room with damp hair. "We need to change hotels."

"Why?" Nic asked.

"The tango targeting you and Grace knows where we're staying. Two attacks in less than six hours? We're not safe here."

"We can't leave the area yet," Mason said from the recliner where he was stretched out. Nicole had formed a makeshift ice pack for him to press against his side.

"We won't." Trent dropped onto the couch beside Grace. "We'll find a new place outside the city."

"The person hunting for us will still be able to find us."

"Not if I register under a different identity."

Grace frowned. "You have to have an ID."

His lips curved. "I have ID. Some Fortress provided, some I procured myself in case I need to be off the grid."

She stared at his handsome face. Where did he get a fake ID? She wouldn't know where to start if she needed one. Her lips curved. Good thing Trent had skills from the darker side of life.

"I don't want to know that," Mason said. "Can't be good for my continued freedom to know that and not report it." He would have said more, but Trent's cell phone rang.

The SEAL checked the screen and grimaced. "Ethan. I'll take this on the balcony. The rest of you pack your bags. We'll check out as soon as you're finished."

CHAPTER TWENTY-ONE

Trent closed the French door behind himself as he answered the Otter Creek police chief's call. "St. Claire."

"Can you talk?"

He sat in the nearest chair, checking to be sure no one else was on a nearby balcony to eavesdrop on the conversation. "Yes, sir."

"I'm not your commander, Trent. I'm calling as a friend."

Right. A friend with a world of experience in Special Forces and a legendary tracking ability. Word in the special operations circles was that Ethan Blackhawk could track anyone in any weather condition or terrain. A bent or bruised blade of grass or a scuff of dirt told him volumes. Law enforcement agencies all over the country still called him in to track lost or abducted children.

"I heard Mason was hurt this morning. How is he?"

Figuring Mase's parole officer wanted more information than that, Trent summarized the doctor's opinion on the construction worker's injuries, then moved on to report the events surrounding Grace and Nicole since their arrival in Dumas. "Randall didn't show up at the office or answer his phone. Grace and Nicole were to sign papers last night so their inheritance from Mrs. Bowen could be released to them. That didn't happen because of Devin's poisoning."

"So you went to the lawyer's home. What did you find?"

"Simon dead. Single shot to the heart, close range."

"And his wife?"

"Also shot, but alive. Grace did what she could, but isn't sure Judy will survive."

"The detectives have any idea who's behind the attacks?"

Trent gave a short laugh. "Besides us? Not a clue. They're too busy trying to pin the crimes on us to look for the real culprit."

"Won't take them long to eliminate you as the suspects." Ethan's voice hardened. "I assume you have alibis."

"When the detectives get the warrants to check security and traffic cams, they'll have time-stamped proof we were someplace else during the critical times. Barton and Weston will be irritated. They believe Mason is guilty because he's an ex-con and in a relationship with Nicole, and I'm crazy about Grace. According to Barton, my background makes me a prime suspect for murder."

"Based on what?"

"Apparently, I'm money hungry and willing to kill for access to $5 million."

Ethan whistled softly. "That's more motive than most men need to commit murder. What's your next move, Trent?"

"Changing hotels. Too dangerous to stay here."

"Alternate ID?"

Trent didn't answer Ethan's question, a confirmation in itself. At least this way, if Ethan was questioned later about Trent's actions, he could deny knowledge of wrong doing.

Ethan chuckled. "Good enough. Trent, it might be best if Mason returns to Otter Creek."

"I don't think he'll be willing to leave."

"Why not?"

"Grace's sister, Nicole, is here. He won't leave her."

"So the fake relationship isn't fake?"

"I don't think it is anymore. He's aware of the risk of staying."

"Make sure Mason is covered. He's a good man and I don't want him behind bars again. He's come too far to end up with hardened criminals for another stint in prison."

"Yes, sir."

"You might need another person to watch your back. If this does come down to a fight, Mason can't help unless it's in self-defense."

He considered asking for backup while he was in the shower, and Trent was reluctant to bring someone else in unless Mason wasn't able to help. Guess he needed to have a private talk with Rio's cousin. "I'll talk to Mase. Fortress is already aware I may need backup."

"Don't wait too long. Mason will always be the first suspect because of his record."

"How are Serena and Lucas?" The police chief's wife had given birth to their son a few months earlier when Trent was deployed with his unit.

"Fantastic. Lucas is growing fast and Serena is an amazing mother. They're my life."

Longing hit Trent with the force of a tidal wave. He wanted the same for himself, one day soon he hoped. The timing for starting a family depended on how soon Grace felt ready. She would carry the lion's share of the load for their family when he was deployed. Knowing that, would she still be willing to raise a family with him?

When a muffled voice came over the phone's speaker. Ethan paused, then said, "I have to go. I want an update in six hours."

Amusement surged through Trent. Yeah, Ethan wasn't his commanding officer, but he wanted to be kept in the loop just the same. Didn't blame him. "Yes, sir."

"Let me know if I can help." Ethan ended the call.

Trent slid his phone into a pocket. Since he'd never unpacked his Go bag, the operative took a minute to enjoy the quiet. One thing he'd learned on missions over the years, you enjoyed the pockets of peace when you had a chance. Those moments didn't happen often.

The French door opened behind him. Without turning, he knew his visitor was Grace. Trent held out his hand. "Come sit with me."

"What did Ethan say?" she asked as she sat in the chair beside his.

"He's worried about Mason."

"So am I. Do you think Ethan could convince Barton and Weston to let Mason go home?"

"I don't think it would matter if he had permission. Mase won't leave Nicole."

"I'm afraid you're right. She's been trying to convince him to leave since you came out here. He's not having it."

Oh, yeah. Mason Kincaid might not know it yet, but he was a goner. Trent smiled. Couldn't think of anything nicer coming out of this situation. Now if Nicole developed the same feelings for Mase and she moved to Otter Creek, everything would be perfect.

"What do we do now?" Grace asked.

"We can't wait for Barton and Weston to figure out what's going on. They're too focused on us." He stopped as a thought occurred to him. "What about Ron Satterfield?"

"What about him?" Grace's nose wrinkled.

"We haven't heard from him." He grinned. "I thought he would have called you by now to press his case for you to go on a date with him."

"Not funny. I would be happy never to see him again."

"The man has good taste." The smile faded. "I don't share, though."

"Good." She brushed his lips with hers. "I don't, either. Make sure you tell that to the women who hit on you."

"Call the law office. See if Satterfield has access to the papers you and Nicole need to sign."

A moment later when she spoke to the receptionist in the law office, Grace tapped the speaker button. "This is Grace Rutledge. Is Mr. Satterfield available?"

"I'm sorry, Ms. Rutledge. Mr. Satterfield hasn't come in today." The woman's voice sounded frazzled.

Trent's eyes narrowed. Two of the partners hadn't showed up today? "This is Trent St. Claire, Grace's boyfriend. When do you expect him to come in?"

"He should have already been here. Were you able to talk to Mr. Randall?"

"No, ma'am. That's why we wanted to consult with Satterfield. He knows about the forms for Grace and her sister."

"I see. Does Mr. Satterfield have your number?"

"Let me give you my work number. If he agrees, leave his contact information."

Grace turned a troubled gaze toward Trent when the call ended. "I don't like this. The situation was the same with Simon Randall and look how that turned out."

"We need to find Satterfield." Trent called Zane.

"What do you need, Trent?"

"Several things. First, you're on speaker with Grace. I need a new hotel, one outside the city of Dumas." He brought his friend up to speed on what had happened the past twelve hours.

"Someone has a target on your back."

His gaze locked with Grace's. "Mason and I are all that's standing between the attacker and the women."

"Name you want to use?"

Trent thought about his options and chose one of the IDs he'd procured for himself. "Thomas Slater." He took a picture of his credit card in that name and sent it to Zane. "What else can I do to help?"

"We need to find Ron Satterfield. He's a partner in Randall's law firm. He hasn't been in this morning although he was expected. The last time we saw him was at the hospital last night."

"I don't like Ron," Grace said, voice soft. "But I don't want to see him end up dead like Simon, either."

"I understand, sugar. Hold." The sound of keys clicking drifted over the speaker. "Satterfield has three residences listed. One is his family home. Parents are still living there. The other two are in his name alone. One residence is in the mountains, maybe a vacation cabin. The other is on the outskirts of Dumas."

"Whatever hotel you send us to, make sure it's nowhere near Satterfield."

"Same room arrangements?"

"If possible. The suite worked well for us."

More keys clicking. "Done. I'm sending the address and hotel confirmation to your email. What else?"

"I'm sending a bullet casing to the lab. I need it processed, fast."

"Better not be one of the casings at the Randall place. Even Maddox can't keep you out of the pokey if you filched the brass from a crime scene."

"It's from the bullet fired at my SUV. I didn't report the incident. My omission isn't going to be a problem. I need that information, Z." Grace's safety was in jeopardy.

"Let me check one thing." A minute later, Zane said, "Hold off on sending the package to the lab. We have an operative an hour away. I'll divert him to your new hotel and he'll pick up the brass. If we're lucky, we'll have information for you in a few hours."

"Who am I looking for?"

"Adam. He ran through a few exercises with Durango last night. He's on his way to Nashville as we speak."

Excellent. Adam Walker was as tough as shoe leather, well-trained with deadly skills, and a good man to have at your back. The Force Recon soldier was also Zane's brother-in-law.

"Trent, if you need him to help, he'll be happy to stay. The boss doesn't expect him back in town until this weekend."

"I'll talk to him." After he talked to Mason. "If he stays, we'll send the casing to the lab via express mail. A few more hours probably won't make much difference. We have a missing lawyer to track down and Mase needs recovery time. If we're lucky, we'll have a chance to speak to Judy Randall."

Grace shot him a skeptical glance. Yeah, based on what she'd said earlier, he didn't think that likely. Besides, if the Dynamic Duo, as Nicole dubbed them, found anything useful and logged it into their computers, Zane would have it in a matter of minutes.

"Do you know Mrs. Randall's condition?"

"No," Grace said. "I planned to corner one of the nurses when I visited Devin."

"I'll see what I can find out. I'll get back to you." He ended the call.

Trent stood. "Let's see if Mase and Nicole are packed. We need to get out of here." Trent knew in his gut something else was coming.

CHAPTER TWENTY-TWO

Trent slung his Go bag over his shoulder and picked up Grace's small suitcase. Though Mason was sore from his encounter with the truck, he insisted on carrying his and Nicole's luggage to the SUV.

Trent had already settled the bill at the front desk and was reluctant to attract attention by traipsing out the front door with luggage in their hands to his waiting vehicle. No, he'd rather take his quarry by surprise.

He herded the group to the elevator and punched the button for the garage level. Trent figured with everything going on, Barton and Weston had the plainclothes cop watching the hotel to make sure they didn't run. He didn't run from a fight, but he wasn't letting the woman he loved be a sitting duck for someone trying to kill her, either.

When the silver doors slid open, Trent stepped out first and scanned the interior of the garage to make sure it was empty of threats before he let the others leave the safety of the elevator. He unlocked the SUV and stored their bags in the cargo area before climbing behind the steering wheel.

After checking the hotel name and location on his phone, Trent drove from the garage and turned toward downtown Dumas. He spent several minutes turning squares, making sure they weren't followed by either a cop or a criminal. When he was satisfied they were clear, he drove to the new hotel.

His eyebrows soared at the sight of the building. Very nice. He bet the price tag would match the luxury of the place. He'd gladly pay the price, though, if it kept Grace and the others safe.

Trent parked in the garage of the hotel, and they unloaded the SUV. In the lobby, he registered them under his alternate ID and grabbed two key cards.

Inside the suite, Grace and Nicole made noises of approval over the lush, thick carpet, overstuffed sofa, loveseat, and recliner, and full kitchen, complete with an espresso machine. Even Trent had to admit the place was beyond his expectations. Once rooms had been chosen and luggage moved to the appropriate place, they congregated in the living room.

Nicole stared at the gas log fireplace. "I want one of those. Ever since I moved from home, I've missed having gas logs. Nothing beats the warmth they generate without the mess to clean up."

"I can install one for you," Mason said.

"I live in an apartment. I don't think the landlord would appreciate the remodeling job." She smiled at him over her shoulder. "I'll remind you of the offer again when I move into a house, though."

"Deal."

Trent's cell phone signaled an incoming text. He checked the screen, typed in a message. "Adam is here."

"Who is Adam?" Mason asked.

"Adam Walker is Zane Murphy's brother-in-law."

A frown. "Isn't that the guy Zane and the Durango team rescued from a sadistic drug lord a few months ago?"

"The same."

"What's he doing here?"

"Taking a bullet casing to a private crime lab to process. He'll stay if we need him." Trent speared him a pointed look. "Do we need him, Mase?"

Rio's cousin was silent a moment. "Might be a good idea to have someone else here." He grimaced. "So far, I haven't done the best job."

"That's not true," Nicole said.

"Mason, you saved Nic's life." Grace laid her hand on his forearm. "You put your own life at risk to save my sister. Nic has one scratch on her arm while you're bruised all over, and Trent has been able to sleep because of your vigilance. You've been effective."

Mason slid a glance Trent's direction, questions in his eyes. Trent nodded. "She's right. I couldn't have asked for a better partner. The only reason I considered asking Adam to stay is you're banged up and distracted."

The other man's cheeks flamed. "No more distracted than you. I can handle it," he muttered.

Nicole looked puzzled. "Handle what distraction?"

A knock sounded on the door, saving either of them from having to answer Nicole's question. Palming his Sig, Trent checked the peephole and admitted Adam to the suite. "Thanks for the package pickup, Adam."

"No problem. I was in the area." Adam's gaze swept over the others in the room in a threat assessment Trent recognized from his own military training. He doubted that would ever change for either of them.

Trent drew Grace forward. "Grace, this is Adam Walker. Adam, my girlfriend Grace Rutledge."

Adam shook her hand briefly. "Ma'am."

"Please, call me Grace. I've spoken with your brother-in-law, Zane, on the phone a number of times in the last few days. He's been invaluable."

He gave a lopsided smile, the deepest scar on his face restricting his muscle movement. "He's a good man, but don't tell him I said that. He thinks I tolerate him because of Claire. Wouldn't want him to think I like him. Keeps him on his best behavior this way."

Grace smiled. "Adam, this is my sister, Nicole, and Mason Kincaid, Rio's cousin."

Adam greeted both before turning to Trent. "Zane said you might need backup. I'm not due in Nashville for a few days. I'll be glad to assist."

"I could use another person on our team, one who's objective. However, I still need to transport this bullet casing to the lab for testing."

"The lab's an hour away. Give me a sit rep, then I'll take the casing and return."

He studied the operative's face a few seconds, nodded. Adam seemed fully recovered from his ordeal in captivity. Operatives, though, were notorious for ignoring injuries and pushing themselves back in the game long before they were ready or medically cleared.

Trent gestured toward the couch. "Let's talk." When everyone was seated, he brought Adam up to speed.

The Marine whistled softly. "Someone has a target on your backs. Makes me wonder why. What's the game plan?"

"We need to find the missing lawyer." Trent frowned. "At the very least, he knows about the forms Grace and Nicole need to sign."

"Aren't you curious if Clarice is with Ron?" Nicole asked. "They disappeared close to the same time, a fact Weston and Barton failed to mention."

"The thought crossed my mind."

"Maybe they aren't aware he's missing," Grace said.

"Clarice would have to be cold to go off with another man while her husband is fighting for his life in a hospital bed," Mason said.

Trent threaded his fingers through Grace's. "You'd be surprised what people will do with enough incentive."

"You can't deny there were romance vibes between Ron and Clarice when they were in the same room." Nicole rested her head on Mason's shoulder. "Why didn't Devin pick up on it? They were blatant about the interest."

"Maybe Devin sees the interaction so much he ignores the byplay between them," Grace said.

Didn't make sense to Trent. No way would he ignore any man making moves on Grace. He'd confront the interloper and squash any further attempts to take Grace from him.

Adam stood. "Where's the casing?"

Trent handed the plastic bag to his friend along with one of the suite key cards. He inclined his head toward the room he'd just left. "You can store your Go bag in there. Grace and Nicole are in the other bedroom."

Adam shrugged one shoulder. "I'll sleep on the couch or the floor out here." His lips curved. "I've slept on worse."

Trent grunted. Fact of life in the military. You learned to sleep whenever and wherever you had the chance. "No need, man. There are two double beds. Only one of us needs to stay awake each shift. You might as well sleep in comfort."

With a short nod, Adam left to complete his errand.

"What now?" Nicole asked.

He planned to do more digging into the backgrounds on the Randalls, the Bowens, and Satterfield, but he could do that during his night shift with his laptop. Through Fortress, he had access to many databases. If he needed more information, he'd tap Zane or one of the other tech geeks for the work. Something was triggering the attacks and he needed to figure out what before the attacker killed another person.

Trent frowned as another thought occurred. What if the problem stemmed from Grace or Nicole's background or their families? Man, he didn't want to go behind Grace's back to dig into her background. However, she might not be aware of questionable things her family didn't share with her.

"Trent?" Grace's soft voice brought his attention to her. "What is it?"

"Thinking about where to focus."

A skeptical look crossed her face, but she didn't challenge his statement. Yet. His lips quirked. His Grace wouldn't let him get by with that vague answer for long. When she did confront him, he planned to tell her the truth. Though their life together wouldn't be easy, he would be honest with her as long as he wasn't sworn to secrecy because of national security.

He wrapped his arm around her waist. "I want to go to Satterfield's house outside of town. If Satterfield is there, I'll find out why he's not answering his phone and what he knows about Clarice's disappearance."

"And if he's not there?" Nicole asked.

"I'll look around, see if I find anything to help us unravel what's going on."

Her jaw dropped. "You're going to break a window?"

Trent grinned. "Who said anything about breaking glass?"

She blinked. "But how will you get inside the house?"

"Don't ask. You can't tell what you don't know, Nicole." He turned to Mason. "You need to stay here, Mase. I don't plan to get caught, but unexpected things happen during missions. I promised Ethan I'd make sure you were covered. This little field trip isn't one you should go on."

"You need someone to watch your back. If Satterfield is behind this and he manages to take you out, all of us are vulnerable. You can't go by yourself."

"That's why I'm going with him." Grace folded her arms across her chest as if daring Trent to tell her no.

He tugged her tighter against his side. "It's not safe. I might run into trouble."

"That's all the more reason why you need me. You're taking me with you or I'll ask Zane to give me the address and take a taxi. You don't want me to go unprotected, do you?" She unfolded her arms and circled his waist. "I need to do this. Let me do what I can to keep you safe for a change. If there's trouble, I'll do whatever you tell me. I know you can handle the trouble and protect me at the same time."

He sighed. The only way to keep her in the suite was tie her to a chair and he wouldn't do that. "If I take you with me, you have to promise you'll do exactly what I tell you to do, no questions asked. There may not be time to explain until later."

"You have my word." An impish smile curved her lips. "Just don't get used to it. This is a crisis situation with a real possibility of danger. On a normal day, you can expect a protest if I don't agree with something you want."

Trent chuckled. "Understood." He looked at Nicole. "I want you to stay here and watch over Mason while he rests. I'm almost positive no one followed us, but I'm not arrogant enough to assume I didn't make a mistake or miss a tail."

"I don't need a nap," Mason protested.

"So watch a movie. The soreness will grow worse as the day progresses. Do your body a favor and give it a chance to recover. Keep taking the pain meds and step up your fluid intake. Don't leave the suite for any reason. The fewer people know we're here, the better for all of us."

Minutes later, Trent drove from the garage and headed toward the downtown bypass. He'd rather not drive past their old hotel and chance someone recognizing them. The bypass took longer because he had to circle around the city. The good thing was he'd have many opportunities to spot a tail and lose them before they arrived at Ron Satterfield's home.

Trent drove slowly past the house, scanning the area. Not much cover in the front. The curtains were drawn, giving the place a desolate air.

"Doesn't look as though he's home," Grace murmured.

"No car out front, but I noticed a three-car garage in the back. We'll need to check inside, see if there's an empty slot where a vehicle should be." He continued to the corner and turned right. On the next block, Trent parked in the deep shadow of a tree. Grace reached for the door. "Wait."

They sat in the SUV for several minutes while he watched for anyone showing interest in them. No curtains twitched. No vehicles drove past at a snail's pace. There weren't many houses. Unlike his neighborhood in Nashville, the lots in this section of Dumas were large, many of them without fences. Sidewalks connected the lots with the detached garages at the back of the houses, forming an alleyway between the blocks.

"Come on, baby. Let's go for a walk." Time to see if Satterfield was part of the problem or the solution.

CHAPTER TWENTY-THREE

"What do you want me to do?" Grace glanced around, happy to have an active role in protecting Trent for once, and nervous at doing something illegal. Did the police throw you in jail for breaking into a house if you didn't steal anything? She wasn't sure she wanted to know the answer. If Barton or Weston had their way, she and Trent would be behind bars in a heartbeat.

"Relax against me, Grace." Trent slid his arm around her shoulders. When she walked too fast, he slowed her down. "We're taking a walk, not running a race. Slow, relaxed movements are overlooked. The quickest way to draw attention is moving fast."

Easy for him to say. Covert operations were his life. Grace was an upfront kind of woman. This cloak-and-dagger stuff didn't come natural to her.

They walked to the end of the street, turned right, then ambled up the alley between the blocks of houses. A concrete driveway circled Ron's home.

As they drew closer to the house, Grace examined the building's facade. Beautiful stonework, gray with the occasional red intermixed, created an old-world ambience that charmed her. Maybe one day she and Trent would have a house similar to this. She smiled at the thought of filling a large home with children. Trent St. Claire would be an amazing father and her parents longed for grandchildren to spoil.

She paused, glanced at Trent. Her boyfriend had been absent so often in the past year, he hadn't met her family yet.

"What is it?"

"I need to introduce you to my parents."

He nodded. "I'm looking forward to it. What should I know before I see them?"

"They'll grill you. Mom is fiercely protective and Dad was never friendly to the dates I brought home."

"They might have a problem with the secrets I have to keep," he warned.

Probably. But she was confident Trent would win them over.

He guided her behind the house, pace still easy. "Let's see if our friend Ron is home." He knocked on the back door, waited a moment, knocked again. When Ron didn't answer, Trent tugged a pair of thin rubber gloves from his pocket and into place over his hands, then knelt, thin metal tools in his grasp.

Grace stared. Lock picks? "I don't have to worry about breaking a window if I lock myself out," she whispered. "I didn't know you could do that."

He flashed an amused look over his shoulder, stood. "Stay behind me," he murmured, handing her a pair of gloves. Once she'd donned the protection, Trent turned the knob and slipped inside the darkened interior.

Grace closed the door behind herself, glancing around with curiosity. Although nothing appeared out of place in the kitchen, the counters were barren save for a coffee maker. Ron either wasn't a chef or he was too busy to cook. She didn't know anything about a law career, but Grace was friends with a couple of paralegals who told stories about the long hours their bosses kept and the mounds of paperwork that came with the job.

After Trent signaled her to wait in the kitchen, she used the time to search, opening drawers and cabinets as quietly as possible. Her eyebrows rose. Nice cutlery. Real china and crystal. She recognized the china pattern as one her aunt preferred. Grace and Nicole preferred stoneware to delicate place settings. A good thing, too, in light of her feelings for her boyfriend. Just contemplating rough-and-tough Trent sipping coffee from a delicate china cup curved her lips.

Trent returned. "Clear. Ron's not here. Neither is Clarice."

"I hope he's in a good mood if he returns while we're in his house." She opened the refrigerator. Standard bachelor fare. Lots of cold cuts, bread, condiments, sodas, alcohol. No real ingredients to cook meals, confirming her earlier suspicion Ron didn't cook much. "Nothing interesting in the kitchen."

"We need to search the rest of the house. No lights. If we split up, we'll cover ground faster."

"What do I look for?"

"Anything connected to you, Nicole, or Devin. I'll take the first floor, you take the second. Thirty minutes tops. If something happens, hide and wait for me to come to you."

Grace nodded and hurried from the kitchen. On the second floor, she found four bedrooms and two bathrooms. Although she felt uncomfortable searching the master bedroom, Grace forced herself to look through the dresser, nightstand, and closet. She grabbed her cell phone and knelt on the floor. She didn't think a light would show if she kept the beam pointed toward the floor. Raising the bed skirt, she turned on her flashlight app.

The only thing under the bed was a shoe box. Grace almost ignored the container, figuring Ron ran out of closet space for shoes. Checking would only take a minute, though.

She stretched out her arm and grabbed the box. Still covered by the bed skirt, Grace lifted the lid and shined the light on the contents of the box. Her gasp filled the otherwise silent room, her cheeks heating. Oh, man. She didn't want those images burned in her brain. How would she look Ron in the face after seeing too much of him?

Pushing back the tide of distaste, she dropped the lid and stood, box clutched in her hands. She should show Trent. Once he saw proof of their suspicions, she would return the box to its hiding place under the bed.

The next bedroom was a little used guest room. Didn't feel lived in like the master bedroom. Pretty but lifeless. The third bedroom doubled as an exercise room. A treadmill, an elliptical, and some kind of weight system with a metal frame and pulleys and cables everywhere.

The fourth bedroom served as an entertainment room. Huge television, several comfortable reclining chairs in black leather, a fully-decked out bar with a mirror and lights. Ron's DVD collection was extensive, befitting the obvious investment in his television screen.

Nothing interesting in the bathrooms. Disappointed she hadn't found anything to help them, Grace descended the stairs in search of Trent. Paper rustling drew her to the room at the end of the hall.

She stopped in the doorway of an office, box propped on her hip. "Find anything?" she asked.

"Yeah. You?" He looked up. "What do you have?"

"A box of pictures." She grimaced. "Take a look, then I'll return them to the place where I found them."

"What kind of pictures?"

"The kind I'd love to erase from my brain."

He took the box from her hands and set it on the desktop. Lifting the lid, Trent stilled, whistled softly. "I see what you mean. Looks like you and Nicole were right. Clarice and Ron are involved."

He upended the box and started skimming the photos before tossing them back inside. Studying one picture for a few seconds, he held it out to Grace. "Look at this one."

"Do I have to?"

"It's not like the others."

Grace took the photo from his hand. Shock held her immobile for a moment. Clarice and Ron were hunters? "Never saw that coming." Was it possible Clarice was simply doing the girlfriend thing of supporting her boyfriend's hobby?

No, she decided. Clarice had her own gun and seemed comfortable holding it. Her free hand rested on the head of a deer, not something Grace would do in a million years. She'd seen enough results of gun violence in the ER to make the prospect of shooting an animal unpleasant. "Devin's wife doesn't seem the type to go tromping through the woods and fire a shotgun."

Trent chuckled. "First, you don't tromp through the woods to hunt, not if you want to be a successful hunter. Second, she's not holding a shotgun. That's a rifle."

"There's a difference?"

"A big one, babe."

"I wonder if Devin shares her passion for hunting."

"Next time you see him, ask. Might be interesting to see his reaction to your question." He turned back to the desk and continued glancing at pictures and returning them to the box. "The interest in hunting explains Ron's home in the mountains."

"And here I thought the place might be a vacation getaway, leaving the stress of the city and job behind."

"The house would serve that purpose as well. Ron hunts prey in the courtroom and in the woods. When you hunt, you have to push everything else aside and focus on the task at hand. Cornered prey can turn on you. Makes the hunt that much more dangerous."

"Experience talking?"

"Oh, yeah," he murmured. Finished with the photos, Trent replaced the lid. "Where did you find these?"

"Under his bed. I'll return them." Grace hurried up the stairs, cognizant of the thirty-minute deadline approaching fast. She slid the box under the bed skirt, then returned to the office. "What now?"

Trent picked up several pieces of paper, stuffed them into the pocket of his black cargoes, and secured the opening.

"I thought we weren't taking anything from here."

He inclined his head toward the copier in the corner. "I made copies of the originals. Ron won't know we have them."

"What are they?"

"I'll show you later." He grabbed the originals of the documents and returned them to a desk drawer. Once again, he pulled out the lock picks and secured the drawer.

The doorbell chimed.

Grace's heart raced. "Oh, no." Had a neighbor seen them at the back of the house and come to investigate? If so, would he announce himself by ringing a doorbell?

"Door's locked and obviously it's not Ron." Trent strode to the window facing the driveway at the front of the house and eased the curtain aside. He uttered a low growl.

"Who is it?"

"Weston and Barton."

Worse than a neighbor. Man, she so didn't want to see the inside of a jail cell. If she was arrested for breaking and entering, would the hospital suspend her? And what about Trent? Despite what he let the detectives believe, her boyfriend wasn't on an official mission. If he was arrested, would Maddox terminate Trent's employment? "What should we do?"

He sent her an amused glance. "Nothing. They don't know we're here."

"We're waiting them out?" Grace didn't know if she could, her tension already unbearable.

"I think the detectives are here to find out what Ron knows about the Randalls, maybe ask followup questions concerning Devin's poisoning."

"If they catch us, we'll end up in jail. I don't look good in prison orange."

His laugh was low. "Don't worry. As long as we're quiet, we should be fine. If they do come inside, I'll deal with them."

That was easy for him to say. Grace trembled so much, she feared she would shake apart. How did he do this for a living? And she had thought her job was high stress. What a laugh. If this situation almost did her in, she couldn't imagine how she'd react to guns fired at her and knives brandished in her direction. She already respected Trent and his skills. This tiny insight made her appreciate his courage and strength even more.

"I'd rather not have to handle the detectives any time soon. I spent more time with them than I'm comfortable with."

"Agreed." He eased her against his chest, wrapped his arms around her while keeping an eye on the detectives. "Unfortunately, we'll have more run ins with them, especially if Ron is missing as well as Clarice." He lapsed into silence.

A moment later, he squeezed her gently. "They're leaving. We'll wait a few more minutes, then leave here."

"Are we going straight to the hotel?"

Trent shook his head. "We have to be sure we aren't followed."

"Will you tell me what you found?"

"When we return to the hotel. Saves having to repeat myself." Ten minutes passed. Trent looked at Grace. "Time to go now. People who live around here should return from work soon."

Trent led her to the back door. He signaled her to wait, then opened the door a crack. When he was satisfied, he clasped Grace's hand and they walked out of the house. "Same as before. Slow and easy."

Instead of going back the way they'd come, the two of them continued down the alleyway, passing five more houses before Trent nudged Grace toward the street where the SUV was parked. He slowed them even further, stopping twice to kiss her in a leisurely fashion.

Good grief. She wasn't sure her heart could handle much more. Between Trent's burning kisses and the pressure to run, her heart raced as though she'd completed a marathon.

Finally, they reached the SUV. Trent tapped the remote, unlocking the vehicle. Another kiss, then he tucked her inside and buckled her seatbelt. Sliding behind the wheel, he cranked the engine and drove from the neighborhood. "You were great."

"Thank you for agreeing to let me come with you. The experience was...enlightening."

He cast her a quizzical glance.

"I've never seen you in action on a mission. I don't know how you do this for a living, Trent. I thought my heart would fly out of my chest and we weren't really in any danger."

Her boyfriend huffed. "This was a piece of cake. I hope you never see me in combat mode." His expression darkened. "If you do, it means I failed to protect you."

CHAPTER TWENTY-FOUR

After making sure they hadn't picked up a tail, Trent stopped at a restaurant for takeout. Returning to the parking garage, he escorted Grace to the elevator. "How do you feel about kids?" he asked as the car rose to their floor, keeping his attention on the doors in front of him. Was he rushing her?

Grace's head whipped his direction. "I love them. Why?"

Thank goodness. Yeah, he hadn't been subtle. But the subject of children was important to him, to them. He wanted a family, although not enough to give up the woman of his dreams if she'd been against the idea. Didn't mean he wouldn't have tried to persuade her to reconsider, even stoop to encouraging her to spend time with Del and Ivy's babies when they were born in a few months in an effort to stir Grace's interest in having a child of her own.

Pregnancy could be problematic for his sister who suffered from Sjogren's Syndrome. Might be caveman of him, but he wanted to pass on the name St. Claire to the next generation.

"Given any thought to how many children you might like to have?"

"Two or three."

"Dogs or cats?"

Another surprised glance from Grace. "Dogs. No cats. I'm allergic to them."

Awesome. He was a dog man himself, but he would have tolerated a feline in order for his kids to have a pet while they grew up.

"Where is all this going, honey?" Her gentle voice caused the region around his heart to warm.

"Future plans." He refused to say more at the moment. Besides, Grace was a smart woman. He'd already told her he loved her. The next logical step was marriage.

The elevator arrived at their floor and the doors slid open. Trent shoved the key card into the slot and twisted the knob.

His eyebrows shot up at the sight of Weston and Barton standing in the living room, facing Mason and Nicole. How did the detectives know where to find them? Had he made a mistake? His gut clenched at the possibility he might have endangered the woman he loved through carelessness.

Beside him, Grace stiffened. Trent pressed the palm of his free hand against her lower back, silently urging his girlfriend not to panic. The Dynamic Duo couldn't know he and Grace had been in Satterfield's house. Otherwise, they wouldn't have left after getting no response to their knocks. Grace needed to relax or the men would wonder why she was so nervous. "Detectives. What are doing here?"

"Where have you been?" Barton demanded.

Trent held up the bags of food, grateful for fast metabolism. "Buying dinner. Your turn. Why are you here?"

"Follow up."

Really? Trent's eyes narrowed. Looked as though the detectives had something more on their minds than asking the same questions. "Try again."

Weston snorted. "You think you're pretty smart, St. Claire."

A shrug. "You hungry?"

The detectives exchanged glances. "We could eat," Barton muttered. "Haven't had a chance to stop for food since we were at the hospital when Mr. Bowen was brought in."

Long day. He'd had his share of those. "Sit down. I bought plenty of food." Trent set the bags on the breakfast bar. "Only one stipulation, gentlemen. No shop talk while we eat."

The cops sat on the loveseat, leaving the sofa and recliner for the rest of them. "I'll get the soft drinks." Mason stood. "I'll bring a variety. You can choose what you want."

"I'll go with you," Nicole said.

While they were gone, Trent emptied the food bags. The scent of barbecued chicken, coleslaw, baked beans, and spiced apple slices made his mouth water. A third bag contained plates, utensils, and napkins.

Mason and Nicole distributed the soft drinks, then chose to sit at the breakfast bar while Trent and Grace ate their meals sitting on the sofa.

To their credit, the detectives kept the conversation to neutral topics. Once they finished the meal, Trent and Mason packed up the remaining food and stored it in the refrigerator. They had just enough food for Adam if he was hungry when he returned.

"Have you located Clarice?" Grace asked.

"Not yet." Weston pulled a notebook from his pocket along with a pen. "We're following a few leads."

Trent translated that into they didn't have anything to go on. If they did know something, the two men wouldn't be here, harassing them. "What do you want?"

"Guess the truce is over." Barton's smile held no warmth or humor, more a baring of teeth.

"What do you know about an attorney named Ron Satterfield?" Weston's pen was poised over his pad.

"Not much." Trent threaded his fingers through Grace's. Her hand trembled, the cold from her skin seeping into his own. "We met him at the Randall home. That's when we learned he's a partner in Simon's law firm."

Nicole twisted in her seat to stare at the detectives. "Do you know how Judy is?"

When both men's expressions went blank, Trent knew the sweet woman who had opened her home to them two evenings before was gone.

"She didn't make it," Barton said.

Nicole pressed her face against Mason's shoulder. He wrapped his arms around her and pressed a kiss to the top of her head.

"Oh, no," Grace whispered. "I don't understand why someone would kill her and Simon."

"You tell us, Ms. Rutledge."

"If I knew why they were targets, I'd share the information. Simon and Judy were great people and didn't deserve what happened to them."

"You don't have a clue what's going on, do you?" Nicole's voice conveyed her contempt for the two officers. "What about looking for the real culprit instead of going for an easy solution that's wrong? You're so convinced we're guilty, you aren't willing to accept the possibility that someone else might be responsible for the killing spree."

Mason laid one finger gently on her lips. When she glanced his way, he shook his head.

"Nic has a point." Grace tightened her hand around Trent's. "You have no proof we're guilty of hurting Devin or the Randalls, yet you persist in digging deeper, ignoring other people with motive to hurt them."

"Yeah, see, that's the thing that bugs us." Barton sneered. "You and your sister have the motive, means, and opportunity. Other people, not so much."

"Have you looked?" Mason asked.

"Sure, straight at you and lover-boy here," he said, inclining his head toward Trent.

Perfect. Just what Trent didn't want to hear. "This is getting us nowhere. Did you want to ask anything else? We can't help you with information we don't have about Satterfield."

"So you haven't seen him?" Weston held up his hand to his partner, halting any response he might have spat out at Trent and the others.

"Not since the night we transported Devin to the hospital."

At that moment, the door to the suite opened and Adam strode inside. His face betrayed no response to seeing the other two men in the suite although he nodded to acknowledge their presence.

"Detectives Weston and Barton, this is my friend, Adam. He's helping with protection. Adam, these are the detectives investigating Devin's poisoning and the murders of Simon and Judy Randall."

"Sorry to hear about Mrs. Randall." Adam slid his Go bag off his shoulder and stashed it inside the bedroom door where he'd be sleeping. When he returned, Trent told him about the meal waiting for him in the refrigerator.

Barton angled his chin toward the other operative. "What's his story?"

"A mission gone bad and, no, he can't tell you about it. The information is classified. Anything else you want to know, Barton?"

Another showing of teeth. "How long have you known about the life insurance policy on your girlfriend?"

CHAPTER TWENTY-FIVE

Trent's heart skipped a beat. Oh, man. Not good news. "Life insurance policy?"

"Don't play innocent with us." Weston stared at Trent, his gaze intent and jaw tight. "Barton tells me you're a Navy SEAL with serious connections. Do you think you can sell that innocent act? How long have you known someone would benefit from her death?"

"Contrary to what you believe, I have no idea what you're talking about." Trent didn't like how this was shaking out. Who was doing this? He needed to uncover the culprit soon or his beautiful Grace would be seeing the inside of a jail cell. All of them might end up in a jail cell before this investigation was finished.

One thing he knew in his gut. Whoever was behind this meant to take out all three of Mrs. Bowen's offspring or at least make that appear to be the case.

Barton sneered. "So much for you being the best." He shifted his gaze to Grace. "If you're smart, Blondie, you'll find a new champion. This one's liable to land you in jail."

"What life insurance policy are you talking about?" Nicole asked.

"The one taken out by Devin Bowen on Blondie along with a separate one on you." His gaze slid to Mason. "Makes me wonder how much your boyfriend values your life."

"Knock it off. My boyfriend is not a killer."

"The same can't be said of St. Claire."

Trent tightened his grip on Grace's hand to keep her from adding more raw emotion to the mix. "When were the policies taken out?" When the detective just smiled, Trent resisted the urge to roll his eyes. So the cops were playing power games. Fine. He'd go around law enforcement to find out what he needed. He needed to move fast. Sooner or later, Barton and Weston would discover the insurance policies he'd found in Satterfield's office, policies he believed Grace and Nicole knew nothing about.

"Look, Detective Barton," Grace said. "It matters when the policies were taken out. Nic and I didn't know Mrs. Bowen was our birth mother until Monday."

The two detectives exchanged glances again. "You can prove your claim?" This from Weston.

She retrieved her purse, pulled out a piece of paper, and handed it to the detective. "This is what Simon Randall gave me in his office Monday morning."

Nicole slid down from her stool, dug out her own paper, and gave it to Barton. "Mrs. Bowen specified in her will that we weren't to be notified of her identity until ninety days after her death. Ninety days was Monday. We didn't know Devin existed until two days ago."

"Hope you don't expect me to take your word for that," Barton said. "Someone could have leaked the news long before Monday. I bet St. Claire and his cronies would have no problem devising a plan to rid the world of a threat to his woman."

The policemen examined the letters carefully. Weston stood. "I'll be back in a minute." He left the suite with both letters in one hand, his cell phone clutched in the other.

Trent's cell signaled an incoming text. He checked his screen, stood. With a glance at Adam, who nodded his agreement to watch over the others, Trent walked into the bedroom he shared with the other men and closed the door.

"What do you have for me, Zane?"

"Nothing good. We had the lab fast track your bullet casing."

"And?"

"Got nothing. No prints. No matches in the system."

So the gun hadn't been used in a crime until yesterday. "Not a surprise. Nothing has been easy or straightforward to this point. You could have simply texted that information. What else do you have?"

"Either Grace or someone posing as her has been making inquiries about buying land and building a house on the outskirts of Otter Creek."

Trent frowned. He supposed his girlfriend could have been investigating that. She'd told him she wanted something of her own. Her not discussing the idea with him did surprise Trent. She'd started using him as a sounding board not long after they started dating. Had to admit it bothered him a little that she pursued the idea without at least telling him she was thinking about a house. If it was her.

Now that he wanted to marry her sooner than later, a house instead of an apartment might be a great idea. According to Mason, there was a building boom in town and a shortage of laborers. Building a new house might take as much as six or eight months to complete.

What about his job? A knot formed in his stomach. Trent loved his work. His body, however, was starting to slow down. His time in the SEALs and his years in black ops were taking their toll. Beyond that, leaving Grace was becoming harder and harder to handle. He missed her with a bone deep ache while he was gone. Couldn't sleep much, appetite suppressed. Yeah, he was totally gone over his woman. Couldn't deny the truth and didn't want to. She'd burrowed deep into his heart and become as necessary to him as breathing.

"I don't know if Grace is thinking of building a house, Z. She hasn't mentioned it, although we haven't had much time alone since I've been home."

And there was that word again. Home. Had Otter Creek become home when he wasn't looking? Perhaps he was associating the town with Grace. He would live anywhere as long as he was with the love of his life.

"Here's the other problem. It's not just a regular house, buddy. The plan mentioned in the email to Elliott Construction is for a 6,000 square foot home. There's no way Grace could afford a house that large based on her income alone. Elliott estimated the house would cost well over $1 million to build."

Knowing the amount of money her birth mother had set aside for her, she could pay for the home in cash. Unfortunately for the person setting up the women, the time line didn't fit in the scheme unless they had prior knowledge of the bequest. "Then it's definitely not Grace. She didn't know about the money from Mrs. Bowen until Monday. What about Nicole? Anything odd with her?"

"Funny you should ask. Apparently, Nicole has been bitten by wanderlust. She's planning to travel around the world for the next several months."

Trent's lips curled. "And leave her boyfriend behind? Can't see that happening."

"The boyfriend-girlfriend thing is fake."

"Not so fake anymore. Someone is out to make the sisters look guilty of murdering the Randalls and attempting to kill their half brother."

"Wait, murdering the Randalls, plural? I thought you said Simon passed away, but not his wife."

"Mrs. Randall didn't survive the shooting."

Zane growled.

"Something else you need to know." Trent explained about the insurance policies on the three siblings, and Devin's missing wife and lawyer.

The Fortress tech guru whistled. "What do you want me to do?"

"First, find a copy of the original insurance policies. We need to know when the policies were taken out. Second, I need to locate Clarice and Ron Satterfield. They both have questions to answer."

"I'll start searching for them. Unless they're off the grid, I'll find them. Do you think they're together?"

"Found pictures that confirmed it and, according to Grace and Nicole, they were giving off couple vibes the other night." Though he hadn't chimed in on that discussion, Trent noticed the atmosphere of intimacy the two created when they were in the same vicinity.

Like Mason, he felt for Devin. Had to bite seeing your wife cozying up to another man. Why wasn't Devin more upset? Trent would never allow another man to make moves on his Grace.

"With her husband in the room to watch them interact? Cold. I'll let you know as soon as I come up with anything. Did Adam stop by?"

"Yeah. He dropped off the package. He'll be staying for a few days."

Zane was silent a moment. "You can't talk freely?"

"Nope." He dropped his voice further. "Barton and Weston are here."

"How did they find you?"

"Don't know, but I'm going to find out. Do me a favor and make some inquiries at Fortress. I want to know if someone gave out too much information."

"I can't see one of our own putting you at risk, Trent."

"Neither can I, but I need to be sure. I think the information came from this end, though." If he had to guess, he'd say it was Nicole. She didn't know exactly what Trent did or how seriously he took security. He figured one of the detectives used intimidation tactics to discover the location of their new hotel. "Later, Z."

He slid the phone into his pocket, making a mental note to call Maddox during his turn at night watch. He'd promised to keep his boss apprised of the situation. Trent grimaced. Ethan needed the latest as well. Wouldn't be wise to tick off Mason's parole officer. The police chief made a formidable enemy.

When he returned to the living room, Weston was handing the letters from Mrs. Bowen to Grace and her sister.

"We'll be in touch," the detective said. "Don't leave town."

"No more moving," Barton snapped.

"Can't guarantee either one." Trent folded his arms across his chest. "We have jobs. This visit to Dumas was supposed to be short term. We'll stay here as long as Grace and Nicole are safe and our employers allow. I will let you know when we leave."

"Listen, St. Claire, I could toss the lot of you in jail."

"We'd already be in a jail cell if you had proof we were guilty of a crime."

"Barton." Weston tilted his chin toward the door. "We'll see ourselves out," he murmured. Another glare from Barton, and the two detectives left.

"Why won't they leave us alone?" Nicole scowled. "We told them everything we know."

"Your names keep surfacing in their investigation," Adam said. "No chance that's a coincidence."

"How did they know where to find us?" Grace asked.

Nicole's face flushed.

"Nicole?" Mason frowned. "What's wrong?"

"You talked to one of the detectives, didn't you?" Grace groaned. "Oh, Nic."

The other woman flinched. "I'm sorry. Barton didn't give me a choice."

Mason clasped her hand. "Why did you tell them where we are?" When she refused to say anything, he sighed. "They threatened me."

"Barton said he would take you in, tell the judge you were a flight risk, and make sure you wouldn't get bail unless I told him. I couldn't let him do that to you, not again."

"The detective was blowing smoke, Nicole." Adam stood and tossed his trash in the garbage can. "Now Mason's safety and yours has been compromised."

Nicole paled. "The police wouldn't tell anyone. Would they?"

"Police stations aren't secure. Wouldn't be surprised if word leaks again."

"How could you, Nic?" Grace dragged her hands through her hair, rumpling the strands. "Trent can't be on anyone's radar. It's not safe for people to know where he's staying."

"What are you talking about? He can't live off the grid."

"It's okay, baby," Trent murmured. He didn't want her to say something in anger she might regret later.

"No, it's not. She has to know how this works. I love you too much to lose you because we compromised your safety, Trent." She moved two steps closer to Nicole. "There are evil people who have a bullet with Trent's name on it. If they find out where he is, his sister Darcy, her husband Rio, plus Rio's teammates and their wives are all in danger from these people. If they find Trent, they find me, you, and Mason."

"You're serious?" Nicole whispered.

"Trent's a SEAL and still works missions in ugly places around the world with Fortress. His enemies would love nothing better than to kill him and anyone he cares about."

Tears pooled in the other woman's eyes when she looked at Trent. "I'm sorry, Trent. I was trying to protect Mason."

The construction worker hooked his arm around Nicole's shoulders and tucked her against his side. "I can handle whatever I have to. My main concern is you and your safety. Don't put yourself at risk again."

"What should we do now?" Grace asked Trent. "Do we need to find another hotel?"

"We should be safe enough for tonight. If we have to stay another night in Dumas, we'll move to another hotel further out, maybe in the next town." Trent sighed. "All of you should sit down. We need to talk."

"Bad news?" Adam asked.

"Someone is going to a lot of trouble to set up Grace and Nicole." When the others were seated, Trent summarized the information Zane had provided.

"A house?" Grace's voice soared. "That's ridiculous. I can't afford to buy a house, especially not one that large."

Trent raised his eyebrow.

"Well, all right, I can afford it now, but I couldn't two days ago. I haven't thought about buying or building a house."

"I like the idea of traveling around the world." Nicole smiled. "I might do that when I retire. If you need it confirmed, Trent, I haven't been looking into the travel possibility, either."

"There's more, isn't there?" Adam glanced over his shoulder from where he been keeping watch out the French doors.

"We need to unravel this mess, fast. Not only does Devin have insurance policies on Grace and Nicole, they have one on him. If he dies, they get the Bowen estate plus the money from their birth mother, and the insurance pays $2 million to each of the sisters."

CHAPTER TWENTY-SIX

Grace pressed her hands to her cheeks. "This is crazy. How do we confirm or deny any of this? The Dynamic Duo won't believe anything we say. They already decided we're guilty."

"We need to talk to Devin." Nicole's expression said more than her words. Grim determination showed on her face. "If he's not behind this, then he's in as much danger as we are. I don't like him, but I don't wish him ill, either."

"Wonder how he feels about jail." Grace spun to face Trent. "Is it safe enough for us to go to the hospital to see him?"

Trent's resistance to the idea was obvious based on the lack of expression on her boyfriend's face. Instead of disagreeing, Trent rubbed his bristled jaw and said, "I don't like the risk, but any hope of talking to him will come through you and Nicole."

"He might know something that helps. At the very least, we can warn him about the real possibility of recuperating in jail. The detectives are convinced of our guilt. Sooner or later, they'll turn questioning eyes toward

Devin and wonder if he's in cahoots with someone else to knock us off."

"You're saying he poisoned himself?" Mason asked, sounding skeptical.

Considering that possibility made Grace's stomach churn. If he had, Devin was lucky she'd insisted he go to the hospital instead of assuming his illness was a stomach bug. Then again, he may have convinced Clarice to take him before it was too late. "Something to consider."

"Stupid thing to do. Wouldn't take much to miscalculate and kill yourself by accident." Adam stretched out in the recliner, a grimace on his face.

Grace observed his stiff movements. "Back?" she guessed.

"Leg. Tweaked a hamstring yesterday. Durango doesn't hold back for themselves or anyone else."

She could imagine. Those men were in top physical shape and ran the bodyguard recruits into the ground to improve their stamina in case the worst possible circumstances occurred.

Grace found her bottle of pain reliever and shook a couple into her palm for the hurting operative. "I'll get water for you."

He waved that aside. "Don't bother." Adam tossed the pills into his mouth and swallowed them dry.

Trent pulled out his keys. "Are you staying here, Nicole, or going to the hospital as well?"

She snatched up her purse. "Going. I want to hear what Devin has to say for himself."

Adam straightened in the chair. "I'll drive my vehicle, watch your six."

Within minutes, the two-vehicle caravan began the drive to the hospital. Trent glanced in the rearview mirror at Mason. "Time to check in with Ethan. If I use my cell, the call will go through the audio system."

"That's fine. It's not like I have any secrets."

A moment later, Ethan Blackhawk's voice filled the cab of the SUV. "Sit rep."

"You're on speaker with Grace, Nicole, and Mason. We're on the way to the hospital to see Devin Bowen."

"Something new there?"

"You could say that." Trent updated the police chief, making sure he knew Mason was out of the loop on questionable activities.

"Mason, how do you feel after that truck sideswiped you?" Ethan asked.

"Sore, stiff. Glad to be alive."

A baby cried in the background and Grace's heart melted. Ethan must be at home with his son. "How is Lucas?" she asked.

A chuckle. "In fine form. He has a great pair of lungs. We're having a male bonding hour because Serena is delivering baked goods to the bookstore."

"We won't keep you," Trent said. "What time do you want Mason's next check in?"

"Six tomorrow morning unless something happens I need to know about. Mason, watch your back. The detectives would love to pin something on you and toss you behind bars."

"They made that clear."

"Don't give them anything to use. My wife likes you and I hate to see her cry."

Trent ended the call with Ethan as he turned into the parking lot of the hospital. Grace was surprised the lot was full. She was used to Otter Creek's rhythm. At this time of evening, Memorial's parking lot had plenty of empty places available. This lot, though, was still full. Trent found a place in the corner. Adam parked a short distance away and jogged to their SUV.

"Anything?" Trent asked.

"Nope. I'll stay out here, make sure no one messes with your ride."

Grace breathed a sigh of relief. Maybe they were catching a break. Suited her. They were due for one. Inside the hospital, she crossed the ER lobby to the desk and asked about Devin.

"He's still in critical care, Ms. Rutledge." The woman glanced at Nicole. "You and your sister can see him with your husbands. One couple at a time, though."

Grace's cheeks burned, but she didn't correct the woman's incorrect assumption. One day soon, if she had her way, Trent would be her husband. She had waited what seemed like a lifetime. She wanted to marry that man.

They rode the elevator to the fifth floor and passed the nurses' desk. Grace waved at the woman on duty, one she recognized from the night they'd brought in Devin. She inclined her head toward the open doorway to their right. "Nic, do you and Mason want to sit in the waiting room?"

She shook her head. "I want to hear what he says."

"Sweetheart, you and Nicole go in. Mason and I will stand outside his room where we can hear what he says." Trent brushed his lips over hers. "See what you can find out."

When Grace walked into the small room with Nicole a step behind, she pulled up short at the sight of the scrub-clad man hovering near the IV stand, syringe in hand. He turned as they entered, capped the needle of the full syringe, and shoved it into his pocket. Behind his surgical mask, he mumbled something Grace didn't catch and left the room.

She frowned, watching him leave. That was strange. Why hadn't he administered the meds or asked them to wait until he finished?

Grace continued across the room. She and Nic stopped at their brother's bedside. "Devin?"

He stirred, his lips curving. "Clarice. I knew you would come." Devin slowly lifted his eyelids. When his eyes focused on Grace, the smile morphed into a frown. "What are you doing here?"

"Checking on you. You were so sick."

"Thanks to you," he muttered.

"Hey," Nicole snapped. "You're lucky Grace insisted we take you to the hospital. She saved your life, Devin."

"Right. Guess that's the least she could do since she tried to kill me."

Grace frowned. "Who told you that?"

"Clarice. Where is she? Did you hurt her, too?"

"Your wife is wrong. If I was guilty of trying to kill you, I would have let you go home to die."

"There's no evidence we tried to kill you." Nic sat in the chair beside his bed. "The detectives have been trying to pin everything on us and can't."

"Devin, do you know any reason someone would hurt you?" Grace asked.

"Besides you, no."

"We didn't try to kill you, but someone is going to a lot of trouble to make it seem that way."

"Why should I believe you?"

"Because the same person is trying to make you appear guilty as well."

Devin frowned. "What are you talking about? I'm not guilty of anything."

"Won't look that way to the police. In fact," Grace said, "I'm surprised they haven't already been by to ask more questions."

"About what?"

"The life insurance policy you took out on us."

"I didn't take a policy out on you two. How could I? I didn't know you existed until Monday."

"We only have your word for that," Nic pointed out. "What if you did know? Would have been easy to arrange the policies."

"We seem to have taken a life insurance policy on you, too." Grace watched Devin carefully for any signs that he already knew the information. His shock convinced her Devin wasn't the one behind the attacks.

"This doesn't make sense. I'm not guilty of anything."

"Neither are we. Somebody is trying to frame all three of us. He also attempted to kill Trent and Mason in the past twelve hours. So you need to think hard, Devin. Who has reason to want you dead?"

Grace noted his heart rate spike on the monitor. She clasped his hand. "Devin, look at me." When he focused on her face, she said, "We'll figure it out and stop them. Trent won't rest until he's uncovered the culprit."

"He doesn't know me. Why would he help?"

"He hates injustice." That truth was why Trent continued to fight against terrorists. Sure, the Navy had trained him well to do his job, spending a ton of money on the training. He could have walked away from that life to do something else. Instead, he chose to stay and continue to wage war on those who preyed on the innocent.

"Where is Clarice?" His gaze flicked to the open doorway, locking on Trent and Mason. "I thought she would be here."

Grace and Nic exchanged glances. Oh, boy. Did they tell him his wife was missing? She looked at Trent and saw an almost imperceptible head shake. Deflect, then. She didn't have a choice. "We haven't seen her since we brought you to the hospital." She smiled. "She doesn't like us much so you shouldn't be surprised we haven't spoken to her."

"She doesn't mean anything by it, you know."

Could have fooled her. If she had to guess, Grace would say Devin's wife hated her and Nicole. "Why do you say that?"

"Clarice grew up on welfare. She worries about not having enough money."

"Understandable." Didn't excuse her rude behavior, but at least it made sense. "She doesn't have anything to worry about from us, Devin."

He snorted. "How can you say that? The Bowen estate is on the table."

"That's your inheritance. Your mother wanted you to have control of the company. If she'd meant for Nic and I to share in the estate, she would have said so in her letters to us."

Devin was silent a moment. "She named the company after you two," he said softly. "G & N Chemicals stands for Grace and Nicole."

"I think it was her way of acknowledging our existence," Nic said. "But we weren't part of your family. We'll be forever grateful that she chose such good families for us, Devin. We grew up loved. Our families dote on us, treat us as though we were blood kin. We couldn't ask for more than that."

He studied each of them in turn. "You really mean that, don't you?"

"Absolutely. We were two of the lucky ones. We didn't grow up in foster care."

Time to wrap this up, Grace thought. Devin looked tired. "Do you need anything before we leave you to rest?"

"I would kill for a soft drink. Something with caffeine. I have a massive headache from not drinking enough coffee."

Grace smiled. "You probably don't want too much coffee right now. Your system won't like it. I'll see if I can find you something. Is it all right if Trent and Mason visit with you for a minute?"

He looked resigned. "Sure."

The two women left the room. "Trent, I need to find him a soft drink."

"I saw a vending machine in the hall near the waiting room," Mason said. "It's around the corner."

"I'll go, Grace," Nicole said. "I could use some caffeine myself. Stay and talk to the nursing staff. Find out how Devin's really doing and when he'll be able to go home."

"I can get it," Mason said.

"You should talk to Devin. I'll be gone for a minute. Besides, you might find out more than we did."

"Go easy, though," Grace said. "He's getting tired."

When Mason hesitated, Nicole clasped his hand briefly. "Go on. I'll be fine. I promise. I'll be gone for a minute, tops." With that, she strode through the doorway and turned the corner.

"I'll wait for her," Mason murmured to Trent. "See what information you can learn from Devin."

Grace walked to the desk to talk to Candy, the nurse she'd become friends with. "How's it going, Candy?"

"Kind of dull, I'm happy to say." A broad smile curved the woman's lips. "Your brother is doing much better this evening."

"He looks good. Any word on when he'll be released?"

"He'll go to a private room tomorrow morning. If he continues to improve, I heard the doctor say Mr. Bowen might go home the day after tomorrow."

"Devin will be happy to hear that."

A blood-curdling scream ripped through the quiet of the critical care unit.

CHAPTER TWENTY-SEVEN

Trent glanced up in time to see Mason sprint through the doorway Nicole had passed minutes before. He raced from Devin's room and followed Mason, Grace a few steps behind Trent.

Mason turned the corner. "Nicole?" He skidded to a stop, looked over his shoulder, panic in his eyes. "She's not at the vending machine."

Though no one else was in the hall, a door slammed nearby, the sound echoing. Trent scanned the corridor, saw the sign indicating the stairwell. "Stairs." He prayed they were in time, that she was still in the building. Grace's sister had only been out of their sight for maybe two minutes. Unfortunately, a lot of bad things could happen in two minutes or less.

The construction worker shoved opened the door before Trent could stop him. "Nicole!" He ran into the stairwell and out of sight.

Trent made sure Grace was behind him as they approached the stairwell. "Wait until I tell you it's safe." He was grateful she didn't argue with him. He cleared the threshold and peered down the stairs, his hand hovering near the Sig secured in his mid-back holster.

His stomach knotted. Nicole lay crumpled at the bottom of a flight of stairs, unmoving. A quick scan assured him no one else was in the vicinity. "Grace, Nicole's hurt."

"Nicole? Talk to me, sweetheart." Mason dropped to his knees beside her, brushing her hair from her face. "Where do you hurt?"

No response. Surprised Grace hadn't already shoved past him, Trent looked back. His heart skipped a beat when he realized she wasn't there. She'd been right behind him. Had someone grabbed her while his attention had been on Nicole? He spun on his heel to retrace his steps when she darted into the stairwell again.

She ran past him. "I told Candy to find a couple orderlies with a stretcher. They should be here soon."

Smart lady. He followed her down the stairs, on alert in case there was another problem or an attempt to grab Grace. On the landing below, Nicole moaned, stirred.

"Nicole?" Mason covered her hand with his without moving her arm. "Come on, baby. Wake up."

"Nic? It's Grace. Where do you hurt?"

"Arm. Hurts bad enough I want to throw up. Massive headache."

Trent looked at the arm near Mason. Looked normal to him. When he checked the other one, he winced. Trent wasn't a medic, but even he couldn't miss the fact her arm was broken.

Grace checked both arms. Nicole hissed when Grace touched the broken one. "Sorry. Anything else hurt, Nic?"

"Left ankle."

A moment later, Grace said, "Looks like a sprain. What about your back or hips?"

"They ache, but nothing like the arm."

"At least you can feel them. Did you hit your head when you fell?"

She shook her head, winced. "I don't remember. I think I blacked out for a minute or two."

"What were you doing in the stairwell?" Trent asked.

"Some guy dressed in scrubs and a mask grabbed me at the vending machine. He dragged me into the stairwell. I fought him off, but lost my footing and tumbled down the stairs."

He heard footsteps running their direction and figured he had only a few more seconds to find out what he could. "Did he say anything to you?"

"Does 'Come with me now or you die' count?"

Trent grinned. Hurting or not, she still had that snarky sense of humor. "Did you recognize his voice?"

"The creep whispered. It could have been my father and I wouldn't have recognized his voice."

The orderlies appeared on the landing above them and started down the stairs with the gurney.

"Nic, the orderlies are going to use a backboard to lift you onto the gurney. Don't try to help. Let them do the work." Grace moved out of the way. "Broken right arm and left ankle sprain. Not sure if she has any other injuries."

Minutes later, the orderlies carried the stretcher bearing Nicole up the stairs with a grim-faced Mason right behind them.

"Are you okay?" Trent wrapped his arm around Grace's waist as they followed.

"I think the guy who grabbed Nic was in Devin's hospital room when we arrived."

He remembered seeing the man who looked like one of hundreds of medical personnel who worked in this hospital. Nothing about him stood out. "Would you recognize him if you saw him again?"

She shook her head. "Scrubs and surgical mask, like Nic said. He had a full syringe in his hand. Instead of finishing his job, he mumbled something and left without administering the meds."

He wanted to know what was in the syringe. Probably nothing good. "How bad is Nicole?"

"The break is one of the worst I've seen. She'll have to have surgery to repair the damage." Grace sighed. "She's not going to be happy about that. Nic will be off work for several more days and her boss isn't the most understanding guy around. I'm afraid she'll lose her job."

He and Grace waited in the ER waiting room with Mason. The construction worker paced, something Trent would have been doing if Grace was the one being examined by a doctor. Again he wondered how deep Mason's feelings ran. Yeah, it was fast, but Trent understood how it could be when the right woman crossed your path. One look at Grace, and he'd been a goner.

An hour later, the doctor who treated Devin walked into the room. "Ms. Copeland needs surgery on her arm."

"Can I see her before she goes to surgery?" Mason asked.

Speculation lit the doctor's gaze. "She's asking for you, Mason. Don't expect her to talk much. She's been given medicine to make her sleepy in preparation for the surgery. She'll be in and out."

"I understand."

"How are you doing? No repercussions from the truck incident?"

He waved the doctor's concern aside. "I'm fine. When can I see Nicole?"

"Better go now. They'll come take her soon."

Mason hurried from the room.

"Cute couple," the doctor commented. "I'd hoped not to see you folks again, at least not under these circumstances."

"Same here," Trent said. "What are the extent of her injuries?"

"Broken arm, sprained ankle, couple of cracked ribs, a concussion. She's lucky the injuries weren't worse. The good news is she'll recover fully."

"Can we see her a minute?" Grace asked.

A slow smile spread across the doctor's face. "If her boyfriend will give you time with her. I wouldn't take bets on that one."

Trent escorted Grace to the exam room. They walked in to see Mason bent over Nicole, his mouth close to her ear. She was nodding at whatever he was saying.

"Nic." Grace crossed the room to her sister's bedside. "How do you feel?"

"Good. Real good. The drugs they gave me work great. Did you catch the guy?"

"No, sugar." Trent squeezed her uninjured arm. "Adam didn't see him leave the hospital. I'll be talking to security while you're in surgery. With luck, we'll score a picture of him without the mask." Doubtful but worth a shot anyway.

Two orderlies arrived.

Mason stroked Nicole's cheek. "We'll be here when you wake up." A brief kiss, and the two men took her away.

"Come on." Trent clapped Mason on the shoulder. "Let's get some coffee while we wait."

"It should be me having surgery. I should have insisted on going for the soft drink for Devin."

"Mason, there's something you should know about Nic," Grace said. "She's stubborn and has an independent streak a mile wide. You can't protect her from everything. No one could have guessed a trip to the vending machine would turn out like this."

"She's a fighter, Mase." Trent squeezed his shoulder. "If she hadn't been, the creep would have abducted her from the hospital. There's no telling where she would be now. The doc said she's going to recover. Hold on to that."

"Nicole will have to stay overnight?" Mason asked Grace.

"At least."

"I'm staying with her. She's vulnerable here. No one is going to hurt her again."

"I didn't expect any different."

After taking a soft drink with caffeine to Devin, they got themselves coffee from the cafeteria and returned to the waiting room to wait for word on Nicole's surgery. Two hours later, a different doctor walked into the room. "Ms. Copeland's family?"

The three of them stood.

"I'm Dr. Wilson, the orthopedist who operated on Ms. Copeland. She did great. Her arm was broken in two places. We had to use pins to hold the bone in place. She's in recovery. You can go back, but she's groggy and will be for a while."

After they walked into the recovery room, Grace stayed back with Trent, allowing Mason a couple minutes alone with Nicole before they walked over.

"Hey." Nicole gave them a small smile, her gaze unfocused.

"Looking good, beautiful." Trent patted her shoulder as he peered at her arm, splinted with metal bars and the pins holding her bones in place so she could heal.

"Liar. When can I get out of here?"

"Not for a while, Nic." Grace squeezed her hand.

"I feel fine."

"Trust me. That's the drugs talking. You won't feel fine after they wear off."

For the next hour, Nicole kept falling asleep, then waking up again. By the time she was taken to a private room, she was more alert. "Are you going back to the hotel now?" she asked.

"I'm staying with you." Mason clasped her hand. "No one will hurt you again, Nicole. I promise you that."

She smiled, then glanced at Grace and Trent. "What about you two?"

Trent eyed Mason. "Need backup, Mase?"

"I've got this. Get some rest. Find this creep, Trent. If you don't, I will."

CHAPTER TWENTY-EIGHT

Trent held Grace's hand as he drove through the quiet streets of Dumas. Night had fallen hours before while they waited for Nicole's surgery to be completed. Though she hadn't said as much, his girlfriend had to be exhausted. From experience, he knew the adrenaline rush had faded hours ago, leaving behind bone-deep exhaustion in its wake.

"He's falling in love with her," Grace murmured as Trent parked in the hotel garage, close to the elevator.

Yeah, he figured as much. "What about her? Does she feel the same?" If Nicole rejected Mason, she would gut him. His own blood ran cold at the thought of Grace ever rejecting him.

"She hasn't said, but I've never seen her this content. Mason is good for her."

"I know my next question is premature, but I'm asking anyway. Is she willing to move to Otter Creek?" He turned off the engine. "He can't move without jumping through a lot of legal hoops. Worse, because he's got a record, not many employers will give him a chance to prove himself trustworthy. Mase is a good man, and he's made a good life for himself in Otter Creek."

"I'll find out." A grin appeared. "I've been after her to move to Otter Creek. Maybe now I finally have the leverage I need to seal the deal."

When Trent, Grace, and Adam returned to the suite. Adam disappeared into the second bedroom and closed the door. He had the second watch of the night. Trent suspected the silent operative was also giving him time alone with Grace. His friend slept little at night since his captivity and torture months ago.

Trent wrapped his arms around Grace and drew her close. "I'll be in the living room the first part of the night. Adam takes over the watch at 2:00. I'll be close if you need me."

"We have to stop this man. To do that, we need to find him. How are we going to find a nameless, faceless ghost, Trent?"

He leaned down and kissed her, slow and deep, before answering her question. "The head of security at the hospital will send me a copy of the footage from cameras in the corridors and parking lots. I'll review them during my watch, see if I can ID this guy. I'll call Zane, see if he has anything new for me. We'll go from there."

"What can I do to help?" Her eyes gleamed, determination shining in their depths.

"Rest. Tomorrow, we're hunting for a killer."

A slow smile spread over her face. "We? You'll let me help?"

As if he could stop her, especially after this creep injured Nicole. "And if I said I meant Adam, not you?"

"I'd be ticked off. He hurt my sister. No one gets by with that."

"That's what I figured. Adam will be giving Mason a break at the hospital for a few hours tomorrow. Even if Mase won't leave for long, getting out of the room and walking around a bit will be good for him. He'll feel more comfortable if Adam is protecting her. Besides, Nicole might need Mase to run an errand or sneak food in."

"I didn't hear that."

Trent chuckled. "Rest, baby." He brushed a soft kiss over her lips. "I love you, Grace. More than I can say."

"I love you, too, Trent. Thanks for taking a leap of faith and asking me for a date last year."

"Best decision I ever made, my love." Knowing his control was at the breaking point, he nudged her toward her bedroom, forcing himself to stay in place.

Once she'd closed the door to her room, Trent turned the lights down in the suite's living area. He didn't need overhead lights with his computer screen backlit.

Grabbing his laptop, he settled on the couch, Sig within easy reach. He booted up his computer and checked his email. Just like the security chief promised, the hospital camera footage was in his inbox.

Anticipation zinging through his system, for the next hour Trent watched the silent feed. Because he couldn't narrow down the time the thug entered the hospital with the information he had so far, Trent was forced to watch several hours of footage sped up.

Only one man caught his attention. This one entered the hospital about fifteen minutes before Trent and the others arrived, already clad in scrubs, mask, and surgical cap. No one else entering the hospital on the hours of security footage he watched did the same.

He frowned. Something about this guy seemed familiar. But what? It's not like he could see any part of his face.

Something about his walk, though, told Trent he'd seen the man before noticing him in Devin's room. He copied that part of the footage in a separate file. Over the next hour, he tracked the man's movements through the hospital, a game of virtual hide-and-seek.

With the mask on his face, no one would recognize him. Trent hoped he removed his mask when he left the hospital, but didn't hold out much hope of that happening.

When his vision blurred, Trent decided it was time for a break, grabbed his cell phone, and called Zane.

"What do you need?"

Weeks of uninterrupted time with Grace. A million of her kisses. A lifetime of safety for her and their future children. A job where he didn't have to leave her for weeks at a time. "About six hours of uninterrupted sleep. You got any?"

A snort. "Check with me after I retire in fifty years. What's going on, Trent? Late for you to call and gab."

He checked the time, winced. "Sorry, man. Tell Claire I owe her dinner when I'm back in Nashville."

"Deal. Prepare to pay up. She has great taste."

"Hmm. That's not what Adam says."

Zane chuckled. "My brother-in-law is not shy about sharing that information. Tell me something I don't know."

"Someone tried to take out Devin Bowen a few hours ago. When he failed, he attempted to abduct Nicole. She fought him off, but fell down a flight of stairs."

"She all right?"

"Broken arm, cracked ribs, but she'll recover. Had to surgically repair the arm."

"Oh, man. Grace wasn't hurt?"

"No." But it could have been his girlfriend. Next time, she might not be so lucky. "Have anything new for me?"

"I've been doing some research."

"And?"

"Found confirmation that Clarice Bowen and Ron Satterfield are having an affair. They haven't been as careful as they should be for the past year. There's a trail of credit card receipts for hotel rooms and vacation getaways for two on dates when Bowen was occupied somewhere else. The interesting thing is all the reservations are in Mrs.

Bowen's name, but the food, champagne, flowers, chocolate, and couples massages were on Satterfield's card. That's not counting the number of meals they shared in Dumas. I can't figure out how a neighbor or friend hasn't run across them on one of their many trysts and informed Devin."

Trent frowned. Based on what he'd overheard Devin tell Grace and Nicole, he was surprised she would jeopardize her marriage and the income generated by G & N Chemicals. If Devin found out about Satterfield, Clarice stood to lose everything. Money, status, security. Didn't add up for her to take such a risk. "Did you learn anything else?"

"Satterfield is a trust fund baby. His parents are deceased as of five years ago. Left him with a sizable amount of money at the time."

"How does the account look now?"

"Anemic. The lawyer bought his way into a partnership at the law firm, then proceeded to systematically live like he's much richer than he is. He's blown through ninety percent of his trust fund. At the rate he's spending, Satterfield has about a year left. After that, he'll be stuck living on his salary."

Trent grunted. That would hurt. Cutting back ingrained spending habits was hard to do. So why was Clarice with this clown? Maybe she didn't know he skated on thin ice financially. What did he have to offer her that Devin couldn't? "Hospital security sent me footage from the cameras around the time of Nicole's attack. When I finish tracking the man through the hospital, I'll send you a copy. See if you can ID this mutt. So far, I'm not having much luck. He's smart, covered his face and hair with surgical gear before he came into the hospital."

"And that made him stand out. Did he have hospital ID on his clothes?"

Trent frowned. "Yeah, I did see a tag. I doubt it's real."

"Maybe not. I'll track it anyway, see what turns up. How's Adam?"

"Sleeping right now. He'll keep a discreet eye on Mason and Nicole for a few hours tomorrow while Grace and I look for Satterfield and Clarice."

"You sure you want to include Grace in this snipe hunt? If you corner the tango, he'll fight back."

"I don't have a choice, Z. I can't leave her unprotected at the hotel."

"What about stashing her with Adam at the hospital? She could visit with her sister."

"If I thought she'd stay there, I would choose that option. Grace is worried about me not having anyone at my back to protect me."

Zane was quiet a moment. "Do you know what a gift she is?" he asked, his voice soft. "Most women want nothing to do with our work. Yours is fighting for the right to protect you, to be part of your world on a small scale."

"I won't ever take the gift or the woman for granted. I didn't believe I'd find anyone who could handle my career choice until I met Grace. I'm in love with her, Zane. As soon as I can convince her to take a chance on a lifetime with me, I'm marrying her."

"Congratulations, Trent. Grace Rutledge is a treasure worth protecting. Just watch your step, buddy. The cops aren't going to like you interfering in their case."

"At the moment, they're convinced the four of us are guilty of murder."

"Then don't give them an excuse to look deeper."

Trent ended the call and returned to scouring the security footage. The short break from the screen had cleared his vision and his mind. Another hour passed when his concentration was broken by Grace's door opening.

He set aside his laptop, grabbed his Sig and stood, concern tightening his gut. "What's wrong?"

"Can't sleep. Do you mind company?"

"Of course not." Trent slid his weapon back into his holster. "Come sit with me. I need to finish scanning the security footage from the hospital. Want to help? Fair warning, though. It's about as exciting as watching paint dry."

In answer, she sat on the couch. She wore tennis shoes, yoga pants, and one of his Navy t-shirts. His lips twitched. He'd wondered where that shirt had gone to. Made him feel good that Grace had stolen his shirt to use for sleepwear, as if she wanted him close to her heart even while she slept.

Trent resumed his seat on the couch and grabbed his laptop. With a touch of his finger, he restarted the video feed of the corridors leading to the critical care unit. The man Trent followed on the security feed appeared on the screen.

Grace leaned closer to the laptop. "There." She pointed to the masked man. "That's the guy I saw in Devin's room."

"How can you tell?" he asked, curious about her observation skills. He was convinced this was the man who hurt Nicole as well. "He looks like hundreds of other men in scrubs to me."

"Look at the way he holds his left hand. The guy in Devin's room had the same nervous twitch. Can you zoom in on his shoes?"

He turned on his mouse and shifted the view on the screen. Trent focused on the shoes and enhanced the picture. He frowned. "Dress shoes."

"No intern, physician, nurse, or orderly wears dress shoes while working. Too easy to slip and you'd kill your feet before your shift was finished."

Pleased, he pressed a hard kiss to her mouth. "You're amazing. Good job. I missed the shoes and the hand motion." He'd been more interested in catching the face without the mask. Now he was a step ahead of the game.

"Did you talk to Zane?"

He gave her a summary of the information the Fortress tech guru passed on to him.

Sorrow shadowed her features. "I feel bad for Devin. He'll be devastated when he learns the truth about Clarice and Ron."

At that moment, the fire alarm went off.

CHAPTER TWENTY-NINE

Grace's hand clenched over Trent's. The fire alarm was deafening in the early morning hours. From the corridor, she heard doors opening and slamming shut, shouts of fear, people running down the hall. Some raced for the elevators. Still others headed for the stairs.

The door to the second bedroom opened. Adam strode out, looking alert and rested, Go bag in his hand.

"Grace, are you still packed?" Trent asked as he pulled her to her feet.

"Yes. So is Nicole. We took your warning to heart." Trent had warned her and Nic to keep their bags ready to grab at a moment's notice in case of trouble. Good thing she and her sister paid attention to his advice. "Are we leaving?"

He nodded. "This might be a coincidence."

"Might not be one. Can't take a chance with your safety on the line, Grace," Adam said. He laid down his bag, returned to the bedroom, and brought out the bags belonging to Trent and Mason.

Grace grabbed her suitcase and Nic's. A quick glance around assured her neither she nor her sister had left anything behind. She shrugged into a sweatshirt she'd left lying at the foot of her bed. Nothing she could do about covering her legs with more substantial clothing. She wouldn't be in the cold night air for long. She tugged Nic's rolling suitcase with one hand and carried her own with the other.

In the living room, Trent finished zipping his bag and slung it over one shoulder. "I'll take your suitcase."

"What about checking out? If the fire is real, we can't stop to do that." Would they be in trouble for leaving without officially checking out? She blew out a breath. Giving the Dynamic Duo an excuse to take them to the police station again was the last thing they needed to do. On the other hand, she wasn't willing to risk their safety, either. What if Adam was right and this wasn't a coincidence?

"The front desk has my credit card information. I'll call after you're safe, tell them to charge the card for expenses." He and Adam tossed their key cards onto the breakfast bar where they would be seen by the maid when she came to clean the room.

"We're taking the stairs to the garage," he murmured. "When we reach the door to the garage, press your back flat against the wall and wait for my signal."

Grace's stomach churned. She hated Trent's life was in danger to protect her. If this was a trap and the killer waited for them, she knew Trent would take a bullet to save her.

Her cheeks burned as she carried Nic's suitcase down the steps so it wouldn't make noise and announce their presence. She wanted to laugh at herself. Really? The fire alarms blared and people poured into the stairwell from every floor. Who would hear the noise of Nic's suitcase bumping along from step to step? At least this way, no one would trip over the bag.

On the way down the stairs, Trent and Adam kept her sandwiched between them. Once they reached the ground floor, the other people left the hotel exiting through the main lobby. A couple more landings, and Grace and the others were alone in that part of the staircase.

At the exit to the garage, Trent reached back and nudged Grace against the wall. He gave some kind of hand signal to Adam who immediately stepped in front of Grace, holding a big black gun by his thigh, attention shifting between the staircase behind them and the door in front of Trent.

She set Nic's suitcase down at her side and prayed the killer, if he was here, kept his attention focused on the front of the hotel and not on the stairwell garage entrance.

Trent twisted the knob with his left hand, eased the door open a crack. A moment later, he moved into the garage with noiseless steps.

Grace's hands fisted at her sides. She wanted to dart into the cavernous concrete interior and run to the safety of the SUV. Unfortunately, she'd be more a hindrance than a help if there was gunfire. She didn't want Trent's attention divided between his surroundings and her.

Time crawled, her need to see if Trent was safe hard to conquer. Finally, the door opened again and Trent motioned for her and Adam to follow him. Relief made her knees weak. Thank goodness. Maybe they'd escape this latest crisis without further injury to any of them.

"I'll follow you," Adam murmured and unlocked his SUV. "If something happens, take off. I'll run interference." With those words, he dropped his bag on the front passenger seat, made sure another weapon and extra magazines were within easy reach, and climbed behind the wheel.

A sick feeling settled in the pit of her stomach at his words. Once Grace was secure inside Trent's SUV, he cranked the engine and backed from the parking spot. "Don't unbuckle your seatbelt, but I want you to sit as low in the seat as you can."

She scooted low enough she couldn't see over the dashboard.

"Perfect. I'm going to drive out of here, nice and easy. Do you remember why?"

Teeth chattering, she stuttered out, "Because fast movements draw attention."

He flashed her a look of approval, then returned his attention to his driving. "Here we go." He made a right turn onto the street. "So far, we're clear. Wait until I tell you it's safe before you sit up."

Grace's teeth continued to chatter, nerves, adrenaline dump, and cold temperature outside to blame for her physical reaction. Man, she so hated this. Why couldn't she be more like Trent? She envied his calm demeanor and quiet confidence. She felt as though her teeth were going to chatter right out of her head.

Another sideways glance from Trent and he turned up the heat and hit the button to activate the heater in her seat.

"Is Adam okay?" she asked, shuddering as the warmth penetrated her back.

A hand squeeze. "He's fine. From what I can tell, no one noticed us leaving the garage."

They rode in silence for a few miles. Grace frowned. The route Trent had chosen was taking them farther out of the city. "Where are we going?"

"Out of town. There must be a leak in the Dumas Police department."

"What about Nic and Mason? Are they safe?" Worry for her sister's safety swelled. Nic was vulnerable and Mason would stand between her and danger just as Trent or Adam would do for Grace. "Maybe we should send Adam to them." When Trent didn't answer, she twisted in her seat to see his jaw clenched and his gaze shifting from the rearview mirror to the side mirror.

Her free hand clenched the door handle. "Trent, what's wrong?"

"Might have a tail." He activated his Blue Tooth and called Adam.

"There are two vehicles," the other man said as soon as he picked up. "A black pickup and a light-colored SUV."

Trent growled. "I'd planned to relocate outside of town. Too risky to do that with the tail. We'd be too easy to follow in the darkness of the countryside. Take the next exit, hop right back on the interstate, and head into town. Once we lose these clowns, we need to find another hotel in a nearby town. Stay connected so we can communicate."

"Copy that. Grace?"

"Yes?" Her voice sounded tight to her own ears.

"Don't worry. We'll get you to safety." He sounded certain of the outcome.

"I know, Adam. I'm more concerned about Nic and Mason. What if there's a third person out there who might hurt them?"

Silence as the other operative considered her words. "I don't know Mason, but if it were my woman in the hospital, I wouldn't be sleeping. I suspect he's wide awake, watching for trouble."

Logical. Trent's friend was right. After the attack on Nic, the construction worker would be on high alert for potential threats.

"Trent, these guys are gaining ground."

"Roger that. Exit is in five hundred yards." Trent glanced at Grace. "You okay?"

"Just peachy. Let's lose these creeps so I can fall apart somewhere safe."

"You won't break, love. You're too strong."

"Doesn't feel like it at the moment."

Trent guided the SUV onto the exit ramp, turned left, shot under the overpass, and zoomed up the entrance ramp with Adam following close behind. Neither of the men spoke aside from giving status updates.

Grace didn't say anything for fear she would distract them. She really wanted to warn Mason to be on extra alert. Hopefully, Nic was sleeping, though. Grabbing her phone, Grace shot off a text to Mason explaining about the fire alarm and warning him to be vigilant. He responded within seconds, including a picture of a sleeping Nicole. She noticed their clasped hands at the bottom of the picture and smiled. Even deeply asleep, her sister was holding tight to the construction worker's hand.

"Everything all right?" Trent asked.

"I told Mason about the fire alarm and warned him to be careful. He sent me a picture of Nic sleeping."

"And that made you smile?"

"Sleep is the best thing for her. I'm smiling because their clasped hands were in the picture as well."

He nodded and returned his attention to the road and the mirrors. Traffic increased as they neared Dumas. When the SUVs drove into the heart of downtown, Trent said, "Adam, get into the lane beside me. At the next light, we separate."

"Copy."

Tension tightened Grace's muscles. How did Trent and Adam pull off this kind of stuff all the time? They acted like it was nothing while she worried about all the things that might go wrong. A driver turning in front of them, a blocked intersection that allowed their pursuers to catch up with them, an ill-timed light, an accident. The possibilities were endless and all equally worrisome.

She considered the attitude of the men as Trent and Adam reached the intersection and turned opposite directions. The two operatives were treating the whole situation as a mission. They came up with a plan and followed it. Something told her if the plan derailed, they would adjust and go to the next option, that they'd never give up. Had to be their military training.

Trent maneuvered through traffic like a shark gliding through water, efficient and controlled. Such a direct contrast to the panic that had enveloped her when she faced the truck bearing down on her a few short nights ago. She hadn't handled things nearly as well.

She glanced out the rear window. One pair of headlights trailed them. As she watched, the vehicle fell back further.

Trent took a quick right and sped up the street before turning right again at the next corner, taking them back the direction they'd been driving. Two blocks later, he turned left at the next two corners. For ten more minutes, he ran through a series of maneuvers until he spotted a street with several restaurants still open.

Grace shook her head. Otter Creek practically rolled up the sidewalks at eight o'clock each night, six on Sundays. Having restaurants open late aside from Delaney's was unheard of.

After a glance in the rearview mirror, Trent swung into the parking lot of the busiest restaurant, and parked in a shadowed space near the back with easy access to the alley behind the restaurant. He turned off the engine. "Get down on the floorboard, sweetheart. No matter what happens, you stay there."

"What about you?"

Instead of replying, he palmed his gun, eased open the door, and crouched beside the SUV. He closed the door, but didn't push it all the way shut.

Tension in the cab of the vehicle was thick enough to cut with a knife. She listened, but heard nothing except the thud of her own heartbeat in her ears.

After what seemed endless minutes, the beam of headlights slowly moving past the vehicles in the lot lit the interior of Trent's SUV. Grace froze, hardly daring to breath. Was this a restaurant patron or the person who had been following them?

If this was one of their pursuers, Trent was in the open and exposed to danger.

CHAPTER THIRTY

Trent waited in the darkness, crouched on the balls of his feet, weight balanced. The cold breeze brought scents of cooking food, booze, urine, and vomit, an unappetizing mix. He registered everything around him, a predator waiting for its prey, his focus absolute.

A truck creeped down the street. Trent's eyes narrowed. Was this vehicle one of those pursuing them or someone looking for a parking space in the crowded lot?

The vehicle swung into the parking lot and trolled for a space. The closer the truck came to their location, the more convinced he became this wasn't a hungry patron. The driver passed three empty slots to angle toward the back where his SUV was parked.

He ignored the vibration in his pocket from his cell phone. Trent checked to be sure Grace had followed his instruction, pleased that he couldn't see her fair hair or her gorgeous eyes peering at him through the windshield. He adjusted his position to put more of the engine block between himself and the threat slowly cruising his direction.

He aimed his Sig, waited. Sure enough, just as he suspected, the black truck stopped directly behind Trent's SUV. Engine still running, the driver opened the door, dome light kicking on. Tall, blond, male.

Feet shod with expensive black loafers, the man walked toward the driver's side of the SUV with deliberate steps.

"That's far enough," Trent said, Sig aimed at the target's center mass. One shot and this clown would be down. He wanted to ask questions, find out what he wanted. If this man made a move to threaten Grace in any way, he was a dead man. "Get your hands where I can see them."

A pause. "St. Claire? Is that you?"

Trent scowled, stood, his weapon still trained on the lawyer. "Where have you been for the past two days, Satterfield?"

"I needed to get away. Been working long, hard hours. I had the time coming at work so I took it." He moved two steps closer. "Not that it's any of your business."

Long, hard hours, huh? Satterfield wouldn't have said that if he'd been on one of Trent's deployments. No time to sleep. If you didn't stay ahead of the enemy, you died. "It's definitely my business when you're following us. So tell me, Ron, what do you want?" If Satterfield was smart, he wouldn't mention anything about wanting Grace. Trent would have to strenuously object to this man trying to poach his girlfriend.

"Relax. I don't have any nefarious intentions where you or your friends are concerned. I saw you by chance as I drove into town. I wanted to see how Grace was doing after that disaster of a dinner at the Randalls the other night." His lip curled. "I wish now I'd never gone."

Trent's hand tightened around the Sig's grip. "Grace is fine. Do you know about Judy Randall?"

"Yeah." Satterfield's voice came out rough. "I was sorry to hear about her death. Judy was kind to me."

But not Simon? "When did you return to town, Ron?"

"A few minutes ago. I arrived in time to clean up and dress for work. What's with the third degree, St. Claire?"

"Someone targeted me and my friends over the last two days. You've been conveniently out of touch."

"Hey, wait a minute. You're accusing me of trying to hurt you? No way, man. Is Grace all right?"

Trent clamped down on his temper. Barely. "Aside from the injuries from her wreck, she's fine. Nicole's in the hospital with a broken arm. Someone took a shot at me. Mason dodged out of the way of a speeding truck." He paused. "A black truck like the one you drive, Satterfield. Know anything about that?"

"Driving a truck isn't a crime," he protested. "I happen to like them and they're popular. There are so many on the road that my truck looks like hundreds of others in Dumas. You can't prove my truck was the one following you or aiming for Mason."

"Except that you're here minutes after I arrived in this parking lot and I don't believe in coincidence, Satterfield. We need the papers Randall wanted Grace and Nicole to sign. Find them or print off new copies so my girlfriend can put this behind her."

"In a hurry?"

"Grace has to work tomorrow evening. No one else at the law firm seems to know where the forms are located." Something Trent found curious.

"I'll take care of it when I go in later this morning. I know where Simon saved the file and I have his password memorized."

Trent's lips curved. Maybe he'd pass the word of Satterfield's location along to the Dynamic Duo since they'd been interested in talking to the lawyer. "Have you seen Clarice?"

Ron's body stilled. "Why?"

"The detectives investigating Devin's poisoning and the deaths of the Randalls are looking for her. They have many questions for Clarice. You'd be wise to point them in her direction."

The lawyer glanced around. "Where's Grace?" Satterfield's eyes narrowed, suspicion rife in his expression. "You shouldn't leave her by herself. This isn't the best part of town. She's not safe here."

"Who said I brought her with me?" he asked, voice soft.

A snort from the other man. "I don't ever see one of you without the other one."

"She's safe." That was all the information he'd give. "She's mine, Satterfield. I don't share."

"I didn't see a ring on her finger."

Trent bared his teeth. "You don't want to push me. This is the only warning you get. Another piece of free advice. Talk to the cops. The detectives are anxious to get your take on the dinner at the Randall home as well as Clarice's observations. I'll be in touch with you later this morning to get the forms."

"Grace and Nicole have to sign the forms in front of me." A shrug. "Rules."

"Nicole may be out of commission for a few days. She can't leave the hospital until the doctor releases her."

"I'll take the forms to the hospital, have her and Grace take care of the legalities there."

"Find the forms and we'll talk."

"How do I get in touch with you?"

"You don't. I'll contact you."

A snort. "You don't trust me?"

"Not a chance."

Trent's cell phone vibrated again. He ignored it, not taking his gaze from the lawyer who looked entirely too relaxed.

Satterfield chuckled. "Smart. I like a good challenge. Too bad for you, you aren't smart enough."

The back of Trent's neck prickled with awareness. Displaced air had him twisting to face the threat he felt approaching. Too late, he realized Satterfield wasn't the real threat. The prissy lawyer was the distraction.

A single gunshot followed by an explosion of pain. The force of the bullet's impact threw Trent back against his SUV. He fought to stay on his feet. Lost. He slid to the ground and into darkness.

CHAPTER THIRTY-ONE

Grace jerked, breath caught in her throat. A gunshot? Her eyes widened in horror at the sight of Trent falling against the SUV and sliding out of sight. He'd been shot. There was no other explanation. Ron shot Trent.

The creepy lawyer stood there, laughing. Rage filled Grace. She had to help Trent despite his instruction to stay in the vehicle no matter what. She could lose him if she didn't.

She yanked out her phone and sent a text to Zane, hoping he could get help to them before it was too late. After placing a call to him so he could hear what was going on, Grace shoved her phone into her pocket and zipped the opening.

She reached for the door handle, determined to render aid to her boyfriend even if she had to fight off Ron Satterfield to do it. Those lessons in self defense she'd been putting off? If she survived the encounter with Satterfield, signing up for lessons was her first priority.

As Grace's fingers brushed the chrome finish, the door was yanked open. "There you are," came a cheerful voice through the opening. "Been looking all over for you. Get out, Grace or I'll shoot you where you're hiding like the coward you are."

Dragging her gaze away from the barrel of the black gun gleaming in the weak glow of a streetlight, Grace raised her head to stare at Clarice Bowen. Thankful she'd been able to text and call Zane before the door opened, she slowly climbed from the safety of the SUV. "You don't want to do this, Clarice."

"On the contrary, I can't think of anything that will make me happier than to rid myself of you. You've ruined all my plans, you know." She tilted her head. "The question is, how much do you care about your boyfriend? Is he just a boy toy or does he mean more to you?"

Did Grace admit she would die to protect him? Clarice already had that end in mind for her and maybe Nic, too. Adam couldn't be far away. All she had to do was stall and stay alive long enough for Trent and Adam to find her. She trusted Mason to protect Nic if someone else involved tried to hurt her sister.

Was it possible Devin poisoned himself in an attempt to look innocent? Her blood ran cold. If so, Nic was in as much danger.

She backed away from Devin's wife, a desperate need to help Trent burning in her gut. He might be dying a few feet away from her.

Grace fought off a wave of grief. Later. She'd deal with her emotions when he was safe. Trent had to be alive. She wanted the chance to fall apart in his arms. She wouldn't accept another outcome.

"Where are you going, little troublemaker?" Clarice stalked after her. "You can't slip away from us. There's nowhere to run."

"Don't worry, darling. Grace wants to check on her man." Ron's voice was filled with disdain. "The big, bad Navy SEAL who isn't so bad after all. You took him down with one shot."

"We don't have time for this," Clarice said. "We have to hurry. The sun will rise soon. That means more traffic and people moving about."

Trent had a first aid kit in his cargo hold. Grace saw it when he loaded their bags for the trip to Dumas. While Clarice and Ron argued, Grace opened the hatch and grabbed the kit. A bigger first aid kit than the ones civilians used. Made sense in light of the career choice of Trent and his friends.

After closing the hatch, she shoved past Ron and hurried to Trent's side. She dropped to her knees. Her boyfriend was slumped on his side, unmoving, blood pooling under him.

Too much blood. She had to stop the flow of red or he'd bleed out before help arrived. When Grace eased him to his back, he groaned. "Sweetheart?" she whispered. "Talk to me, Trent."

No response.

She grabbed Trent's knife and sliced open his shirt. The blade rent the material with ease. She shoved aside the remnants of his shirt and examined the wound. A bullet had gone through his shoulder.

Grace opened the medical kit. Bandages, supplies to field stitch wounds, antibiotics, pain killers. Everything she needed except the time to use the supplies, because Ron was striding toward her, his expression hard. She only had seconds before they either took her to another location or killed her where she knelt.

Her gaze fell on a handful of white packets. QuikClot. She grabbed two, ripped open one and poured the contents into his wound. Rolling Trent onto his uninjured side, she dumped the white powder from the second packet onto the exit wound and prayed what she'd done would keep him alive until help arrived.

Grace leaned over his body as if checking her work and depressed the button at the side of Trent's watch, a button that sent an emergency alert to Fortress along with his GPS coordinates. He'd told her about that feature of his watch on his last trip home.

Ron yanked Grace to her feet and pressed a gun to her side hard enough to leave a bruise. Nice. The two lovebirds had matching weaponry. What she wouldn't give to have one of Trent's guns in her hands. Wouldn't do her any good, though. Her yoga pants didn't have pockets and the weight in her sweatshirt would give her away.

"Come quietly to my truck and climb into the backseat," Ron said in her ear, his voice a fraction above a growl. "If you make a peep, Clarice will put a bullet in your boyfriend's head."

She glanced back to see Devin's wife now standing beside Trent, the barrel of her gun pointed at the injured SEAL. "Please, don't hurt him more than you already have. You wanted me. Leave Trent alone."

Clarice smiled. "You're a weak woman, Grace Rutledge. That's going to work to my advantage."

Not weak. A woman who desperately loved the injured man at her feet and would do anything to give him a chance for survival.

Ron shoved Grace toward his truck. He jerked open the back door and motioned for her to climb in. "Face down on the floor, baby."

"Don't call me that," she snapped. "The only man who has that right is lying in a pool of blood in a dirty parking lot. How did you find us at Cutter's?" Would Zane understand the message she was sending him?

"Easy, sweet cheeks. I put a tracker on your boyfriend's vehicle when Clarice and I came to visit poor, sick Devin."

Another shove from Ron sent her flying into the frame of the open back door. Grace yelped, the pain so bad tears stung her eyes. Her face was already bruised on that side.

Grace did as he directed and crawled onto the floorboard. Hard hands wrenched her arms behind her back. Thin, flexible ties bound her wrists together. Zip ties? She wiggled her wrists. No way she was getting out of the restraints without help. Something else she'd have Trent teach her.

"Don't give me a reason to stop this truck, Grace," he murmured, trailing his fingers down her arm. "You won't like my response. I'm not squeamish about hurting you so don't test me." The door slammed behind her. Seconds later, Ron climbed behind the wheel and drove from the lot.

Grace tried to keep track of the turns, but there were so many, the effort was futile. Instead, she turned her attention to searching the floorboard for anything she could use to defend herself or to free her hands.

Each time the truck passed under a street light, she visually searched another section of the floor. Her jaw clenched. Nothing. Just her luck Ron was a neat freak. At the next fast turn, Grace rolled to her side and scooted as close as possible to the front seats. With the darkness so absolute in the back, she couldn't see. Maybe she'd be able to check for something useful with her hands. If only she had longer arms.

Worry for Trent made breathing nearly impossible for Grace. Losing the man she adored would kill her. No. She couldn't think about that or she would be paralyzed with grief. Focus meant a better chance for survival.

Grace searched the carpet under the passenger seat with her hands until her fingers bumped against something skinny and metal. Frowning, she moved the object closer until she could grasp it with her hand. A screw driver. Not as good as a knife, but she'd take it. There were several places on the body with soft tissue.

All she needed to do now was free her hands to use the tool. What she wouldn't give for even a fraction of Trent's knowledge or experience right now. Since she didn't have either, Grace settled for twisting her sweatshirt around until she could slip the tool into her empty pocket and zip it closed.

"What are you doing back there?" Ron glared at her over the top of his seat.

"The floorboard is uncomfortable. Since you tied my hands, I'm rolling around every time you turn a corner."

"Guess you'll have a few more bruises to accompany the ones I already gave you."

"Where are you taking me?"

A pause. "I don't suppose it matters if you know. You won't be telling anyone. We're going to my cabin where we won't be interrupted."

Had Zane heard? She prayed he had and would send Adam or someone else to rescue her. "You won't get away with this, Ron."

The lawyer laughed. "I already have, lady. I already have."

CHAPTER THIRTY-TWO

A familiar raw pain speared through the darkness and dragged Trent back to the surface of consciousness. He held himself still, fighting off the burgeoning nausea and waiting for the noises around him to sort themselves out.

"Trent, wake up, man." The sharp words helped clear some of the fog from his thoughts.

Adam. He frowned. They'd separated so they could ditch their followers. Drawing in a deep breath, Trent forced his eyelids upward to see the other operative crouched beside him, weapon in hand as he scanned the area. His pulse pounded in his ears. Where was Grace? "Grace?"

"Gone. Satterfield and Clarice Bowen took her at gunpoint. Zane contacted me, said for you to call him on his secondary number as soon as you were able."

Trent tried to move, groaned at the effort.

"Easy." Adam laid his Sig on the ground within easy reach and helped Trent to a sit up and lean against his SUV. "Don't undo your woman's work."

His gaze dropped to his shoulder, noted the liberal use of QuikClot. "Through and through?"

"Yeah. You lost a lot of blood before she stopped the bleeding."

"How long since they took her?"

"About fifteen minutes. They were gone when I arrived and found you on the ground, out cold."

"Get me up. I have to find her."

"Whoa!" Adam pressed a hand to Trent's chest to hold him in place. "You're not going anywhere except a hospital, Trent. The wound is bad, man."

He glared at his friend. "If the woman you loved had been kidnapped, would you go to the hospital before you rescued her?"

"Look, I understand. Grace is in trouble and she belongs to you. I don't have the time or skills to stitch you. Grace couldn't disinfect your wound before using the clotting agent. I'm not a medic, Trent, but even I know you probably need surgery to repair the damage."

"Fine." He tipped his chin at the open first-aid kit. "Throw some gauze over both sides and tape it. Once we have Grace, I'll go to the hospital and let the doc patch me up." Rio could do it if he were here. He wasn't. That meant improvising.

Instead of arguing further, Adam found the duct tape and two packs of sterile gauze. He grabbed his Ka-Bar and sliced off the rest of Trent's shirt. After a quick cleanup job, he ripped open one packet of gauze. "Hold this in place until I can slap some tape over it," he muttered.

Between the two of them, they managed a decent patch job. Good thing Clarice had hit his left shoulder. His lips curled. The crazy woman had aimed for his heart and missed. Trent had full range of motion in his right arm and was able to use his left even though movement was painful. All he cared about was finding his girlfriend before Satterfield or Bowen hurt her. The possibility of them shooting Grace made him want to hurl all over Adam's combat boots.

Adam shut the first-aid kit and stood, reaching down to haul Trent to his feet with one hand. "We'll need to take my SUV. Satterfield attached a tracker to yours and we don't have time to find it."

They unloaded Trent's SUV in under a minute, locked it, then climbed into Adam's vehicle. "Did you see which direction they took Grace?" Trent asked as the other operative drove from the lot.

A head shake. "Call Zane. He'll tell you what we know."

Curious about the vague answer, Trent dug his cell phone from his pocket and called Zane. "It's Trent."

"How bad is your shoulder?"

"Don't know or care." Nothing mattered to him but saving Grace. "What can you tell me about Grace?"

"Your girlfriend is amazing. She saved your life."

He glanced at Adam who was driving them away from downtown Dumas at speeds well over the legal limit. "So I hear."

"Grace is one smart cookie, Trent. She sent me a text when you were shot, then called me. The phone is in her pocket so I can hear everything going on. She's with Satterfield in his truck. They're headed for his cabin."

Trent scowled. "How did he find her? I told her to stay inside the SUV."

"Clarice found her and forced her out at gunpoint. While Clarice and Satterfield were yammering, Grace got your med kit and did what she could to patch your shoulder."

"She should have made a run for it." His hand fisted. Why hadn't she saved herself?

"The Bowen broad threatened to shoot you in the head. Your girlfriend bargained for your life. She dumped QuikClot into your wound and activated the emergency signal on your watch. If I wasn't already married to the love of my life, I'd make a play for Grace myself."

She traded her life for his? His stomach lurched in protest at the risk she was taking, depending on him and the others to rescue her in time to save her life. "She should have protected herself."

"Grace protected the man she loved with the only thing available to her. Her own life."

Trent's eyes burned. If he lost Grace, his life would be over. He'd shatter on the inside. "Is she all right?"

A pause.

No. Just no. "Tell me."

"Satterfield isn't being gentle with her, Trent. He either hit her or shoved her into something hard enough to make her cry out in pain. From what I can tell, she's in the backseat on the floorboard, hands restrained."

Fury exploded in Trent's gut. Satterfield was a dead man. "Can you talk to her?"

"Possibly. There's a lot of road noise. If she speaks to me directly, I can pass her a message. Otherwise, I'm afraid to draw attention to the phone. If they discover and take it, you have no way of knowing what you're walking into."

"Tell her to stall, to do whatever it takes to survive until I get there. Make sure she knows I'm alive and coming for her."

"I'll try." Zane ended the call.

Trent turned his face toward the side window and wiped his eyes. Grief hit him, the weight nearly crushing in its intensity. He'd miscalculated. Trent had suspected Devin of being behind the attacks and possibly Clarice. He never considered the lawyer a threat to anything but his pride. Yet Satterfield might be the biggest threat of them all.

"You're a lucky man." Adam changed lanes and zoomed onto the Interstate entrance ramp. "If you don't marry that woman as soon as you're out of the hospital, you don't deserve to have her."

"Agreed." Trent waged a battle with his emotions for long minutes. Finally, he said, "After this, she may decide my life is too dangerous for her to live with." And he wouldn't blame her.

A snort from the driver. "No way, man. Your girlfriend is strong enough to take on anything life with you entails, including terrorists and wannabe terrorists. She won't cut and run."

Trent believed that as well. Would Grace consider him worth the risk? He'd do anything for her, he realized. If she wanted him to quit working for Fortress, he'd suck it up and find another career to support them financially. Trent loved his job. He loved Grace more.

They rode in silence for another thirty minutes when Zane called. "Is Grace safe?" Trent asked in greeting.

"So far. She found a screwdriver on the floorboard and she's hidden it in her pocket."

Thank God. Trent drew in a shuddering breath. "Did she say anything else?"

"She said to pass on two messages. Satterfield shoved her face first into the side of his truck and her eye is swelling shut. She didn't want you to be unprepared when you saw her face."

Love for Grace swelled in his gut. She knew how he'd react when he saw the injury. His Grace had known to prepare him ahead of time to help his control. "And the other message?"

"She loves you." A pause. "Gotta go. The road noise stopped. I'll contact you soon."

Trent dragged his hand down his face, wishing Adam could drive faster. Impossible. The operative was already pushing ninety. Not attracting the attention of law enforcement yet was a miracle. "How much farther?"

"Twenty miles," he said, his expression grim.

Twenty miles was a long way when the last fifteen were curvy mountain roads they couldn't navigate at ninety miles an hour. Trent prayed they wouldn't arrive too late.

CHAPTER THIRTY-THREE

Satterfield's truck slowed to a stop. Thank goodness. Grace slumped against the back of the seats. The last few miles had been torturous, akin to riding over a washboard. Her relief was short lived, however.

Ron climbed from behind the wheel and opened the back door. "Out, Grace." When she couldn't sit up on her own because of the restraints and the awkward position she was in, Ron reached inside the cab of the truck and yanked her out.

Grace lost her balance and cried out as she fell on the bruised side of her rib cage. If she survived this ordeal, Grace knew she'd be bruised from head to toe.

"On your feet," Clarice ordered. "It's cold out here and we have business before I deal with you."

Sounded as though Devin's wife had a permanent solution in mind. Stall. She needed to stall. "I need help. My balance is off with my hands tied."

An exasperated sigh. "If you're so helpless, what on earth does St. Claire see in you? He needs someone more like me, a capable, strong woman."

"Hey," Ron protested, a scowl forming on his face. "I don't want you thinking about him that way. The only man you need is me."

"Of course, sweetie." Clarice patted his arm, the pat one you'd give a puppy. "I didn't mean to insult your male ego."

Grace struggled to sit up, biting back the groans wanting to escape. Giving away how much pain she was in wasn't smart.

She watched the other two interact and wondered if Ron realized Clarice patronized him. The adoration in his eyes as he looked at Devin's wife told Grace the lawyer was in over his head and didn't have a clue he needed rescuing. The other woman was using him.

"Bring her along to the cabin." Clarice turned and strode toward the log structure.

"Let's go." Ron lifted Grace to her feet and clamped a hand over her arm.

Too bad. She'd debated whether or not she could run into the nearby forest and escape. With Ron's hand gripping her arm, Grace didn't stand much chance of wrenching free. "What does she want with me? I don't have anything of value."

A snort. "On the contrary, sweet cheeks. You and your sister have shares in G & N Chemical as well as a great deal of money."

Grace stumbled over a rock in the darkness and would have gone down if not for Ron's painful hold. "That's not true. Mrs. Bowen left us money. The stock shares all belong to Devin. That's his company now, not ours."

She jerked to a halt as a thought formed in her brain, whipped her head around to look Ron in the face. "She's going to kill Devin, isn't she?"

"For a smart woman, you're slow. She already tried, would have succeeded if you hadn't interfered." A sneer curled his lips. "Clarice is going to exact her revenge on you for spoiling her plans."

"Tell me something I don't know, like why she believes Nic and I have shares in G & N. We don't. Mr. Randall made that clear."

"He didn't tell you if something happens to Devin, you and your sister inherit G & N. Mrs. Bowen didn't want the company to pass out of family hands."

So Clarice had made a desperate gamble and grabbed Grace. Whatever plan she'd hatched had to involve Nic. It wouldn't be enough to kill only one of the sisters. Cold chills surged up her spine. Clarice was going after Nic.

"She's crazy," Grace said flatly. "Mason is watching over Nic. Clarice doesn't stand a chance against him." The construction worker seemed very protective of Nic. There was definitely a romance blooming between the couple. Whether it was enough to win Nic's heart was another story.

"And what about you, sweet Grace? Doesn't your SEAL think you're worth the trouble?" He huffed out a laugh. "If he's still alive. By the time anyone finds him, he'll probably be dead, bled out on the cold, hard ground, wondering why his favorite nurse didn't help him."

Grace hung her head as if defeated, worried Ron would see the truth on her face. She wasn't a good liar, a good thing in most circumstances. Not this one. If she gave away the knowledge that Trent was alive and coming for her, Trent and Adam would lose the element of surprise. Plus, Clarice and Ron would know Grace had somehow managed to get a message out. If one of them searched Grace, she'd lose her cell phone and her connection to Zane.

That phone was her lifeline and the only way for Fortress to track her location. Trent's friend was pinging her cell phone signal to keep tabs on her. If she was separated from her phone, her chances of survival dropped dramatically.

Shoving her into motion, Ron forced her toward the cabin.

"You won't get away with this," Grace said. "You can't kill eight people without anyone connecting the murders and coming up with you and Clarice."

Another harsh laugh. "Not eight, honey, seven. Poor Devin is going to be the fall guy now. Since you saved his pathetic life, Clarice decided to use that to our advantage."

"But that doesn't make sense. Devin doesn't have motive to kill all of us."

"Oh, that's the beauty of Clarice's plan. It seems old Devin has been skimming from the company, and you and Nicole found out along with your boyfriends and the Randalls. He had to cover his tracks."

"It won't work."

"Already is. Clarice owns a few shares of stock herself, a gift from her mother-in-law. No one questions her when she comes to visit Devin or some of the others in the company. She has her husband's passwords and shares them with a friend of hers, one who learned some interesting skills that aren't entirely legal. Let's just say he's magic with numbers and accounts."

"That's why G & N is short of money. Clarice has been stealing it. Where is the money going?"

"Offshore bank account in the Caymans. No one asks questions in the islands." Another laugh. "We'll live well the rest of our lives. I'll enjoy living on the beach somewhere and not having to work another day."

"What about all the people who work for the company?" Outrage filled Grace. "They'll lose everything, their livelihood, their pension and insurance. Devin stands to lose more than the rest. G & N is his legacy from his mother. He'll lose the business and go to prison for years."

"So?" Another shove.

"It's not fair, Ron. Devin is innocent. He hasn't done anything wrong except fall in love with a black widow."

She sent him a pointed glance. "They eat their mates. You might be the next man to miscalculate her true motives, you know."

Uncertainty clouded his gaze for a moment, then he shook his head. "She loves me. Clarice would never hurt me."

And Ron thought she was slow and stupid. Clarice Bowen didn't love anyone but herself and the bundles of money she'd stolen from G & N. "Why doesn't she divorce Devin instead of framing him for murder and fraud? Would have been simpler."

The lawyer shook his head. "Can't. Devin forced Clarice to sign a pre-nuptial agreement. If she divorces him, she gets nothing."

And neither did Ron if Clarice didn't inherit. "And if he dies?"

"Everything goes to you and Nicole. If, however, Devin goes to prison and you two are dead, Clarice would have control of the company. She hates everything G & N stands for. You don't understand what she's been through. Devin's not a good husband, Grace, no matter how he appears on the surface. He's controlling, abusive physically and mentally. She's a virtual prisoner in her own home, even if the cage is a gilded one. Clarice can't take any more pressure. I'm afraid she'll crack under the strain."

Good grief. Clarice did a masterful job sucking Ron into her delusions. If there had been physical abuse in the Bowen home, Zane would have unearthed that information pretty fast. According to Trent, his friend had seen nothing in Clarice's medical records except two visits to the hospital, once for pneumonia, then for a sprained ankle. If there had been ongoing physical abuse, chances were good X-rays would have shown fractures or broken bones.

Ron Satterfield was a lost cause. Nothing would convince him of the truth except his lover's actions. Grace almost felt sorry for him. Almost. The two of them had killed the Randalls and tried to murder Grace and the others. Ron and Clarice deserved whatever punishment was meted out to them.

The lawyer propelled her up the wooden porch steps and into the house. A quick glance around showed the vacation home was decorated in the typical heavy log and leather furniture of rustic dwellings. The wood floors were covered by large area rugs and pictures decorated the mantel. Clarice and Ron beamed at her from the snapshots.

Shew. Guess Devin hadn't been out here or he might have objected. If Grace had been cozied up to another man in photos like this, Trent would have been furious. Thinking of the man she loved cause a keening deep in her soul for the SEAL who was essential to her. She wanted a lifetime with Trent St. Claire. To reach that goal, she had to survive the next few minutes.

Ron shut and locked the door, then pushed Grace toward the kitchen. Clarice waited, leaning against a counter, a drink in her hand. She motioned to the chair in the center of the room.

"Sit, Grace. Let's talk."

Talk. Right. That's why there was a plastic sheet on the floor under the chair. She swallowed hard. How far away were Trent and Adam? Lacking any choice in the matter, Grace sat.

"Tell me what I want to know, sign your shares over to me, and I'll let you leave." Clarice smiled although her eyes were cold as ice. "Nothing could be simpler."

The other woman was a stone-cold liar. "What do you want to know?"

"Tell me where your sister is. I need to talk to her as well. Once we come to an understanding about how things should be, you'll both be free to get on with your lives. If your boyfriends don't have any better taste in women, they deserve the two of you."

Free to get on with their lives? Another lie. "I don't know where Nic is."

Anticipation lit Clarice's gaze. "You're not telling me the truth. Did I tell you there's a penalty for lying to me?"

Grace shook her head. Oh, goodness. This was going to be bad. Hurry, Trent.

She set her drink aside and lifted a knife from the counter, the blade gleaming in the overhead light. "Ron and I are a great team, Grace. He's very strong, always working out at the gym. He used to be a boxer in college. My man knows how to inflict the most painful damage without killing you. I, on the other hand, enjoy working with knives. I've very good at it. Of course, you won't look the same when I've finished with you. Your handsome man will be looking for other female companionship."

"Ron said you hated G & N Chemicals and I suppose you hate your husband as well. If you've already been taking money from the company, why don't you clean out the accounts and disappear? You're smart enough to escape before the feds are on to you. You wouldn't need to play this game with Devin or the rest of us."

Laughter spilled from Clarice. "Please, this is so much more fun. Watching G & N implode will devastate Dev and thrill me. I hated Gayle and everything she stood for just like she hated me. Nothing will make me happier than to destroy the very thing she loved the most along with her precious son. And you're going to help me do it. What irony."

While Clarice droned on about her cleverness, Grace took in the large room, trying not to be obvious. A door to her left led outside. No way to know if the door was locked, but at least she didn't see a deadbolt. If only her hands weren't bound. Right now, she was hampered and off balance. If she fell, Ron and Clarice would be on her in a heartbeat.

Clarice sighed. "You aren't paying attention to me, Grace." She flicked a glance at Ron who twisted and backhanded Grace.

The momentum behind the slap sent Grace tumbling to the floor. Tears stung her eyes. Man, that smarted. With one eye swelling, she had to protect the other one so she could see if she had a chance to run. The lawyer picked her up and dropped her back on the chair.

"Let's try this again." Clarice sipped her drink. "Where is Nicole?"

"I don't know. Did Ron tell you he hurt Nic?"

The glass thudded on the counter. "Is that true?"

"An accident," Ron said. "She wouldn't come willingly. The broad fought with me and lost her balance. She fell down a flight of stairs."

"That doesn't sound so bad."

"Her broken arm needed surgery to repair." Her sister was lucky she wasn't hurt worse.

"So she's in the hospital?" Clarice's eyes brightened.

"She might have been released by now. If the doctor think she's strong enough, it's possible he released her."

"Where would she go? To the hotel?"

How much longer before Trent arrived? "We took our belongings with us when we left the hotel." Grace eyed Clarice and Ron in turn. "There was never a fire at the hotel, was there?"

"Very good. Took you long enough."

So she didn't think like a criminal. At least Trent and Adam had suspected the truth as soon as the alarm blared. "If she left the hospital, I don't know where Mason would have taken her."

"Call her or her boyfriend."

"I don't have my phone. It's in Trent's SUV." She prayed they didn't see the lie on her face.

A scowl from her captor. "What woman leaves her purse behind?"

"The kind who wants to keep her boyfriend from dying."

Clarice shrugged. "No matter. I'll find her. I always get what I want." She straightened from the counter and motioned toward the breakfast bar. "The form to sign over your shares to me is there. Hurry up. I have other things to do."

"Untie me." Grace stood. Although loathe to put her back to Clarice, she needed her hands free. "I'll sign if you don't hurt me anymore." Griped her to have to beg Clarice for mercy. She reminded herself that every minute she stalled, Trent was one minute closer.

"That's more like it." The other woman picked up the knife again.

So much damage that blade could do. Grace held her breath as Clarice approached, expecting to feel the cold bite of steel in her flesh at any moment. After a slight tug, the only thing she felt was the zip tie falling away from her wrists.

She sucked in a gulp of air as blood flow returned to the inflamed joints, her tendons aching from Ron's rough treatment. Ron shoved her toward the bar. A pen lay beside the single sheet of paper.

"Sign it and all this will be over. You'll be a free woman."

Grace glared at Devin's wife. If she escaped, the form would be invalid since she was signing under duress. No. When she escaped. Snatching up the pen, she signed the paper with a flourish.

In her peripheral vision, she noticed salt and pepper shakers by her hand. She might not have a gun or a knife, but pepper in the eyes and nose was painful. Better than nothing. So who should be the recipient of the pepper? Ron, she decided. He was the stronger of the two of them. If she had to defend herself against Clarice, she could always use the screw driver. Not much defense against a knife.

She laid down the pen and slid the form across the smooth surface. "Since I'm free to go, may I have a drink before I start walking out of here?"

A snort from Ron.

"Something cold, please," Grace clarified. "I don't like tap water or warm soft drinks."

Clarice's eyebrow rose, but she turned toward the refrigerator.

Grace leaned on the bar, using her body to block the sight of her hand curling around the pepper shaker and unscrewing the metal top from Ron. The moment Clarice opened the refrigerator and peered inside the appliance, Grace snatched the shaker off the counter and chucked the contents of the shaker into Ron's face.

She raced the few steps to the door, flung it open, and ran.

CHAPTER THIRTY-FOUR

Trent answered his cell with a whisper. "Go." The cold air nipped his skin, the sun's rays too weak yet to offer heat. He and Adam had opted to run the last quarter mile to negate the possibility of Satterfield and Bowen hearing their approach to the cabin and possibly hurting their hostage. Surrounded by woods, the two Special Forces soldiers were moving fast, closing in on Grace's location. The desire to sprint to her side without regard for his own safety was a drumbeat in Trent's blood and took every bit of his training and discipline to quell the urge. He'd be no good to his girlfriend if he was dead.

"Grace escaped, but Satterfield and Bowen are chasing her down."

His heart lurched. If they caught her now, Trent would be too late to save her. He couldn't let that happen. "Location?"

"Sent the tracker coordinates to your phone. You have your pack?"

"Copy."

"Good. She's running full out toward a cliff. If she doesn't see it in time to stop, Adam may have to rappel down to her."

A cliff? Trent pushed himself faster. "Drop distance?" He fought off the weakness threatening to stop him in his tracks. If he gave in, Grace would die. Trent knew he needed blood and fluids, the hot ache of his body telling him a round of antibiotics was in his future as well. As soon as his wife-to-be was safe he'd seek medical attention, not while danger stalked at Grace's heels.

"Not so far that she wouldn't survive a fall as long as she landed right. However, the cliff face is almost straight up, too steep for Grace to climb out on her own. One more thing. Bowen's next target is Nicole. I've already notified Rio. He's on his way to Dumas. He'll take over the watch at the hospital although the doctor's notes indicate he'll release Grace's sister later this morning."

"Copy that." He checked the coordinates, then shoved his phone into his pocket, and summarized Zane's information for Adam who ran easily beside him.

"Split up?"

A nod. "Take the left." Trent's jaw tightened. "Grace is heading for a cliff. If she falls, we'll have to rappel down to get her. Z says the pitch is too steep for her to climb up unaided."

With a nod, Adam slipped into the still mostly dark forest. Not even a leaf stirred at his passing. Soon, the Marine was out of sight.

Trent veered to the right, hand wrapped around the grip of his Sig. Training and instinct guided his steps through the rough terrain. His Grace didn't have the skill to navigate this race through the early morning light without injuring herself, another thing to hold against the two killers on her trail.

He'd capture them alive if possible. If not, Trent wouldn't lose sleep over it, though he'd likely be spending a long time answering questions from the Dynamic Duo. As long as Grace was safe, he'd endure anything he had to.

A faint voice carried on the breeze. Trent frowned, listening. Female. He corrected his course slightly to the left and moved cautiously forward. The angry words berated someone in the woods. Definitely not Grace. He'd never heard his girlfriend raise her voice to anyone. Fifty more feet and the words became clear.

"I told you to keep an eye on her." The strident tones belonged to Clarice Bowen. "You let her escape. She's a scared, spineless woman, and injured to boot. There's no excuse for your inability to hold on to her."

"Stop nagging. My eyes still burn from the pepper she threw in my face."

Despite the circumstances, amusement made Trent's lips curve up. Pepper? Good job, baby, he praised her silently.

"Oh, quit whining. I washed them out. After she's dead, we'll go to the store and find eye drops for you. Just a few more minutes, sweetie."

Trent's smile faded, disgusted at their interaction.

"There." Ron's voice rose. "I see her."

"She's limping." Mocking laughter rang out in the silence of the forest. "Not so much of a threat, are you, Grace?" Clarice taunted. "Run faster. Maybe I'll let you escape."

Trent's jaw clenched.

"Stop shouting," Ron said. "Someone might hear you and come to investigate. I'm not killing anyone else. Grace and Nicole are the last ones. If you want the other boyfriend dead, kill him yourself."

"There isn't anyone around to hear. That's why I chose this spot to take care of business. Are you really leaving Mason to me?" Her voice dropped into almost a purr.

Like that was going to happen. Devin's wife didn't know who she was dealing with. Mason was a gentle man, but he wasn't a pushover. Being in prison for 13 years had taught him to take care of himself and those he cared about. He wouldn't be duped by Clarice or leave Grace's sister unprotected.

"Maybe you should have found someone else to do your dirty work, Clarice. There are plenty of people who hire out."

"They also have loose lips. Never mind. I already took care of the SEAL. I can handle a thug and Nicole. I'll go to the left, cut Grace off," Clarice told Ron. "We'll box her in and end this. If you catch up with her first, don't wait for me. Kill her. We need to find her sister and take care of her, too. Once she learns her sister is dead, she'll come out of hiding soon enough and I'll be waiting for her and her lovestruck bodyguard."

Clarice jogged to the left, her movements telegraphing her location clearly. Adam wouldn't have any problem locating the woman and dealing with her. Devin's wife wouldn't see him coming. The Marine was at the top of his game, his skills world-class.

Trent turned his attention to the man bearing down on Grace with ground-eating strides. He angled his approach to intersect with Satterfield. Ahead of the lawyer, Grace stumbled, fell to her knees. She tossed a quick glance over her shoulder, scrambled to her feet, and took off again.

Trent increased his speed, no longer bothering to hide his approach. With his dark clothes, Ron wouldn't see him until he broke out of the tree cover. He leaped over a fallen log, skirted a large oak tree, and dashed out of the tree line as the lawyer reached for Grace.

"Satterfield!"

Instead of turning to face Trent, the other man lengthened his stride, leaped onto Grace's back, and took her to the ground. She tried to wiggle out from under Ron's weight and failed.

As he ran to his girlfriend's aid, Trent shrugged his pack off with a grimace, and tossed it aside. He couldn't afford to have his movements hampered any further. The duct tape had kept him from bleeding out, but it wasn't flexible. Adam had been more interested in getting on the road than his taping finesse.

Satterfield grabbed a fist full of Grace's hair and yanked her head back, gun pressed to her temple. "Get up," he growled out. He dragged her to her feet, her body shielding most of him from Trent.

"Stop right there, St. Claire." The lawyer retreated several steps, forcing Grace to retreat with him.

"You don't want to do this, Satterfield." Trent shifted his position, looking for a better angle on the man holding Grace. "You can't escape us."

A frown. "Us?"

"Did you think I'd come out here alone? I didn't know how many people Clarice had duped into doing her bidding." He gave Ron a mocking smile, hoping to goad the lawyer into focusing all that anger on Trent. "Guess you're the only one foolish enough to believe her lies."

Satterfield's cheeks flushed. "Why aren't you dead?"

"Your lover is a bad shot." He shifted a few more inches to the left. His blood ran cold at the sight of the land dropping off to nothing mere feet behind Satterfield. If he slipped off, he'd take Grace with him.

"Stop moving," Ron snapped. "I'll shoot her if you move one more step."

"And lose your leverage to control me?" Trent shook his head. "I don't think so."

Satterfield retreated another foot, forcing Grace backward.

"I'm the bigger threat, Ron. If you shoot Grace, I'll drop you where you're standing and I won't miss. Do yourself a favor. Let my girlfriend walk away. Tell Clarice you killed her. How will she know you showed compassion to an innocent woman?"

A snort. "You must take me for an idiot. If I let her leave, you'll kill me."

He still didn't have a good angle and didn't want to shoot Grace by accident. Time for another tactic. "There isn't another option unless you lay down the weapon and give yourself up. I'll make sure you leave these woods alive." He tilted his head. "Unless you have a better plan to end this stalemate."

Satterfield was silent a moment. "I'll let Grace go on one condition."

Satisfaction zinged through Trent's body, already knew where Satterfield would go with his offer. "Name it."

"You take her place. I'll kill you instead."

CHAPTER THIRTY-FIVE

"No!" Grace wouldn't allow Trent to sacrifice himself for her. Ron might not have noticed how pale her boyfriend was, but Grace had. As a woman crazy in love with Trent St. Claire, she believed he would prevail. As a nurse, however, she wasn't sure he could handle a healthy lawyer desperate enough to fight a Navy SEAL, even one who was injured. "Don't."

Her boyfriend ignored her heartfelt plea, gaze fixed on his opponent. "Clarice will demand proof of Grace's death."

Ron shifted his stance, edging further away from Trent. "I'll tell her I pushed Grace over the side of the cliff and her body is too far down to see."

Cliff? Grace clawed at Ron's restraining arm. Oh, man. Not good. A cold sweat broke out over her body. No wonder Trent had been bargaining so hard. Ron was planning to use the natural drop off to kill her instead of using his gun. From his perspective, what was one more death? He'd already killed two people and tried to kill Grace and the rest of them. "Ron, don't do this. Clarice isn't worth losing your life over."

"I told you. All I have to do is leave the country with her and the money, and we'll be set for life. No worries, no more pressure, nothing but time on our hands and a lifetime of being together."

"That's what this is about?" Trent asked, moving a few inches closer. "Money and a woman who cheated on her husband? You're a lawyer. You make a good living, certainly more than Grace and Nicole. Why didn't you just take their trust fund and disappear without Clarice? Ten million bucks is plenty to live on for years."

A short laugh from the man behind Grace. "What money?"

Several pieces fell into place for her. "You stole the trust funds."

"Mrs. Bowen set them up right after you and your sister were born. There hadn't been account activity for years except for all that lovely interest accruing. The old lady croaked before I had everything in place for Clarice and I to leave."

"When you ran out of time, you decided to kill us before we tried to withdraw the funds." She dug her nails deeper into his skin. "You're the one who forced me off the road. What about the Randalls? Did you have anything to do with their deaths?" Positive of the answer she'd receive, Grace pushed for confirmation anyway. Hopefully, Zane was recording the conversation.

"Randall found out, didn't he?" Trent's face paled further, his voice a little weaker. Ron probably didn't realize the difference since he didn't know Trent. Grace did. The contrast between his voice on a normal day and this one scared her.

"Simon checked the balance in the accounts. When he called me to ask me about it, I realized I couldn't wait any more. I was on the verge of being turned in to the cops. That couldn't happen if I wanted a life with Clarice."

Cold rage filled Grace. "You killed Simon and Judy. They were a sweet couple. How could you do something so despicable?" Before the sound of her last word faded, she felt the muscles in Ron's body harden against her own.

"Easy, sweet cheeks. I'm not a nice man." With that, he tightened his hold on her and shifted his weight.

"No!" Trent lunged forward, but he wasn't fast enough. Ron twisted and flung Grace over the side of the cliff.

She screamed, flailing, searching blindly for anything to stop her freefall into the dark abyss below. Grace hit a ledge, her hands grabbing onto an outcropping of rock shaped like a cone. Her momentum sent the lower half of her body sliding off, leaving her dangling in mid-air. She fought the panic exploding in her gut. She hated heights with a white-hot passion. Later. She'd give herself permission to fall apart after her feet were on solid ground.

Dirt and small rocks rained down from above. Vile curses from Ron reached her ears as well as the sound of fists connecting with human flesh. "Trent!"

Seconds later, two gunshots were fired off, in rapid succession, and Ron fell over the side of the cliff. His body missed Grace by inches.

"Grace!" Trent's head peered over the edge. Relief flooded his face when he saw her. "Don't move."

"Hurry. I'm losing my grip." Even as she said the words, her hand slid and she scrambled to readjust her hold. Grace couldn't keep this up for long. She wasn't a rock climber.

"Hold on, baby. I'm coming to get you."

She refused to look down, an exercise in terror that would end her chance of marrying the man of her dreams. Grace couldn't think of anything worse than losing her life on the rocks at the bottom of this cliff.

More pebbles and dirt fell from above. Blinking the grit from her eyes, she chanced a quick glance, saw Trent descending the cliff face at amazing speed. Shocking he could move that fluidly even though he'd been shot in the shoulder.

Trent stopped his downward trajectory when he reached her side, then dropped a bit more until he was slightly below her. He did something she couldn't see with his harness, then said, "Do you trust me?"

She nodded, sucking in a ragged breath.

"Here's how we're going to do this. I have a second harness I'll attach to my own. I'm going to slip this on you and we'll rappel down to the bottom of this rock face."

"I'm afraid of heights," she whispered.

"Me, too. I won't let you fall."

"What about your shoulder?"

He was silent a few seconds. "We shouldn't delay long. I can't handle climbing to the top, but I should be able to get us both to the ground in one piece. If my arm stops working, we'll just hang out here and wait for Adam to lower us to the ground."

Hang out on the side of the cliff? "When we get off this mountain, don't make plans to take me camping."

He gave a mock sigh as he slipped the harness up her legs and made sure it was secure. "Too bad, beautiful. I was planning to beg you to marry me while we were on a wilderness retreat. At least there, no one else would bother us and we could turn off our phones so I won't have to worry about Fortress tracking me down for another mission."

Her heart lurched into a wild, erratic rhythm. He thought about proposing to her? "Ask me now. We're alone and can't answer phones."

"No way, Ms. Rutledge. I don't have my speech worked out nor do I have a ring that will knock your socks off."

"Trent! Ask me already."

He chuckled as he clipped her harness to his. "I love you, Grace Rutledge. Will you marry me?"

"Yes. Now get me off this mountain."

"Whatever you say, sweetheart. I want you to wrap your arm around my neck and let go of the rock. I've got you now. I promise I won't let you fall."

She glanced at his beloved face. "How will we go down the side? I don't see how you can rappel with me in front of you."

"Easy. Hug me tight, then let me do all the work."

"Trent!" Adam looked over the side of the cliff. "You and Grace okay?"

"I can't make the climb and you won't be able to pull me up along with Grace. Our combined weight is too much for one man."

"Agreed. Safest for both of you to rappel to the ground. Let me know when you're ready. I'll make sure you reach the ground, haul up the ropes, then retrieve the SUV. There's a dirt road a quarter mile to the right. I'll drive to meet you and take you to the hospital."

"Copy that." Trent glanced down into Grace's eyes. "You ready, honey?"

"More than. How do we do this?"

"Since you're not a fan of heights, don't look down. Just look at my face, nowhere else."

Not a hardship as far as she was concerned. Grace remembered many nights when she'd longed to see Trent's beloved face while he'd been on some unknown continent in a third-world viper's nest, tracking kidnapping victims or hunting down terrorists.

As they started their descent, Grace said, "Did I tell you the first time I saw you, I thought you were a male model?"

A startled look crossed his face. "No." His cheeks flushed, the color a stark contrast to the icy pallor of his skin. "Must have been a shock when you learned what I do for a living."

"I think you're even better looking now," she murmured.

"My face is still the same and so is my body, although it's beat up right now."

"Now I know the heart of the man. I'm so in love with you, Trent St. Claire. I'm glad you let me catch you."

He huffed out a surprised laugh. A moment later, their feet touched the ground.

Grace sagged against Trent for a second. Safe. They were safe. Knowing her boyfriend was weaker than he wanted to admit, she kissed him gently and straightened. "Thank you for saving my life."

When he didn't bother replying, just concentrated on unhooking the harnesses and the ropes with carefully controlled movements, Grace's stomach twisted into a knot. "How can I help?"

"You heard Adam. The dirt road is to the right. If I go down, find Adam and get yourself to safety. We don't know if Clarice and Ron were working with a third person. I can't lose you, Grace."

No way was that happening. She wouldn't leave him alone. What if someone else was out here who might harm Trent while he was unconscious? She could stall until Adam arrived. Trent's friend would find her. Of that she had no doubt.

"Come on." She wrapped her arm around his waist and urged him to move. His arm settled heavily across her shoulder. Thankfully, the sunlight was stronger, giving them more warmth and better light to navigate the rough landscape.

Twice Trent stumbled and almost dropped to his knees. He righted himself at the last instant with Grace's help and continued forward at his plodding pace. So not like him. She'd jogged with him many times when he was home from deployments. Her SEAL was fast. This snail's pace wasn't normal for the Trent she loved.

As they walked, Trent's breathing grew more ragged and his temperature rose higher. She'd give anything for water. Trent needed fluids and antibiotics. Both were in short supply in this mountainous region. Unfortunately, the hospital was a good distance from here.

Maybe Zane could help. Grace unzipped the pocket of her sweatshirt and pulled out her phone. The screen lit up. Amazing. She was still connected to Trent's friend. "Zane?"

"How are you, sugar?" he answered immediately.

"Banged up. Ron got in a few good hits. I'm more worried about Trent."

"What do you need?"

"I don't know what resources Fortress has, but Trent needed to be at the hospital an hour ago. He's lost a lot of blood. He's still mobile, but I don't think he will be for long. His pulse rate is too fast, breathing ragged, temperature elevated. I don't have fluids and I'm afraid he needs blood."

"Hold."

"I'm fine," Trent muttered and stumbled again, this time going down on one knee. After a several gasping breaths, he struggled to his feet and continued toward the road.

"You need medical treatment. Sit down and rest a minute. I don't hear anyone coming." Surely they would be safe for five blessed minutes while he caught his breath.

The SEAL shook his head, putting one foot in front of the other in increasingly erratic steps. "Can't. I'm moving on sheer adrenaline and will. If I stop, I won't get up again. Can't leave you vulnerable."

Stubborn man. Good thing she adored him. She had a feeling their life together would never be dull.

"Grace?"

"I'm here, Zane."

"I contacted a friend who owes Fortress a favor. A chopper is on the way to you. Should arrive in fifteen minutes."

She took at the wooded terrain. "I'm not a pilot, but I don't think there is a place for the helicopter to land. We're in the middle of a forest."

"I sent Adam the coordinates of the nearest clearing. The pilot will fly you and Trent directly to the hospital in Dumas. The ER has been alerted and will be ready for him. They also promised to have a surgeon on standby if Trent needs surgery."

Grace suspected he would. Relief swept through her at his words. "Thank you, Zane."

"Glad to be of assistance. When Trent is back on his feet, tell him to bring you to Nashville. I'm looking forward to meeting you."

"I'd like that. Should I keep our call connected?"

"Until you're in the helicopter. I've also notified Weston and Barton. They will arrive at Satterfield's cabin within the hour to start processing the crime scene. Heads up, though. They were not happy no one had notified them of your kidnapping."

Yeah? She hadn't been too thrilled about that fact herself. Her face felt hot and swollen. No doubt she looked like a battered woman. "Have you talked to Adam? What happened to Clarice?"

"He didn't have a problem capturing her. She's currently trussed to the trunk of a tree with plenty of duct tape. Adam assured me she wasn't going anywhere."

"Good. I'm putting the phone back in my pocket now."

"Give me regular updates, sugar."

Grace adjusted her hold for a firmer grip on Trent. "Zane is sending a helicopter. You'll be at the hospital soon."

Instead of replying, Trent groaned and sank to his knees, taking Grace with him.

"Trent!" When he started to keel over, she braced him with her shoulder and eased him to the ground. "Sweetheart, talk to me." Nothing. Grace checked his pulse. She dug out her phone again. "Zane, I need Adam. Trent's down and his pulse is weak."

"Copy that."

Agonizing minutes later, Adam ran full tilt from the thick trees. "Grace!" The other operative crouched beside Trent. "The SUV is just over that ridge. Go. I'll be right behind you with Trent."

Grace leaped to her feet and started toward the trees at a fast clip. In less than a minute, Adam caught up with her, Trent over one shoulder with his arms hanging limp.

"Pick up the pace. Helo's waiting."

She broke into a jog, praying she didn't face plant on the rock-strewn ground. With her eye almost swollen shut, her depth perception was off. Finally, they broke out of the line of trees. The SUV was parked fifty feet in front of them.

Once Adam settled Trent in the backseat, Grace climbed inside and knelt beside him to keep him from rolling onto the floor. The tires squealed as Adam raced to the landing site.

Trent's eyelids lifted slightly. "Grace," he whispered.

"I'm here. You'll be fine." She would accept nothing else. He was the other half of her soul. "We'll be at the hospital in a few minutes."

He blinked, frowned. "He hurt you."

"Yes. Soft tissue damage. I'll heal."

"Make sure the doc checks you out."

"I will. I promise."

A slight nod and his eyes closed again.

"Trent?"

Silence.

"Almost there," Adam murmured. "Two minutes. I'll load him into the helo, then head back to Satterfield's place.

I need to meet the cops on site. Rio will be at the hospital soon. He'll take over the protection detail."

"Thank you, Adam. For everything."

"Anytime. Make sure I receive an invitation to the wedding."

Her eyes stung with tears. "I'm planning to marry this man as soon as possible."

"Good. He deserves the best, and that's you."

She gave a watery laugh. "Our wedding pictures will look a fright. My face is bruised and swollen, and there's no telling what shape Trent will be in. But I don't want to wait anymore." Grace wanted the right to claim the St. Claire name, to come home at night to the man she loved when he wasn't deployed.

"So take the wedding pictures later after you've healed. I'm sure my sister would be thrilled to take them for you."

Zane's wife was a photographer? Perfect. "That's a great idea."

"I'll talk to her, ask if she'll put some ideas together for your photo shoot. Claire is a creative genius when it comes to pictures."

Seconds later, Adam parked. He opened the back door and hoisted Trent over his shoulder again and carted him to the waiting helicopter. After settling him inside, Adam placed her beside Trent, closed the door, and moved away from the helicopter.

And then she and Trent were airborne. Grace watched over him on the fifteen-minute flight, and prayed.

CHAPTER THIRTY-SIX

Grace paced the waiting room, sick with worry and so antsy she couldn't sit still. Trent had been in the exam room with the doctor for what seemed like forever. She knew the ER staff were working as fast as possible to evaluate him and still her skin crawled with the overwhelming need to rush into the room and demand an update. But she didn't work here and at the moment she'd be in their way. After his surgery, though, Grace intended to play the almost-wife card and camp out by his bed. No one would force her to leave his side.

Footsteps had her spinning on her heel. Grace's gaze locked with the nurse she'd made friends with over the past few days. She hurried to the other woman's side. "How is he?"

"Headed for surgery in a minute. Want to see him before they take him?"

Too choked up to speak, she nodded and trailed her friend. Trent's eyes were closed when Grace reached his bedside. After scanning the monitors showing his vitals and finding the results reassuring, she clasped the hand of his uninjured arm between her palms. "Trent."

He stirred. "Baby? You okay?" His words were soft, slurred. The love of her life didn't handle drugs well. The cocktail the doctor had given him in preparation for surgery had hit him hard.

"I'm safe. Don't worry about me. The doctor is going to take good care of you. The next time I see you will be in recovery after they repair your shoulder."

"See a doctor?"

Her lips curved. Her SEAL had a one-track mind. "Not yet."

Trent's brow knitted.

"I'll have one of the doctors check me while you're in surgery. It will help distract me."

The lines of his forehead smoothed. "Stay with me," he murmured.

She trailed her fingers over Trent's cheek. "You just try and get rid of me, St. Claire. You asked me to marry you on that mountain and I'm holding you to it."

The orderlies came in to take him to the surgical floor. Grace leaned down and brushed a kiss over Trent's lips. "I love you. I'll be by your side when you wake up, love."

"Love you." And he succumbed to the medication.

Blinking back tears, she stepped to the side and watched the orderlies maneuver the bed from the room and into the elevator. Knowing he'd be angry with her if she didn't take care of herself, Grace found her friend and asked to see a physician. Minutes later, she was ushered into the same exam room where Trent had been.

A redhead hurried inside the room. "Ms. Rutledge, I'm Dr. Karen Lively. I understand you were a kidnapping victim."

"That's right."

Dr. Lively studied Grace's face. "Did the police rescue you or did you escape on your own?"

"My boyfriend rescued me."

"Wow. Is he a cop?"

Grace considered what she could say to answer the woman's question without compromising Trent's safety and decided on a partial truth. "Military."

"Did your boyfriend hurt you, Ms. Rutledge?"

"Absolutely not. Trent would never lay a hand on me in anger. Detectives Weston and Barton with the Dumas PD are aware of the kidnapping. Verify my story with them." Grace realized Dr. Lively was looking out for her best interests, but she hated that the other woman believed the worst of Trent even for a moment.

When she returned to the waiting room, she had confirmation of what she already suspected. Soft tissue damage. More bruises to add to the collection she already had from the car accident. Painful, but temporary. Grace dropped into the nearest seat to wait for word on the outcome of the surgery.

Twenty minutes later, Rio and Darcy walked into the room. "Grace!"

Grace stood and found herself enveloped in a tight hug. "Darcy, it's my fault. I'm so sorry." Her voice broke on the last word.

"You didn't shoot my brother," Darcy said as she released Grace.

"He was injured protecting me."

Rio wrapped his arm around her shoulder and hugged her to his side. "Grace, Trent would do it again in a heartbeat. No one means more to him than you. From what Zane said, you saved my brother-in-law's life. If you hadn't been there, he would have bled out in that parking lot. We owe you a debt we'll never be able to repay."

His gentle words set off a cascade of tears that Grace couldn't stem no matter how hard she tried. Rio nudged her back into her seat. Darcy sat beside her and gathered her close. When the storm of tears passed, Rio crouched in front of her with a bottle of water. "Drink. You're dehydrated." Rio handed a second one to his wife. He waited until Grace drank a quarter of the liquid before he asked, "How long has Trent been in surgery?"

"Over an hour." Seemed longer. "He lost a lot of blood, was weak, and still he fought off Ron Satterfield and rappelled down a cliff with me holding on for dear life." She'd never felt so helpless and useless in her life. She couldn't do anything to assist him in saving their lives.

"He never does anything half way." Darcy patted Grace's hand.

A scrubs-clad man with a surgical cap came into the room. "St. Claire family?"

The three of them stood.

"Mr. St. Claire is in recovery. The bullet did quite a bit of damage in there. He'll need therapy to regain full motion."

"Recovery time?" Rio asked.

"Four to six months at least, maybe longer. Depends on how he responds to treatment and his diligence in doing the exercises. We have several physical therapists we recommend. All of them are local and some do in-home therapy if he prefers that."

"We'll line up the physical therapy. We're not from Dumas." He held out his hand. "Thank you."

With a nod, the doctor said, "You can see him now. One of the nurses at the desk will tell you where to go."

He was going to recover. Tension drained from her muscles. Extended therapy, but he'd recover. Grace intended to make sure he did every exercise, rested, and ate properly.

"Wait here," Rio murmured. He went to the desk and spoke to the nurse. Armed with instructions, he led Grace and Darcy to the bank of elevators.

In the recovery room, Trent occupied the third bed to the right. Grace dried her tears with the sleeve of her shirt, not wanting to alarm Trent if he was aware enough to notice them. She trailed her fingers lightly over his cheek. "Trent?"

He sighed, nuzzled her hand. "Grace."

"I'm here, love. So are Rio and Darcy."

A slight frown. His eyelids raised a fraction. "Darce?"

"Hey." His sister clasped his hand. "Laying down on the job, huh?"

"Shouldn't be here. You hate hospitals."

"Simple solution to that problem, bro. Stop being injured and I won't have to keep coming."

His lips curved slightly as he drifted off again. For the next hour, Grace and the others talked quietly. She brought them up to speed on the events of the past twenty-four hours. Rio answered phone calls and texts from Trent's boss, his teammates, and his friends.

Finally, Trent was moved to a private room. When his eyes grew heavy again, Grace said, "I'm going to check on Nic and Mason. I'll be back in a few minutes."

He flicked a glance at Rio.

"No." The medic's jaw clenched. "I'm not leaving you. Between the two of you, you're more vulnerable than she is right now."

"I'll stay with St. Claire," a deep masculine voice said from the doorway. "Go with Grace, Rio."

Grace's gaze locked with icy blue eyes. The buzz-cut blond man strode into the room as if he owned it. One of Trent's teammates? No. Somehow he wore authority like a second skin. Could this be Brent Maddox, the man Trent worked for?

Rio's eyebrows soared. "I thought you were in Washington, D.C. this week, Maddox."

"Cut out early when I heard about Trent's injury. Go check on your cousin, Rio."

"Yes, sir." He looked at his wife. "You staying here?"

She shook her head. "I want to see for myself that Mason is all right. The Kincaid men tend to blow off injuries."

Rio grinned instead of denying what all of them knew to be the truth.

The three of them went to Nic's room and found Mason sitting in a chair by her bedside, his hand wrapped around hers. The construction worker's face filled with fury when he saw Grace. "Who hurt you?"

Nic's head snapped around. She gasped. "What happened?"

"Long story."

"Sit down and talk. I'm not going anywhere."

Grace gave her sister the condensed version of events, ending with, "The good news is Trent will be all right. He'll need extensive therapy, though."

"You could have been killed," Mason said.

"That was Ron's intent." She shuddered. "I thought I was going to die when he threw me off the cliff." An experience she would be reliving in her nightmares for years to come. She might have to take Trent up on his offer to find her a trauma counselor.

"So what happens now?"

"Adam met the detectives at Ron's cabin. According to him, Weston and Barton arrested Clarice and are collecting evidence. Zane supplied them with a copy of the recording he made from my phone call to him. Clarice and Ron said plenty to incriminate themselves and prove we had nothing to do with the crimes dogging our steps."

"We can go back to Otter Creek now?" Mason asked.

"After the detectives take our statements. I'm ready to see the last of this town." Grace eyed her sister. "What about you, Nic? You planning to return to Otter Creek?"

Nicole's expression darkened. "I can take as long as I want to recover."

"What's wrong, Nic?"

"I lost my job. My former boss said he can't have an employee who isn't dependable or responsible."

Rio whistled softly.

Oh, man. Grace's heart hurt for her sister. "I'm sorry. Why don't you stay at my apartment for a while? Heal while you decide what your next move is." She wasn't above a little matchmaking. The relationship between Mason and Nicole would grow much slower if they lived in different towns.

Nic glanced at Mason who winked at her. She turned back to Grace. "I've been thinking about a career change." She gave a short laugh. "Would have been an easier choice if I had the five million from Mrs. Bowen."

"We'll find it," Rio said. "I'll ask Zane to start searching. He can follow any electronic trail. What would you do with the money?"

"Tell them what you've been considering," Mason encouraged.

"I'd like to open a pet grooming business in Otter Creek." Silence greeted her statement. Nic glanced nervously from one to the other. "I haven't seen one in town when I visited Grace. Do you think anyone would be interested in a local shop?"

"You have experience in pet grooming?" Rio asked.

"I spent every summer in college working in the grooming department of a local pet shop. Now, I work part-time as a groomer. I don't really need the money. I have a lot of fun working with the animals."

"I think it's a great idea," Darcy said, her smile wide. "PSI is training search and rescue dogs. The handlers will love having a local place manned by someone the staff at PSI trusts."

"I've heard more than one person complaining about having to take their pets to another town for grooming." Rio looked thoughtful. "I say go for it. We'll spread the word for you."

"But won't the police need the money Ron took as evidence of his crime?"

"Maybe. Fortress has a lot of pull. We'll see if we can't get around that problem." He laid his hand on Nic's shoulder. "In the meantime, I'd start making a business plan and planning your move to Otter Creek."

CHAPTER THIRTY-SEVEN

"What does the doc say about your shoulder?" Maddox asked, his intense gaze locked on Trent. He lounged back in the chair beside Trent's hospital bed.

"I'll regain full motion, but I'll need extensive rehab."

"Recovery time?"

"Maybe six months." Less if he had anything to say about it. The possibility of being off work that length of time made his gut rebel.

"Where do you plan to recuperate?"

"Otter Creek." Trent hadn't hesitated. He'd missed Grace so much on this last deployment he wouldn't give up extra time with her, banged up shoulder or not.

Maddox was silent a moment, watching him with rapt attention. "Would you be open to a reassignment?"

Trent blinked, his throat tightening. "Sir?" Was Maddox going to saddle him with a desk job?

"The dorms on PSI's campus will be finished in a couple weeks. I plan to double the size of our classes. To do that, I need another unit like Durango to help with the training. Cahill and his team can use the assistance. You interested?"

He stared. Stay in Otter Creek permanently? Darcy would be over the moon. And Grace? Man, he couldn't wait to see her face when he told her. "Permanent reassignment?" he asked to be sure.

"Yes. You and your team would rotate missions with Durango so one of the teams is always in residence at PSI. If the demand for our services continues to grow at the current pace, I'll soon be adding a third team on site."

"Why us? Why not a different team?"

"Because your heart's in Otter Creek, Trent, and I can't afford to burn out my best units. Your team and Durango have been going out on too many missions. PSI has two teams graduating from the program in a week with another five gearing up to start training the week after."

"Is this a way to ease me into early retirement?" Trent knew he'd been injured more than most of the other operatives aside from the members of Durango. Then again, he'd been on many of the most dangerous missions Fortress had carried out. He was team leader, didn't know to do anything different than lead his teammates into battle.

Maddox snorted. "It's a way to keep from losing one of my best operatives. If you keep working at the same pace as the last few years, Grace will be a widow before she's forty. I'm not letting that happen."

Relief swept through him. Maddox wasn't easing him out. "And when I am ready to stop taking active missions?"

"PSI is your permanent assignment until you retire, period. You have too much experience to waste it. Your training will keep our future operatives alive. Think about it. Talk to Grace. If you both agree this is the best decision for the two of you, I'll inform your teammates of the assignment change."

"What if they don't want to make the transition?"

"I've already touched base with them, sounded them out. Your team will follow wherever you lead, Trent.

Remember, they're about the same age as you and have similar battle scars. I don't think there will be a problem."

"If there is any push back, talk to Adam about taking my place."

A nod.

A knock sounded on the door to the hallway. Maddox placed himself between Trent and the door, Sig in his hand.

"It's Rio," said the medic. He pushed open the door and waved Darcy and Grace inside the room. His eyes narrowed as he studied Trent's face. "Everything okay, Trent?"

He looked at Grace. "I need to talk to Grace." An unspoken demand for the rest of them to get out of his room. His decision concerned her as well. He could guess what her answer would be, though. Their conversations and texts throughout his last deployment reflected the increasing loneliness each of them felt at the separations.

"We'll wait in the hall," Maddox said and herded the other two out the door.

When he and Grace were alone, Trent held out his hand. "Come here, love."

"What's wrong?" She sat on the chair by his bed.

"Nothing. You're too far away, though." He patted the bed. "I need to ask you a question."

Grace sat by his hip. "You already asked and I said yes."

Trent grinned. "I remember. Should have made you do the asking."

"Don't think I wouldn't have done just that. I can't wait to be your wife. Now, tell me what's going on."

No point in prolonging his news. "What would you say if I told you Maddox offered me a permanent job at PSI?"

She stared for a long moment. "You would be in Otter Creek all the time?"

"My team and I would be sent out on short-term missions like Durango. In fact, we would be switching off missions with them. Maddox wants us to help train new teams for Fortress. This decision concerns you, too. What do you think?"

A slow smile curved her lush lips, lips he wanted to nibble and kiss for a long time once he got out of this bed. "I want that more than anything. To be able to see you more? Nothing could be better." Her smile dimmed. "Don't take the job just for me, love. I'll survive whatever your decision. If this job is what you want, then accept Maddox's offer."

"I love my job, Grace. My team and I provide valuable aid to victims across the globe." He lifted his uninjured arm and brushed her bottom lip with his thumb. "But I love you more than my job. I can't be apart from you for weeks at a time anymore. I'm only half alive without you now. I want this job for me. I want it even more for us."

She leaned down and kissed him. When she drew back, her eyes sparkled. "I love you, Trent."

"Enough to marry me in a few days?" Please say yes, he begged silently. Trent's heart pounded against his rib cage as he awaited her reply.

"As soon as we can obtain a marriage license." When Grace drew back the next time, her lips were swollen and her cheeks flushed. "I want to marry you in Otter Creek. Our wedding might be thrown together fast, but I want our friends and family there to witness our marriage."

Perfect. Trent needed time to buy Grace's engagement ring and their wedding bands. "Do you want Marcus Lang to marry us?" Cornerstone Church's pastor was a friend to both of them and had performed the weddings for each of the members of Durango. Seemed to be a tradition now to have Lang's participation.

"I can't think of anything that would make me happier."

CHAPTER THIRTY-EIGHT

One week later, Trent pulled Grace into his embrace while their rapt audience watched. Her long white dress gleamed under the lights of Cornerstone Church's sanctuary, her eyes lit from within. He'd never seen any woman more beautiful than his Grace.

"I love you, Grace St. Claire," he murmured and took her mouth in a long, deep kiss that had several women in the audience sniffing, including Grace's adoptive mother. When Trent lifted his head, he threaded the fingers of his hand through hers and turned with her to face the auditorium filled with friends and loves ones. So much for a small wedding. Zane's wife, Claire, snapped picture after picture from a distance. When Grace had worried about her face being so bruised, the photographer promised to retouch the photos. Their official wedding pictures would be taken when both Trent and Grace were healed enough to do them justice.

Lang said, "I present to you Trent and Grace St. Claire."

The audience burst into applause as Trent and his bride started down the aisle, followed by Mason and Nicole, their only attendants. Once they cleared the sanctuary doors, Trent stole another series of kisses from the woman who was his heart.

"Hey, now," Rio said, amusement filling his voice. "Save some of that for the honeymoon."

Without breaking the kiss, he slugged the medic in the arm. When he came up for air, he made himself step to his wife's side. He and Grace greeted their well wishers.

Having opted to have a meal catered by Serena Blackhawk assisted by the best cooks in Cornerstone Church, Trent escorted Grace to the table arranged for them at the front of the fellowship hall. He kept an eye on the clock, willing time to go by faster.

Finally, it was time to leave. "It's time, honey," he murmured in her ear.

Despite the bruises slowly fading, her face glowed with happiness. "I'll be ready in ten minutes." Another kiss from his wife and she retreated to the room she'd used to dress for the wedding. Trent slipped out as well to change. Didn't want to wear dress clothes for hours on the plane.

Ten minutes later, she returned to the hall, this time dressed in clothes suitable for their flight to Hawaii. Trent's heart turned over in his chest. He could barely believe this gorgeous woman had agreed to spend the rest of her life with him. "Ready?"

Rio and Darcy walked toward them. "SUV is loaded," the medic said. "The Fortress plane is fueled, pilot is already doing the final pre-flight check." The use of the company plane was a gift from Maddox, his contribution to their wedding day.

With a nod, Trent turned toward the friends and family watching them. "Thank you for sharing this day with us. We'll see you in two weeks."

Darcy hugged them both. "Have fun."

"That's the plan." Trent shook Rio's hand.

Holding hands with Nicole, Mason caught the keys Trent tossed him one handed. "Let's go, Mase."

An hour later, Trent escorted Grace up the stairs to the Lear jet's cabin while Mason loaded their luggage. After hugs from Nicole, the other couple left the plane and the pilot taxied down the runway.

Trent looked at the woman who was now his. "This is just the beginning, you know."

"The beginning of what?"

"Our journey through life together. Now comes the most important part. Creating a bond that can't be broken, one of laughter, trust, and love."

She leaned close and kissed him with soft tenderness. "We began forming that bond the moment we met, love."

Yes, they had, he realized. No other woman understood him like Grace. She owned his heart. "I love you, baby." More than he could ever express in this lifetime. She was home to him and always would be. "Thank you, Grace."

"For what?"

"Giving me you." A gift he didn't deserve but would never take for granted. He'd spend the rest of his life making sure Grace never regretted choosing to share her life with him.

On the Edge

ABOUT THE AUTHOR

Rebecca Deel is a preacher's kid with a black belt in karate. She teaches business classes at a private four-year college near Nashville, Tennessee. She plays the piano at church, writes freelance articles, and runs interference for the family dogs. She's been married to her amazing husband for more than 25 years and is the proud mom of two grown sons. She delivers occasional devotions to the women's group at her church and conducts seminars in personal safety, money management, and writing. Her articles have been published in *ONE Magazine*, *Contact*, and *Co-Laborer*, and she was profiled in the June 2010 Williamson edition of *Nashville Christian Family* magazine. Rebecca completed her Doctor of Arts degree in Economics and wears her favorite Dallas Cowboys sweatshirt when life turns ugly.

For more information on Rebecca . . .
Sign up for Rebecca's newsletter: http://eepurl.com/_B6w9
Visit Rebecca's website: www.rebeccadeelbooks.com

Printed in Great Britain
by Amazon